I'm Not
Cinderella

I'm Not
Cinderella

TARRAH MONTGOMERY

CURRAWONG PRESS

To my own Prince Charming, Ryan.
I'm so lucky to be living in the best fairy tale
I could ever wish for.

Currawong Press
110 South 800 West
Brigham City, Utah 84302
http://walnutspringspress.blogspot.com

Text copyright © 2013 by Tarrah Montgomery
Cover design copyright © 2013 by Currawong Press
Interior design copyright © 2013 by Currawong Press

ISBN: 978-1-59992-892-0

Acknowledgments

It's so fun to be able to thank all of the great people in my life who have supported me and helped me write this novel. I first want to thank my Heavenly Father for all of the blessings he has given me. I also want to thank my biggest cheering squad—my family, who has always been there for me since I was a child and wrote endless stories on all of our extra paper. My mom and my sister, Torie, share my love of everything happily ever after, and I blame them completely for my own fairy-tale addiction. I can't wait until our next girls' trip. I love you guys! I'm thankful for my family now, with my young kids and wonderful, supportive husband. I get my best ideas from them, and my kids help me with their great imaginations. Thank you for giving me my perfect real-life fairy tale, complete with Prince Charming and everything.

I am fortunate to get advice from fellow authors. My uncle, Mike Ramsdell, author of *Train to Potevka,* gave me great counsel and support as I wrote this novel. It's also nice to call him family. I have the best friends in the world who have read my book and laughed at all of the right parts. You guys are the best!

Thanks to Amy Orton for loving my story enough to give me a chance, and thanks to Linda Prince for helping me polish the book and make it the best it could be. What a fun experience it was to work on this novel.

Again, thank you to everyone who has encouraged me along the way. I have the best family, friends, and neighbors in the world, and I am so excited to share this project with you.

Prologue

Once upon a time in a land not so far away, a nobleman lived happily in Idaho with his charming wife and their two young daughters. But no sooner had the oldest daughter turned three than the nobleman left his family. The small family suffered the sad consequences of extinguished love.

This is the story of the oldest daughter—me. With no father in my life and a mother who was the love glum, I tried to fill my life with fairy tales to numb the heartbreak around me. I saw the pain and loneliness in my mother's eyes and wanted so desperately to find what she was lacking. I looked out to the world and wished for the enchantment and fantasy I found in stories. I wished for the one thing I didn't have. Love.

Like many young girls, I dreamed of being a princess. After all, how could reality hope to compete with castles, fairy godmothers, magic dresses, and royal balls? It was normal for a girl to occasionally wish to escape. But with me, it was more than occasionally. In fact, if someone wrote my biography, it would be titled *True Confessions of a Fairy-Tale Junkie.*

My favorite fairy tale was *Cinderella*. It wasn't just the romance that captured my fascination—it was the entire account and the world within the magical story that kept me spellbound. The real world was harsh and uncaring. By living in my fantasy world, I could leave reality and pretend, for a while, that it didn't exist, and that Prince Charming *did* exist.

Every day I wished for Prince Charming.

Chapter 1

My *Cinderella* Obsession— How It All Started Seven Years Ago

For my tenth birthday, Nana gave me a DVD of *The Slipper and the Rose: the Story of Cinderella,* with Gemma Craven as Cinderella, and Richard Chamberlain as the dark, perfect, and handsome Prince Edward.

My *Cinderella* fascination soon turned into a full-fledged addiction. I watched the musical so many times I could recite the lines with the actors. The words often spoke themselves into my head. Sometimes it felt like a window was opening and I could see that world.

As I watched the reunion between Prince Charming and Cinderella in the movie, my heart pounded. I felt the elation of the characters as they sang of their love. If I pressed the PAUSE button, the moment would stand still, waiting to carry on. I would have the uncanny feeling that someone was watching me. Sometimes I actually felt that if I turned my head, Prince Charming would be standing there. (Note to self: Dreaming of and visualizing Prince Charming behind me was probably a huge indicator of my unstable mental state.)

Three Weeks Ago, When I Found Cinderella in My Room (the REAL Cinderella—no kidding!)

One night, the summer I was seventeen, I ventured down the stairs of my grandmother's old farmhouse for a glass of water. In the darkness, I tiptoed down the creaky stairs from my bedroom in the attic. Everyone was asleep except for me, and the wood planks groaned with each careful footstep I took.

"What are you doing?" a voice spoke from behind me.

"Cass, you scared me." I spun around to face my younger sister.

My brown-eyed sibling giggled. "That's what happens when you creep through an old house at night."

"A little warning would have been nice."

At fifteen, Cassidy was already an identical spawn of our mother's beauty. Cass's soft auburn hair bounced in waves along her shoulders, as opposed to my frizzy mass of brown. She was often compared to the beautiful singer and actress Selena Gomez, with her stunning eyes and gorgeous hair—minus the fame and stardom, of course. *Selena's new song is so cool. Makes you want to dance.*

I'm losing focus. Moving on.

"Are you getting a drink?" Cass asked.

"Yeah."

"Me too." She linked arms with me and we continued down the stairs.

I loved the sounds and smells of my nana's old farmhouse. Some people would be irritated with a rickety, handle-with-care kind of home, but I loved the worn feeling, as if years of experience qualified the house to shelter and comfort the people who lived there.

My senses welcomed the home's familiar features—the smell of dust from underneath the stairs, the wind whistling through the loose trim on the windows, the shutters rattling against the house.

Nana had convinced Grandpapa to buy the small farm with their retirement money as a remedy for her childhood nostalgia and to create a haven for their remaining years. After Grandpapa suddenly died a few years back, Nana held firmly to their dream.

The "almost a farm" contained one horse, three milkless cows, a dozen chickens, two stinky pigs, and one barkless dog named Ol' Pete. We were in charge of feeding the cows, gathering the eggs, and slopping the pigs. The chores kept my sister and me busy and were actually soothing once we fell into a rhythm. Ol' Pete, a German shepherd that had wandered onto the farm when I was about seven, followed us around everywhere, attempting to bark and protect us from every little sound or movement. Even a grasshopper was deemed a threat. Ol' Pete was old and his legs were bad—he always limped—but he never swayed from his self-designated battleground.

I loved summer holidays at the farm, despite the chores. This was the place where you took time to sit on a porch swing and enjoy what was around you. All the quirks of Nana's home were a comforting reassurance of what had been the only constant in my life.

Since my father abandoned us when I was three, my younger sister and I had moved constantly with my mother wherever her latest career took us. Each year seemed to bring a new setting and a new challenge of trying to fit in. The only thing that never changed was summers spent with Nana.

My mother only stayed at her mother's house long enough to drop us off. She used the summer months to advance her career. She took required company trips, added referrals to her client list, and caught up on things she had been putting off during the year. She stopped by the house only a handful of times, merely to fret about what she needed to be doing instead. It was a long time before I realized she used her career the same way I used *Cinderella*—to try to fill the emptiness in our lives left by my father.

Our summers at Nana's place in Idaho would have been paradise except for one thing—my mother's guilty conscience. She thought she had to make up for leaving her daughters all summer, so she insisted we help our grandmother with the farm chores to build our character.

"Is Shane coming over again tomorrow night?" Cass asked once we entered the kitchen.

"No," I said. *Ugh, I hope not.*

Shane was my boyfriend. Yes, I actually had a boyfriend—a pretty good catch, too. He had just graduated from high school. And he was really smart, which just had to be a "royal" trait. Right? But no matter how beautiful and brawny he was, he was no substitute for the Prince Charming of my dreams.

"Why not?" Cassidy asked.

"He's having a guys' night with his friends."

"I'm sure he'll be around later."

"No, he won't," I said unconvincingly. "I told him not to come."

"Oh, I'm sure he'll come over after his guys' night."

I had to change the subject. "What are you doing tomorrow night?"

"Nana and I are going to watch *Northanger Abbey.*"

Northanger Abbey was one of my favorite Jane Austen stories. Nana didn't have cable or satellite TV. Her television had three channels: the striped one, the one that showed what you could watch if you had a better TV, and the Spanish channel. Not that we would have chosen to watch it. Instead, we watched anything Jane Austen, Audrey Hepburn, or Doris Day, plus the Rodgers & Hammerstein collection, other classics, and of course, *The Slipper and the Rose.*

We also read a lot of novels, primarily fairy tales. When it rained, all three of us—Nana, my sister, and I—would snuggle into a good book and get lost in the magic. Nana's passion for a good tale could outdo even mine. At night, while I fell asleep in my room after a pleasant escape in one of my books, the light from Nana's reading lamp would seep through my floor grate.

"Don't worry," Cass said. "I'm sure Shane will want to watch it with us when he comes over."

I frowned. "Not funny."

"Girls, what are you doing out of bed in the middle of the night?" Nana asked as she joined us in the kitchen.

My grandmother was the most delightful woman I had ever known. She was wearing a bright yellow nightdress—the brightest lemon yellow I had ever seen anyone wear. Her hair was loosely gathered at the top of her head in a bun. Her appearance shouted her exuberant existence, and she brought the warmth of the sun with her.

Being at her house was like stepping into an enchanted story. She encouraged my imagination and dreams. One thing my imagination noticed was how Nana's life resembled *The Wizard of Oz.* Her name was Dorothy, and she always laughed when I compared her to the classic story, but the similarities were undeniable.

First of all, when Nana was younger, she lived on a farm in Kansas. Never mind the fact that she presently lived on a farm in southern Idaho. Second, Nana had an aunt named Emily, just like in the movie. Third, Nana met my grandfather, her sweetheart, while wearing ruby slippers. Well, they weren't really ruby, and they weren't slippers, but they were red shoes. Papa and Nana met at a dance. He always said he noticed the shoes before he noticed the girl.

"We were just talking about how Shane is coming over tomorrow night," my sister told my grandmother.

Nana raised an eyebrow. "Shane's coming over?"

I nodded, admitting the likelihood.

"Well, we'll have to make him some cookies," she said.

"Even if he does come, he won't be staying for very long," I said.

Nana looked at me disappointedly. "Brinlee, Shane is a nice, handsome fella. You should pay more attention to him. If you continue to avoid him, you'll lose him."

"I know." *Is that a bad thing?*

Nana reached out her hand and smoothed the hair next to my face. "What's the matter, honey?"

With her gentle nature, my grandmother was the complete opposite of my mother. My mother didn't like my fairy-tale passion—

in fact, she discouraged it. She didn't want me daydreaming of living in la-la land (her words). Maybe it was my father's abrupt and brutal departure that left her bitter about happy endings. So, nine months out of the year, I hid my passion. I read or watched my fairy tales secretly at night in my bedroom. The only time I was free to pursue my hobby was during the summer months at Nana's house. There, and only there, I could bask in the euphoric vision of fairy tales and all things happily-ever-after.

Unlike my mother, Nana inspired my hope for love. Sometimes, as we watched an old romantic movie, I caught her wiping tears from her cheeks as she remembered Grandpapa, her true love.

"Brin, what's troubling you?" Nana asked again. There was something about the love in her eyes that always made me want to tell her everything.

Where do I start?

"She compares every boy to Prince Charming and feels she never measures up to Cinderella," my sister said.

I let out a puff of air. She was right, and my grandmother knew it. Even if Shane met my expectations of Prince Charming, I would never meet my expectations of Cinderella.

"Brinlee, you are just as beautiful as any Cinderella." Nana's eyes sparkled. "You have been blessed with an overabundance of humility, so you will never see the beauty you possess."

As a grandmother should and would, Nana always found a way to make me feel like the most beautiful person on the planet. She grasped my hand and led me to the small foyer of the house. After placing her hands on my shoulders, she slowly turned me around to face the antique mirror fastened to the wall.

"Look," she said.

Feeling silly, I turned my head away to protest. With her hands still on my shoulders, she forced my attention to the mirror.

"With open eyes, look," she said gently.

I complied and looked at myself in the mirror. My nose seemed normal, not too pointy or too flat. My cheekbones were adequately high. My slightly slanted green eyes were shaded by long, dark eyelashes. My complexion was my mother's—fair and smooth, except for the freckles sprinkled on my nose.

I stood up straight and inspected my figure. At five feet six inches, I looked normal—ordinarily normal. Disappointingly, I looked nothing like the stunning heroines in my beloved stories. But, at Nana's request, I had looked with open eyes.

Once in the sanctuary of my bedroom, I fell dramatically onto my bed. I wanted to hide in a dream and sleep my worries away. I closed my eyes, replaying my favorite *Cinderella* scenes in my head.

I finally dozed off, but was awakened by a crash at the opposite end of the room. *What was that?* I sat up. As in most really old homes, the attic stretched across the length of the house. It held boxes, suitcases, old furniture and appliances, and holiday decorations. Nana had stacked everything and pushed it to the far end of the attic to make room for my bed and one small sofa. Anything could have fallen off the heap of forgotten items and made the noise I'd heard.

Another crashing sound made me jump to my feet. This time it was louder, as if a heavy object had fallen, like a box of books. Maybe one of the leaning towers of storage was losing its foundation. I decided to survey the damage. After all, what was there to be afraid of—besides rats (which I hate), giant spiders (which I despise), or nasty boxes with mold (which make me cringe)? What else could be hidden among Nana's collections?

Even though the early morning light was beginning to shine through my bedroom window, I turned on the lamp on my nightstand to help light up the darker side of the room. Dust rose from the floor as I carefully stepped closer to the leaning piles of boxes.

A third crash sounded throughout the room.

"Oops," a tiny voice whispered from behind the boxes.

My heart halted along with my feet. "Who's there?"

Silence.

Maybe I was just hearing things. Maybe I was dreaming. *Yes, this is just a bad dream,* I told myself.

After what seemed like an eternity, a small voice spoke again. "I'm sorry."

My hand covered my mouth to stifle a gasp. Panic ran through my veins. What was I supposed to do? What did they say to do in situations like this? Scream? Run? Fight?

But fight what? The person with the tiny voice?

"Please forgive me." The voice was closer.

Not daring to move, I grasped behind me for something, anything to use as a weapon, but my fingers found only air. I watched a girl move from behind the nearest stack of trunks, smiling and beautiful, as she wrung her soot-covered apron.

"I'm so sorry, miss," she said as she pointed to the boxes behind her. "It was dark, and I couldn't see where I was going. I hope I didn't break anything."

Her voice, barely above a whisper, sang as she spoke, and her movements were as smooth as an angel. It was as if she had stepped out of a storybook. She was astonishingly beautiful, if you overlooked her soiled dress and the smudges on her face. Part of her wavy brown hair was pinned behind her head, while the rest covered her shoulders and back.

When I didn't speak, she curtsied. "My name is Gabriella."

So formal, I thought.

Absently, I followed suit and attempted a curtsy. I emphasize the word "attempted," because I clumsily bowed with my foot dangling awkwardly behind me and my hands pinching the seams of my sweatpants.

The girl smiled kindly. "And your name, miss?"

"Oh, sorry. My name is Brinlee."

She curtsied again.

Again?! I thought. *A little repetitive, don't you think?* Still, I did my best to curtsy back.

"I'm pleased to meet you Miss Brinlee," she said.

"I'm pleased to meet you too, Miss Gabriella."

"My friends call me Gabby, but my family calls me Cinderella."

That name—that single, four-syllable word—slapped me back into reality.

K, what is this? Ah! A prank. I wondered who had executed the plan to have someone parade in my room and impersonate Cinderella, my fairy-tale heroine.

"How did you get in my room?" I asked the girl.

She pointed to the boxes behind her. "My entrance was through that door."

"What door?" The only door in the room was the one behind me, leading to the stairway. "Did you come through a window or something?" I narrowed my eyes.

The girl shook her head. "No, the door I passed through is behind those containers."

Frowning, I peered over the stacks and stacks of boxes.

"Before today, the door never opened, no matter how hard I tried," she said. "But today, on this day, it has opened." She stopped, her eyes bright with realization. Her gaze bore into mine. "You have opened it for me. You must be the source."

"What is your deal?" I asked a bit forcefully. "Who put you up to this? Was it Cass? Who was it?" I stepped forward.

She frowned. "I do not know what you mean."

I rubbed my temples. This conversation was going nowhere.

Gabriella, the actress, stepped around me and reached out to the lamp on my nightstand. "What is this? It is very unusual." She pushed on my mattress. "What comfort! I would lie in this bed all day."

She scanned my corner of the attic, then meandered through it, clearly fascinated with every little thing.

What if she really is Cinderella? I wondered. *Wait! What am I thinking?*

"I think I might be having a nervous breakdown," I said.

The girl looked confused. "What is your meaning?"

"You're not supposed to be here. You are only a figment of my imagination."

She tilted her head and looked at me sympathetically. "I am as much a figment of your imagination as you are mine, because I stand here before you."

"But I am a real person. You are only a character in a book." I walked over to my bookshelf and grabbed one of my copies of the Cinderella story. I thrust it into the stranger's hands.

"Yes, this is a book." She placed her hand on mine. "But I am a real person just as you."

I withdrew my hand. *What's happening?* If this wasn't proof of my insanity, then what was it?

"I don't understand. This can't be real," I said. "Where did you come from?"

"My home is in Fenmore Falls. I come from a place very different than yours."

Ya think?

"What do you call this place?" She handed my book back to me.

"We call this place Idaho."

She scrunched her eyebrows. "Idaho?"

I nodded. She seemed to be as bewildered as I was.

"I've never heard of it," she said.

"Tell me something about your world," I challenged her. "Tell me something I couldn't possibly know."

"Well . . ." She paused, and then her eyes brightened. "Just this morning, it was declared that the prince had come home from a long trip overseas. It is expected that there will be a ball to celebrate his return."

Just like the Cinderella story.

"I already knew that," I said. Then I thought of something. "You haven't met the prince yet, have you?"

"Of course not. Why would I have reason to meet the prince? I only saw him one time at the castle."

What if there was some truth to what she said? What if she was who she said she was? *Maybe this is the real Cinderella who is only beginning her fairy-tale story!*

"Tell me something else," I said anxiously.

"My chambermaid, Katie, heard from a very dependable source that the prince's ship had been captured and rummaged by pirates. He, along with only a few of his loyal safeguards, was barely able to escape and return home. The whispers about the tale began today."

She actually appeared to believe what she was telling me.

"Show me the door," I said.

Gabriella appeared to be thrilled at my request. She grabbed my hand and led me to the far wall behind the stacks of old boxes. I followed her while my other hand still clutched the Cinderella book, my thread to realism.

There, leaning against the wall, was a door. Nothing seemed unusual about it—it was simply an old door being stored in the attic.

"This is a broken door," I said.

"It is the way I entered," Gabriella replied. "See? I left it slightly propped open."

I looked to where she pointed, but saw only a leaning door. "This is not a door. Well, I guess it was a door at one time, but it's not now. It's broken and has been taken off its hinges."

Gabriella looked at me thoughtfully.

Determined to illustrate the obvious, I placed my hand on the long-forgotten doorknob. I twisted it and pulled. The doorknob squeaked as I turned it, and then, unexpectedly, the door opened. Instead of staying firm against the wall, it opened as if on hinges.

With the door wide open, I peered inside. The doorway led into another room—a room considerably different from the one I stood in. Long tables were sprinkled with flour, and directly adjacent to the door was a stone fireplace that breathed its heat onto my face.

All the reasons this scene couldn't be real were demolished by the evidence in front of me. I could even smell freshly baked bread.

"I don't understand," I whispered.

"Nor do I," Gabriella said. "All I know is that when I passed through this door, I left my world and entered yours."

Chancing a closer look, I placed one foot onto the packed-dirt floor of her kitchen. My other foot followed. I looked back at Gabriella, who watched from the other side of the miraculous door. Behind her, I could still see the stacks of boxes in my grandmother's attic. Gazing into reality while standing in a fantasy was a pretty weird sensation.

Then, without warning, the door began to close. I scrambled to grab it, but something seemed to force it shut. Perhaps Gabriella, the supposedly sweet angel, had closed the door herself.

"Gabriella! Help me!"

Chapter 2

The Book

The priceless book, a 1912 McLoughlin Brothers edition of *Cinderella,* was a gift from Nana and my sister. The illustrations on the brittle, wrinkled pages were exquisite, particularly the faded portrait of the gentle, beautiful Cinderella sitting next to her hearth.

Inside, I read: "Poor Cinderella got home frightened and out of breath, with no carriage—no horses—no coachman—no pages— and all her old clothes back again. She had none of her finery now, except the other glass slipper."

Stuck in Cinderella's World

Still clutching the Cinderella book in one hand, I struggled to twist the wobbly doorknob. "Gabriella!" I shouted.

I thrust my shoulder against the door. "Ouch!" *That hurt more than I expected. Why does it always work in the movies?*

I pounded on the door. "Gabriella!"

Why couldn't I open the door? And why wasn't she letting me in? More importantly, was she the one who closed the door? Maybe Gabriella saw my world as refuge from her cruel and abusive home, but why would she thrust me into these horrible conditions? I rested my forehead on the door and feebly whispered, "Gabby, please open the door."

"Excuse me, miss," said a male voice.

I twirled around in alarm, dropping my book to the floor. In the doorway to the kitchen stood a tall man whose beauty took my breath away.

"Who are you? Please state your business," he said in a strong voice. He couldn't have been more than a few years older than me, yet his manner exuded authority. He wore white tights, black buckle shoes, knee-length pants, a white shirt, and a jacket. His hair was pulled back into a low ponytail. *Ooh la la!*

Clearly losing patience, he strode toward me and asked again, "Has someone let you in, miss?"

"Oh . . . I'm sorry. I was a little lost for a moment." *Yeah, lost in your gorgeous eyes.* I mentally swooned.

"Who are you?" He stared at my twenty-first-century outfit— hot pink sweatpants and a white T-shirt.

This dude was obviously not going to believe I was invited into this house. So, I went with the truth. "I'm Brinlee. I'm here because of Gabriella."

What if Gabriella didn't live here? Or what if she was hated by everyone in her world and not just her stepmother and stepsisters? *Oh, Brinlee, how did you get in this mess?*

"You're a friend of Cinderella?" The man lifted an eyebrow.

Seriously? They really call her that? "Yes," I answered.

"There was no notice of Cinderella receiving a visitor today." Once more, he looked at my strange clothes. "What was your name again?"

Crap! This guy is not buying it. I need to get out of here. I looked back at the door I'd entered. I already knew it was locked. To the left was another door, this one partly open. It led outside, and I figured if I could sneak out that door I could make a run for it.

"Please wait here while I confer with the lady of the house," Ponytail Man said.

As soon as he turned on his heels and left the room, I bolted through the open door. I ran outside and hurried down a dirt road leading away from the beautiful but scary man. I didn't know what people in this day did with trespassers, and I didn't want to find out. Maybe if I ran fast enough, I'd pass out and awake from this dream.

It was early morning, just as it had been when I left my room in Idaho. The sun was barely making its appearance on the horizon. I ran past a stable and a few houses made of wood. I kept running past a small pond near the side of the road. My lungs burned, but I ran as fast as I could. Thankfully my purple slippers had rubber soles. You never know when you're going to wake up and have to run for your life.

When I finally stopped, I put my hands on my knees and panted just like Ol' Pete. My tongue even hung out while I gasped for air. I didn't know how far I'd run, but just as the dizziness went away and I could focus my eyes again, I felt the earth tremble. Something was coming! I ran to the side of the road and ducked behind a tree. Were there bad guys in Cinderella's story? I didn't know, but I crouched down just in case.

Two men approached on horseback. One of them dove over and toppled the other off his horse about ten feet from me. I sank closer to the ground, wishing I could disappear. The two men wrestled, one of them clawing at the dirt as if in search of something. The other man wore a mask, a black cloth wrapped around the upper part of his face.

Suddenly, the masked man jumped up. "I've got it, old man." He held up what looked like a key. A very large old key.

The first man, who was short and chubby, stood slowly and brushed the dirt off his pants. He looked toward the line of trees where I hid. I stilled my breath and waited until his gaze returned to the masked man. "It is of no consequence," he muttered. "My source will obtain another one."

"Your source?" the other exclaimed. "You have no source. He confessed everything this morning. How do you think I was able to find you so quickly?"

Just then, the portly man jumped at me through the trees like a viper snatching its prey, and brought me to a standing position with a sharp object pointing to my neck.

The masked man's eyes grew wide as he looked at me and then at my captor, and then back at me. "Where did you come from?" he asked, taking a quick inventory of my strange attire and loose hair.

With the knife at my throat I couldn't reply, but I didn't have a suitable answer anyway.

"Give me the key," the man behind me said, tightening his hold.

"Or what, Isaac? You'll kill her?"

I gasped.

The old man chuckled, and I felt his belly shake. I won't even mention his breath. *Eeeew! Where's the Listerine when you need it?*

The masked man stepped forward. I couldn't help but look into his brilliant brown eyes. Somehow I knew the rest of his face would be a masterpiece too. But perhaps he hid his face to hide an awful wound, like the Phantom of the Opera. Or maybe he suffered from an abnormality from birth.

But he had great hair. It was long and brown and tied at the back of his head. *First the guy at Cinderella's house with girl hair, and now this guy.* Anyway, it was pretty. It made you want to run your fingers through it.

Or maybe cut it off. Just a little bit. In his sleep.

K, I'm getting distracted. How could I get distracted with a man holding a knife to my throat? Blame it on the masked man's hair.

His beautiful hair.

Brinlee, stop.

Moving on.

"Not a step closer," said the dude with stinky breath.

"All right, all right." The tall man held up his hands. "What do you want?"

"Give me the key."

"You know I can't do that. How about an exchange? You give me the girl, and I'll give you everything on my horse."

Isaac loosened his grip on me but not enough for me to escape. "Do I have your word?"

I was intrigued. Would this masked man, gorgeous as he was, really trade everything on his horse for me—a girl he didn't know and who dressed funny?

The tall man crossed his arms over his massive chest. I could see his muscles—they were right there, rippling through his open white shirt. When I looked into his eyes, he held my gaze. I wanted to look away but couldn't. He was the most handsome guy I'd ever seen—a serious hottie. And he was certainly the first man I'd ever seen wearing a mask while riding a horse. Somehow, he made the look work even better than Zorro.

The masked man frowned at me, as if remembering where he was. "I give you my word," he told my captor.

Isaac released me and shoved me toward the ground. A hand clenched my forearm and I let out a yell, but then quickly swallowed it. It was the masked man, even more intense up close. But his eyes were no longer soft in wonder. They were hard, staring down at me.

"Are you a witch?"

What?! "What?"

"A witch," he repeated. "Why are you in the woods? And your clothing . . ." He reached a hand to my hair. "Your hair. No one allows his woman to parade around as such."

I slapped his hand away. "I am not a witch. I am from—" I closed my mouth. He wouldn't believe me if I told him. "Look, you big jerk," I said, not caring if my language confused him. "You don't want to know where I'm from. It would freak you out." *It's freakin' me out!*

He leaned back, looking surprised. But then he turned as if sensing Isaac behind him. He spoke to the potbellied man. "You have exactly five minutes before I change my mind and turn you in."

The pudgy man hurried to the masked man's horse and started removing items from the saddlebags. When he had transferred his hoard to his mare, he led her to a tree stump and stood on it to climb into the saddle.

He turned and gave me one last look, staring like he'd never seen a girl in pants, which he probably never had. "Nice doing work with you, Black Rider," he said to the masked man before riding away.

"Well, that was a waste," my rescuer grumbled. He walked to his horse and mounted easily. He reined the animal away and started down the road.

"Wait! You're just going to leave me?"

He stopped his horse and peered down at me. "Miss, I think you've gotten me into enough trouble for today." He started forward again.

I ran toward him. "Please help me. I don't know where I am."

He tilted his head. "You're not my problem anymore."

How rude! "Fine! Be that way. I just hope your conscience lets you sleep tonight, knowing you left a damsel in distress alone in the woods. Who knows? Maybe Isaac will have second thoughts and come back to kidnap the girl he left behind. Then you can wonder if something terrible will befall me." *Befall? Since when do I say "befall"?* Maybe I was suffering from some sort of illness that messed with the language part of my brain.

Black Rider halted his horse. It looked like my guilt trip worked, because he slid off and marched up to me. He pointed his finger at my face. "I'll take you to where you need to go. Nothing more. Understand?"

Wow, can you say "anger management"?

"That is all I ask," I said.

He returned to his horse but did not mount. I ran to his side and waited for him to make a stirrup with his hands, but instead he grabbed me by the waist and lifted me onto the saddle. Sideways, as in sidesaddle. Not wanting to fall off, I quickly swung my right leg over the horse's neck so I could have a leg on each side of the animal.

"Is everything all right?" Black Rider asked me.

"I'm just not used to riding sidesaddle."

He didn't comment but climbed up behind me. He slid his arm around my waist and reached for the reins with his other hand.

I could get used to this, I thought as I felt his warmth behind me.

"Where shall I take you?" he asked.

Even though I'd just escaped Gabriella's kitchen, I now realized it was my only hope of going home. Maybe I could sneak in without the pretty blond boy seeing me, then open the door and return to Nana's house. I could forget any of this ever happened.

"Will you take me to the house over there?" I pointed in the direction of Gabriella's house.

"Sherwood Manor?" Black Rider said.

Um, sure. "Yes."

"Are you a servant?"

Hmm, how do I answer that? "Not really. I'm a friend of someone who lives there."

"So, you're a guest?"

"I guess you could say that." I don't know if being thrust into another realm and locked out of your world made you a guest, but sure—let's go with it.

For a while, we rode along in silence. He let the horse walk slowly, and I guessed the guy wanted me to be as comfortable as possible. Finally, I realized I'd better investigate my whereabouts. "So, you travel this road a lot?" I asked.

"Yes, it is the main road in the kingdom."

"You mean Fenmore Falls?" I asked, remembering what Gabriella had said earlier.

"Of course I mean Fenmore Falls. Where else would I mean?"

Not knowing how to answer, I changed the subject. "Why was the key so important?"

"What key?"

I huffed. "The key you stole from the other guy. You know, the guy you pushed from his horse and rolled around in the dirt with. Does any of that ring a bell?" I knew I was being sarcastic, but he was baiting me.

"It's somewhere safe."

"Like tied to the leather rope around your neck?" I guessed.

His hand left my waist and tugged at the rope in question. "Do I need to be wary of your thievery now?"

"No. I just saw you put it on when he was removing the stuff from your horse."

I shifted my weight to get more comfortable. My elbow leaned into Black Rider's thigh, and he grunted with pain.

"Sorry."

"It's fine."

"Did you get hurt?"

"'Tis a previous wound," he said.

Awkward silence followed. I didn't know if he was mad at me for knowing where he had stashed the key, or because I'd hurt his leg. But I had barely touched it, so the wound must have been serious.

The stillness gave me time to worry. *What should I do with my hands?* I had no idea how to properly ride a horse in tandem. My hands felt awkward on my lap, and the saddle wasn't equipped with a horn to hold on to, so I ended up folding my arms across my chest.

"It's the key to the magazine," Black Rider finally said, startling me after the silence.

My endless study of the history of *Cinderella* had paid off. I remembered that a magazine was a building where weapons and gunpowder were stored. "Why did that guy have it?"

"If that key got in the wrong hands, Fenmore Falls would be doomed. Isaac is just one poor man who was paid handsomely to do just that—put Fenmore Falls in danger."

"So what does that make you? The kingdom's Robin Hood, like Russell Crowe or Kevin Costner?"

Both great actors. Both great movies. Sigh.

"Your speech is unusual," Black Rider said.

I could say the same about you. "I'm not from here." *Obviously.*

"Your clothing is strange."

"Yep, I've noticed."

"And you are unchaperoned," he finished.

"I'm not from here. Did I already say that? 'Cause I'm not. I'm only here for a little bit. Hopefully I'll be going home very soon. I need my sister right now. But she wouldn't be much help. She'd be panicking, probably running around screaming, which is what I feel like doing right now. No, my sister would not be much help. My mother wouldn't be a good choice either. That leaves Nana. Yes, Nana would know what to do. She'd find . . ."

My voice trailed off as I felt Black Rider's chest rumble with laughter. "I take that back. This day was not a waste. You are the most joy I've had in a long time." He continued to laugh.

"Well, I'm glad you're enjoying this," I snapped.

Once he was able to stop laughing, he asked, "What is your name? I must find out the name of the peculiar fairy from the woods."

Well, that was kind of nice. "Brinlee. My name is Brinlee."

"Well, Miss Brinlee, we have arrived at your destination."

I hadn't realized we were at the last bend before Gabriella's house. Just now I could see the outline of the towering manor through the trees. So distracted and enjoying the ride *(yes, I'll admit it was kind of fun),* I also must've missed the pond I'd passed during my escape.

"This is as far as I go." Black Rider stopped his horse and jumped to the ground. I swung my leg over and slid off the horse right into the guy's waiting arms. When I felt his breath on my neck, the hair there stood at attention.

As if he could sense his power over me, he grinned. "Thank you, Miss Brinlee, for the adventure."

I found my voice. "I didn't get your name."

"You know I can't tell you that."

He stepped away and guided his horse a few paces back toward the road.

"How do I know you're the good guy and not the bad guy?" I asked.

"You're still standing with your virtue intact, are you not?"

Eeeew. "But how do I know you're not the bad guy who was paid by the bad guys to get the key?"

"Sometimes you need to trust your instincts, even if they're dressed funny and lurk in the woods."

He mounted his horse and started down the road, then turned to look at me one last time. "Welcome to Fenmore Falls."

See ya, wouldn't want to be ya, I thought in return.

Now, to get back home.

Chapter 3

The Odd and Fascinating World of Cinderella Tales—*Pepelyouga (Cinderella)*
Serbia, 1917

On a high pasture land, near an immense precipice, some maidens were occupied in spinning and attending to their grazing cattle, when an old strange looking man with a white beard reaching down to his girdle approached, and said, "Oh fair maidens, beware of the abyss, for if one of you should drop her spindle down the cliff, her mother would be turned into a cow that very moment!"

So saying the aged man disappeared, and the girls, bewildered by his words, and discussing the strange incident, approached near to the ravine, which had suddenly become interesting to them. They peered curiously over the edge, as though expecting to see some unaccustomed sight, when suddenly the most beautiful of the maidens let her spindle drop from her hand, and before she could recover it, it was bounding from rock to rock into the depths beneath. When she returned home that evening she found her worst fears realized, for her mother stood before the door transformed into a cow.

Thankfully, I hadn't encountered an old man with a white beard on my trip. The last thing I needed was for some weirdo to do some magic and turn my mother into a cow.

With all of the versions of the classic story, I didn't know which one I had stepped into. Ever since the Cinderella story was first told in Chinese in 850 A.D., operas, ballets, and even ice shows had done their own interpretations of it. In each tale, magic help was required. While Cinderella was a servant, she was magically advised, provided for, and fed. Or the magic came from her dead mother, a tree on the mother's grave, a supernatural being, or talking birds. Other sources of magic in Cinderella stories include a goat, a sheep, a cow, and a magic tree that springs up from the remains of a dead animal.

Many of the original Cinderella stories involve birds instead of a fairy godmother. The Brothers Grimm had Cinderella attend the ball three times, with the aid of birds that helped her finish her chores—impossible things her teasing, cruel sisters had demanded her to do, including picking out the lentils they had thrown into the ashes of the fireplace. A French author, Charles Perrault, introduced the most popular version of *Cinderella,* with the fairy godmother who turns a pumpkin into a carriage.

Some accounts were much more gruesome than the cute Disney or Rogers and Hammerstein versions. In one telling, the stepsisters try to squeeze their feet into the glass slipper. And in the Grimms' version, the sisters cut off their toes and heels so their feet can fit into the shoe. The prince rides off with one of the stepsisters, but the birds tell him to look back. Seeing blood on the trail, he realizes the sisters lied, and he is finally able to see Cinderella. *Yeah, a little gross.*

Can you tell I was totally obsessed with the story of Cinderella? The only advantage of switching schools every year with my mother's job was that I could use the same research subject at each school: The History of Cinderella.

Unoriginal, you may say. I say genius. Why waste brain power on something that doesn't matter? Cinderella matters.

Now, On With My Story

After my adventure with Black Rider, I kept to the outlying trees and then sneaked close to Gabriella's house. As indicated by the rumbling of my stomach, I had missed breakfast and had probably been gone from Nana's house for a couple hours. I couldn't wait to get home and help myself to the leftover apple pie in the fridge.

I reached Gabriella's kitchen door and peeked inside to make sure the coast was clear. Though relieved to find the room empty, I was suspicious because I'd seen no one outside. Where were all of the servants? Where was Ponytail Man? I grabbed my Cinderella book from the floor where I'd dropped it, then turned to the infamous door. I tried to turn the knob and wished with all my might that I would be able to see my room on the other side. But the knob did not turn. It did not even move. At all. Not even a hair.

I banged my fist on the door. "Gabriella!" I shouted. I did not care if anyone heard me. I wanted to go home.

"Gabriella!" I shouted again.

"Miss?" a soft voice said.

I turned around to see a young servant girl smiling at me from the kitchen doorway. She had the brownest eyes and the most beautiful golden hair. She curtsied. "The lady of the house always wishes to be informed of who is visiting her household."

"Oh, um, um . . . I'm Brinlee." I scrambled to give reason for my presence. "I'm a friend of Gabriella."

The petite girl smiled. "I'm delighted to meet you, Miss Brinlee. My name is Katie. I'm also a friend of Miss Gabriella."

Ah, the chambermaid. "Yes, Gabriella mentioned you. She said you were the one who told her of the prince's pirate encounter."

The girl held a finger up to her lips and whispered, "Hush. These things must not be spoken out loud. It is only chitchat, nothing of consequence." A grin crept onto her face. "But who shall resist believing the quest of the prince when such exciting gossip is spread?"

I liked her playful attitude.

Noticing the book I held tightly in my hand, Katie asked, "What is that book?"

"Oh, it's nothing," I answered. It was one thing to be visiting the Cinderella story, but how would I explain it to someone who was actually *in* the story?

Katie seemed to want to ask more about the book, but instead she said, "Will you be staying with us long?"

"Um . . ." I looked over my shoulder at the sealed door leading home. "I don't know."

"Come—" she threaded her arm through mine "—Lady Catherine will want to meet you."

Panic rose to my chest. Did she mean Gabriella's stepmother? The evil stepmother? *Okay, this is seriously getting weird.* I kept my arm rigid and refused to move.

"It's best to do it now and just get it over with, Miss Brinlee."

I stepped back to the door and desperately yanked at the knob. *Please, let this door open,* I silently prayed.

"I never understood that," Katie said. "It resembles a door, but it is not. No one knows the reason for its outline upon the wall when the only thing on the opposite side is the garden."

This couldn't be happening. Where was the exit button? I wanted to go home.

"Here." Katie pulled at my arm. "I'll accompany you."

She led me out of the kitchen and into a long, narrow hallway. This had to be a hallucination, yet I felt as if I was actually walking through Cinderella's house with her chambermaid, Katie.

We climbed a set of stairs leading to the second floor, and another to the third floor. The floors and walls of the house were lined entirely with stone. On the third floor, large woven tapestries draped the hallways. There were pictures of knights battling dragons, beautiful groves and gardens, and maidens standing next to rippling pools of water. The tapestries were stunning works of art.

At the end of the hallway, Katie brought me to a tall, wooden door. She knocked and an angry voice said, "Who is it?"

"Sorry to disturb you, milady, but we have a visitor."

There was a moment of silence. Katie smiled at me.

"Come," the voice commanded.

Katie opened the door, and I followed her into the room. My eyes immediately fell on the woman sitting on a chair next to a mirror. Her long, dark hair hung loose—contrary to the storybooks, where the stepmother wore her hair up—and her extraordinary scarlet gown, which matched the room itself, seemed to melt on the floor like butter. The low, wide neckline concealed very little. The sleeves, adorned with ruffles, lace, and bows, clasped her slim arms tightly at the elbow. She was beautiful.

She swiveled around on her perch. "Who are you?"

"Brinlee," I said quickly.

She inspected me with her eyes, starting at my head and moving slowly down to my feet.

Growing uneasy, I looked at my white T-shirt, pink sweatpants, and purple slippers (now covered with dirt and mud from my morning jog). I folded my arms across my chest, with my Cinderella book still in hand. Not that I could hide my outfit, but I wanted to conceal my shaky hands.

The woman stood. "Why are you in my house, Miss . . . Brinlee, was it?"

"She's a friend of Miss Gabriella's, Lady Catherine," Katie said.

The woman shifted her gaze to the chambermaid. "You shall know your place and shall not speak unless you are spoken to."

Attempting to divert the woman's attention from Katie, I said, "I've come to visit my friend, Gabriella."

Lady Catherine's unbearable stare returned to me. "How long have you known Cinderella?"

"I've known her my whole life," I answered in truth.

"Why is it that I've never heard of you? Where are you from?" the woman asked.

"I'm from Idaho."

Lady Catherine stood silent, probably pondering where Idaho might be. "Do you have any important or principal relation?"

She was asking if I was of noble blood. I mentally reviewed my genealogy and said, "My family comes from Wales. I am related to the royal family of Dinefwr Castle." *Very, very distantly.* Did they even know about Wales in this strange world called Fenmore Falls?

Lady Catherine's expression didn't reveal whether she believed me or not. "Where is Cinderella? I haven't seen her all morning," she asked Katie.

Katie looked at me for an answer.

"She's actually at my home in Idaho," I said.

Lady Catherine smirked. "Cinderella has gone to see you, and you have come here to see her. Forgive me for noticing that the arrangement appears to have an error."

"I guess you can say we've sort of made a swap."

Lady Catherine looked at my clothes again. "Well, at least you look prepared to perform Cinderella's household duties." The woman sighed. "In any case, a break from her will be refreshing."

Abruptly, she clapped her hands twice and shouted towards the closed door, "William! Come!"

I jumped at the outburst, wondering if Lady Catherine had Tourette's or something.

Within seconds, hurried footsteps could be heard echoing against the rock floor of the hallway. The door opened to reveal Ponytail Man, and I thought again how perfectly handsome he was.

"Yes, milady?" he said.

"Fetch Miss Brinlee's bags," Lady Catherine ordered. "It looks like she will be staying with us for a while."

I tore my eyes away from the beautiful man and said, "I didn't bring anything with me."

All three occupants of the room looked at me questioningly.

"My luggage isn't here yet," I lied. "I came ahead, anxious to arrive early."

"Very well," Lady Catherine said. "Katie, show Miss Brinlee to Cinderella's room. Since the two of them seem to have exchanged places, it is fitting for Miss Brinlee to fill Cinderella's position." The lady of the house turned to the young man. "You may go, William."

As he took his leave, his eyes lingered in my direction. I almost staggered at the cold, odd sensation I felt from his gaze.

Lady Catherine spoke, seizing my attention. "According to the laws of Christian hospitality, I will not turn you out of my house. However, I have reservations regarding who you truly are."

"Milady—" I began.

"It is unnecessary for you to speak," she interrupted. She took an authoritative step closer. "I don't care how a person like you comes to be a friend of Cinderella. But I shall favor you with a warning—the doings of this household will be held private. Every word breathed within these walls shall remain in this house."

Chills ran up my spine. This stepmother was really as evil as the storybooks said.

When Lady Catherine took another step toward me, I felt her breath hot on my face. "You must follow orders with exactness. Is that understood?"

I nodded. "Yes, milady."

"Good. You may leave." She flicked her hand.

Quickly, Katie grabbed my elbow and led me out of the room.

Once we were in the hall and the door was closed, I exhaled the breath I didn't know I was holding.

"I'm so glad you have come to visit," Katie exclaimed, as if the awful scene with Lady Catherine was a normal occurrence. The chambermaid continued to talk while leading me farther down the hall. "We will have so much fun together. You come from a very different place, and I am anxious for you to share your knowledge with me."

I turned to look at her. No doubt we were very close in age, but oh, how different her life was from mine. For instance, I replaced empty toilet-paper rolls, while she emptied chamber pots . . . that somebody else had used.

I hadn't thought about using the bathroom in this place yet. Suddenly, my bladder taunted me. *Oh, great.*

"What's your story?" I asked Katie. "How old are you? Where are you from?"

"I'm eighteen years old, and I'm from the kingdom, of course. I've lived in this household all my life. My mother does the mending, and my sister helps with the cleaning. My assignment is to assist and serve the ladies of the house."

I had read about chambermaids and lady's maids, but I never imagined meeting one. This was definitely a bizarre dream.

Katie presented me to another set of doors. "This is Miss Gabriella's room."

The girl opened the door. I gazed inside and gasped. "This is amazing!"

With everything drenched in blues, silver, and crystal, the room reminded me of a cloud. Compared to Lady Catherine's gloomy, red room, this one was calm and refreshing. It was exquisite.

"This used to be Miss Gabriella's mother's room. Blue was her favorite," Katie explained.

"It's perfect."

"When Miss Gabby's father died, this part of the manor was left alone. Lady Catherine said it reminded her of the ghost of Miss Gabby's mother. So, this room was left to Miss Gabby. She's kept it the same ever since."

I stepped farther into the peaceful bedroom. The atmosphere spoke of Gabriella—sweet and charming.

"Miss Gabby spends most of her time downstairs in the company of the other servants. I don't know if this room brings her comfort in her mother's memory, or perhaps sorrow."

"Probably both," I said.

I reached out to touch the lace on one of the tables. My fingers glided across the supple silk. *It feels so real.*

Katie said excitedly, "Did Miss Gabby tell you about the ball at the palace?"

This is just like the Cinderella story. "We really are right at the beginning, aren't we?" I murmured.

Katie gave me a funny look. "You say the most curious things."

The large bed beckoned to me. Maybe a little nap would cure my insanity. "I don't feel so good," I said.

"Are you well?"

I shook my head. "I think I should rest a bit." *Then, I will wake up from this nightmare.*

Katie raced to a nearby cupboard and retrieved a white garment. She laid the billowy piece of linen on the bed. "Here is a shift for you. Change into this, and then I'll have Mama wash some new stockings and petticoats for you."

In a sleepy daze, I stared at the nightgown.

"Would you like me to assist you in changing?" Katie asked politely.

"Oh, no, no," I said. "I can change myself, thank you."

"Rest well, then. I'm so glad you've come to visit, Miss Brinlee."

"Thank you, Katie."

After she left, the first thing I did was find a hiding place for my Cinderella book. I climbed onto the fantasy bed and slid the book under the fluffy pillow. Then, I laid my head on the pillow and whispered, "Just a dream. It's just a crazy dream."

As I glided off to sleep, I remembered the words Nana often said to me. "Hold on to your dreams, Brinlee. Don't ever let go."

How ironic.

Chapter 4

Boyfriend Number One—First Breakup: Marty Adams

We were twelve. We were in the same class. Our relationship started in a note and ended likewise. The first said, "Will you go steady with me?" Three weeks later the last one said, "Let's be friends."

I was angry at the boy, and I was angry at myself for being naive enough to think true love existed . . . at the age of twelve. But mostly I was angry at my father. It always came down to him.

Nana was the one who made it all better, like always. On the phone, she said, "Hold on to your dreams, Brinlee. Don't ever let go."

Surprised, I said, "That's the problem. I dream too much."

"Dreams, wishes, hope—they all have the power to fill our lives with happiness. They teach us that there's a reason to rejoice. With hope, we may be assured that the ending of the book of our lives will exceed our greatest expectations."

I thought about her simple words.

"You're the only one who can write your love story," she said. "I've been writing mine, and it's better than any fairy tale."

Later That First Day

No longer able to ignore my hunger pains and the call of my full bladder, I woke up.

"Cass, you better have saved me some apple pie," I grumbled as I stretched my tired legs. I would not be a happy camper if I went downstairs and found the pie tin empty. After my crazy dream, I deserved a sugary snack.

I opened my eyes and found I was not lying in my bed at home. I was still in Gabriella's room. *Oh, come on! Seriously?!*

My eyes quickly scanned my surroundings. "It wasn't a dream," I said out loud.

After a light knock at the door, Katie peeked her head inside. "Are you all right, Miss Brinlee?"

No, I am not all right. I am undoubtedly, certifiably going crazy.

She pointed to my clothes. "You didn't change into your shift."

"I fell asleep before I had time to change."

She smiled. "You appeared tired, Miss Brinlee. I hope you rested well."

She approached the bed and put down a bundle of fabric. "Mama washed some new stockings and petticoats for you. We figured you were about the same size as Miss Gabby."

I stood motionless as she laid out each item. *This isn't happening. This isn't happening. This isn't happening.* Maybe if I said it three times and clicked my heels, I could return home. Or did I have to say "There's no place like home" three times? Wait, wrong fairy tale.

"Miss Brinlee?" Katie looked at me as if she had spoken to me and just realized I wasn't listening. "Are you all right?" She placed her hand on my arm.

This can't be happening. Yet here I am . . . still here. But how?

"Katie, right?" I said.

"Yes, miss."

Questions swirled in my mind. "Where am I?"

She frowned. "You're in Miss Gabriella's room."

I shook my head. "That's not what I meant. What is this place?"

"I don't understand you, Miss Brinlee." Katie scrunched her eyebrows. "You arrived here at Sherwood Manor this morning—don't you remember?"

I ran my fingers through my hair and began to pace. *This isn't real,* I reminded myself.

"Miss Brinlee?" Katie said.

I stopped pacing. "Tell me, where am I?"

She took a step backward, a puzzled expression on her face. "You are in Fenmore Falls. You are in Sherwood Manor, the home of Lady Catherine. You are standing in Miss Gabriella's room."

"Look, you have to tell me," I whispered. "Has there been anyone else like me here before?" I pointed to my clothes. "Someone who dresses funny and talks strange?" *Maybe this is a reality TV show like Survivor or something.*

"No," Katie answered.

Guess not.

I leaned closer to her, close enough to see the darkness of her lashes. "Hmm. For a moment I thought you were wearing mascara."

I raised my hand and pinched the side of her arm.

"Ouch," she exclaimed.

Yep, she is real. "Sorry, I was just checking."

As Katie rubbed her arm, the bedroom door opened. Another girl joining my fantasy world said, "Katie, why didn't you tell us our visitor was awake?"

The newcomer gracefully moved across the room, holding the sides of her elegant pink dress. The movement was like water flowing across the floor as it was poured from a crystal cup. The girl's auburn hair swayed with each perfect stride.

"Forgive me for not introducing myself sooner. I'm Rose."

Delighted not only by her grace, but also her gentleness, I happily returned the gesture. "I'm Brinlee."

Rose unexpectedly squeezed my hand. "Welcome to our home, Miss Brinlee. I hope your stay with us is long."

"Thank you."

Is this one of Cinderella's evil stepsisters? Things seemed quite different in this particular story. For example, Cinderella slept in a cloudlike bedroom instead of on the floor next to the fireplace. But hey, I could get used to this version of the story.

"Katie, have you offered our guest some food?" Rose asked. "She must be famished."

"No, miss." Katie gave a slight curtsy. "I'll go and ask Cook."

I grabbed the chambermaid's arm. "Katie has been so kind and helpful since I arrived," I said. "I don't know what I would have done without her." Not ready to be left alone with the stepsister, I kept hold of Katie's arm.

"Wonderful," Rose said. "I hope you are comfortable during your stay here."

Just then, another young woman entered through the open door. Unlike Rose, she pierced the room with exactness and coldness. "Why must we entertain a guest of Cinderella?" she asked loudly. "She is of no consequence to us."

The haughty girl looked maybe a year older than me, but her cruel countenance made her seem older. I realized she was the other stepsister, and she definitely fit my definition of evil stepsister. Her attitude certainly resembled her mother's.

Rose rolled her eyes. "Show some propriety, Fanny. It would do you some good."

Before I thought about it, I snickered at the evil stepsister's name. "You're kidding."

"What are you cackling about?" Fanny glared at me.

I stammered, trying to erase my smile. "Sorry . . . I was just thinking about something."

"She's our guest, Fanny," Rose said. "Mother says she may be of noble relation."

I grinned. Lady Catherine had believed my claim of regal ancestry.

Fanny straightened a bit. "What is your name?"

I curtsied clumsily. "I'm Brinlee."

Fanny's eyes scornfully evaluated my clothes.

All right, I get it. My clothes are strange. The constant inspections were getting old.

With her index finger, Fanny wiped at my sleeve. Then she held her finger up to scrutinize the soot on it. The ashes must have gotten on my arm when I bumped into the fireplace in the kitchen. "Cinder and ashes, just like Cinderella," she said.

I brushed at the side of my arm to remove the black smudges.

"I think I'll call you Ashlee because you're so fond of wearing ashes," Fanny sneered. "It's only appropriate that you have a fitting name, just like Cinderella's."

Anger boiled within me. "Oh, very clever, Fanny," I said. "How about I just tell you to sit on your fanny and keep your mouth shut, Fanny? Two can play at this game."

The girl's mouth clamped shut.

With a rush, I continued, "I know all about you, Miss Fanny Sherwood." I stepped closer. "You're just like all of the evil stepsisters. You're a selfish brat who's used to getting her way and gets her thrills by slamming everyone else down, but inside you're just a lonely and frightened little girl who's afraid of losing everything, just like when your father died and you were penniless."

I exhaled. *Boy, did that feel good.*

Everyone stared at me in shock. All right, maybe I was a little harsh with Fanny, but she deserved it! If I was going to endure this fantasy, I wasn't going to tolerate someone downsizing my self-worth.

"How did you know about our father?" Rose asked softly.

"I've read so much about you and your family," I said.

Fanny scowled. "What do you mean you've read about us?"

"I mean I've heard so much about you. Gabriella told me about you and your family."

Fanny lowered her eyebrows but said nothing.

Rose pointed to my pants. "Is this the fashion where you come from?"

I looked down at my clothes. Compared to the other girls in the room, with their petticoats, stays, and gowns, I looked like a clown. Not to mention the cinder and ashes on my sleeve.

"These are my work clothes. My proper clothes are coming."

"Katie will help you change into something more appropriate," Rose said. "Won't you, Katie?"

"Yes, miss."

Fanny eyeballed me one more time before rushing toward the door and ordering, "Rose, come!"

Rose smiled but quickly followed her older sister.

When they were gone, Katie said, "Nobody has ever put Miss Fanny in her place like that before."

"Was it terrible of me?" I asked.

"No, miss. It was about time," Katie said with a wink.

I smiled. "She seemed pretty shocked."

Katie giggled. "I will never forget the look on her face. Now, let's get you changed so no one else will question your status."

"Thanks for helping me and being so nice to me. I should only be here a couple of days before Gabriella returns." *I hope.*

"Would you like me to assist you in changing?" Katie asked.

I looked at the numerous pieces of clothing on the bed. I had no idea what most of them were or how to put them on. "I would love your help, Katie. Thank you."

But there was something else I needed to do first—use the bathroom. I didn't think I could hold it any longer. "Can I use the bathroom first?"

Katie looked at the white pot under a nearby table. "I'll give you a moment of privacy."

Great. When was indoor plumbing invented?

Katie returned a few minutes later, after I'd done my business.

'Nough said.

She began giving me an eighteeneth-century makeover. Come to find out, there was an exact order and method of getting dressed. And let me tell you, it was no walk in the park. Personally, I was partial to sweatpants and T-shirts—obviously. They were easy. It took me five seconds flat to find a used pair on the floor and throw them on. But this was different. There was more to it than just a pair of pants and shirt.

First, there was a shift, which was the nightgown. Trimmed with lace, it had a drawstring at the neck and one at each elbow. Second, silk stockings were put on the feet, held up with ribbon-like garters tied just above the knees. Katie's socks were knit, not silk. Perhaps the difference indicated a step in social ranking. Next, was the corset. I knew that corsets—or stays, as they were sometimes called—were mainly used to support the body and remind one of good posture, but all I could think about was the horror stories of women who cinched their waists so tight that their uteruses started to fall out.

Truly! I read about it in a book.

Eventually people got smart and realized that God made women's bodies the way they were for a reason. So, thankfully corsets became extinct. But for now, they were shouting at me loud and clear as Katie tightened one around my waist. Without the series of yet-to-be-invented hooks on the back of the corset, Katie had to lace up the back, and it took quite a while.

No wonder everyone had a chambermaid back then. It would be almost impossible to dress yourself!

For a long time I just stood there, wondering what all the fuss was about. But when the corset began to close around my figure, things started to happen. I became aware of the sturdy fabric surrounding me on all sides. The tough bones pressed into my skin and held me stiff.

I gasped.

"Is it too tight?" Katie asked.

"A little." *It just feels like I'm going to suffocate, that's all.*

Katie finished the laces while I concentrated on my breathing. It wasn't so bad if I held still. And never moved. Not ever again.

The one good thing about the corset was its equivalent to the modern Miracle Bra. It was a tummy tucker, spine corrector, and push-up bra—all in one.

Take that, Victoria's Secret!

Katie walked to the nearest wardrobe and soon returned, holding a pair of shoes. Each was fastened with a buckle and slightly elevated by a heel. "I hope these are your size."

I sat awkwardly on the bed and tried to bend down to slip on the shoes. The corset allowed me to move maybe two inches. *Yeah, that's not going to work.*

Katie cleared her throat. "Miss Brinlee, let me help you."

Clearly, I had to accept. But I wasn't accustomed to having someone serve me, so I felt a bit uncomfortable watching Katie put my shoes on my feet.

After she fastened the second shoe, I stood and found the sturdy footwear quite comfortable.

Katie placed a wrap with a little pocket around my waist. "Here is where you will store your knitting items," she said

Sure, I knit—not.

Then, glory to all, Katie showed me my dress. It was a soft, beautiful green gown with a full skirt and elbow-length sleeves. But before I could put on the dress, there were the petticoats. Two. Since the dress had an open front, it needed one petticoat to fill the gap and another underneath to puff up the skirt. A stomacher, a triangle-shaped piece of fabric, held the front of the dress together with laces.

You'd think I'd be done by now, but Katie was still pulling things out of closets and drawers. She told me there was another hoop petticoat that women of gentry wore on special occasions or when visiting town. She set one out for me in case I needed it later.

Another petticoat? Were these people crazy? I know, let's make women's lives even more uncomfortable and make them walk with not only two fluffy petticoats but three—that'd be fun. Oh, and let's make one of them hooped. *Brilliant!*

Katie put a white neckerchief around the collar of my dress and an apron around my waist. But when she offered me a cap, I said, "Do not put that on my head. Can I just leave my hair down?" *A girl's got to draw the line somewhere.*

"The cap will protect your hair from dust and dirt," Katie said.

"That's all right. I'll take my chances with the dust and dirt."

"Very well, but you'll need your cap and hat when you leave the house. I'll set one on your bed."

When I was finally dressed, I dared to look at myself in the mirror. What I saw took my breath away. For once in my life, I felt fabulous, even magnificent. I was staring at the fulfillment of my longtime wish to be somebody else.

"Miss Gabriella made the dress herself," Katie said from behind me, peeking over my shoulder at my reflection.

"It's beautiful."

It really was amazing. I felt like a princess. One day in this place wouldn't be so bad. *Would it?*

I moved my tongue around my chalky mouth. "I need to clean my teeth. Is that possible?"

"Of course. The instruments are right over there." Katie motioned toward the table by the chamber pot. "There's a fresh block of chalk, along with birch twigs and salt."

"Thank you." *Wait—what did she say?*

"I'll let you finish." Katie turned to leave. "When you're ready, I'll show you to the kitchen so you can get some food."

"Thank you, Katie."

When she left, I walked over to the table and looked at the dental hygiene supplies. I placed some salt and chalk on a birch twig and began to brush. *Somebody's got to teach these people some modern tricks,* I thought. Maybe I could invent toothpaste in this world and become rich. Or become the new Mark Zuckerberg.

But first I needed to learn how to breathe in this corset. Then I'd think about ruling the social-media world.

Chapter 5

Another Cause of My Cinderella Obsession— The Soundtrack to *The Slipper and the Rose*

Suddenly, suddenly it happens and the dream comes true
Wonderfully, beautifully it happens and your world is new
Magically, you're holding the golden prize
Mystically, your castles begin to rise.
("Suddenly It Happens," Image Entertainment [Chatfield, CA: 1976])

The Next Day

When I woke the next morning in Cinderella's room in Sherwood Manor, it took only a few seconds to realize where I was. I decided to pretend this experience was an episode of the *Twilight Zone*—a plot with no explanation and just an experience to watch and enjoy.

Last night, after I ate dinner in the kitchen and banged on the mystery door a couple more times, Rose (the nice stepsister) found me and invited me to accompany Fanny and her to town today. Rose clapped her hands and said, "It will be so much fun. We'll visit the milliner's shop for new gowns for the ball."

I grinned at her animation. "That sounds wonderful." Which was the truth. I was excited to see a real dressmaker's shop, as well as the kingdom of Fenmore Falls. Anticipating the forthcoming ball wouldn't be so bad either.

Katie helped me prepare by following the same long ritual as the day before, but this time dressing me in a purple gown. She gave me a hat decorated with flowers to wear over my cap, and a purple fan that matched the dress. Since I was visiting town, I had to wear the third petticoat—and feel completely like an idiot, with my dress swinging like a bell.

After a light breakfast in the dining room, I followed Rose and Fanny to our transportation at the front of the house. My eyes went wide as I climbed into an honest-to-goodness, prehistoric, horse-drawn carriage.

Even though I understood the evolution of the vehicle, I was still surprised at the discomfort and slow pace of eighteenth-century transportation. This trip was going to take forever. In a car we could probably get to town in ten minutes via the freeway, but in this carriage it was going to take a couple of hours on uneven and rutted roads.

Imitating Fanny and Rose, I crossed my ankles and placed my hands in my lap. After a while, numbness crept into my butt cheeks. The carriage was squeaky and smelly, to boot, and even though it was a covered coach, the sides were open and exposed to the environment. Meaning, dirt and dust. I was grateful Katie had demanded I wear a cap and hat to protect my hair.

To distract myself from the uncomfortable ride, I looked at the beautiful countryside as we passed. This time, since I was not running in my purple slippers, I could enjoy Fenmore Falls' scenery. Sherwood Manor was surrounded by green, rolling hills, framed by an outlying forest. The carriage continued along the road until we passed the pond I'd seen the day before. Soon, we entered the depths of the forest. With my view obstructed by the thick trees, I listened to the birds.

Gabriella's stepsisters and I spoke only a few times during the journey. After what seemed like five hours but was probably only twenty minutes, the carriage halted.

Rose leaned over her sister to peek out the window. "Why are we stopping?"

"Probably an animal on the road," Fanny answered.

When nothing happened for a few more minutes, I peeked out the window to see for myself. I didn't see an animal. But I did see something . . . uh, someone.

Crap! It was Black Rider, the beautiful, brown-eyed bandit from the day before. And oh, did he look even more handsome today.

Crap! I thought again.

Brinlee, get a grip.

I pulled my head into the carriage so he wouldn't see me. He was talking to the driver of our carriage. What did he want? *Oh please, oh please, I hope he's just asking for directions and not stealing from the rich to give to the poor.*

"What's going on out there?" Rose asked me.

"Someone's talking to the driver."

"Who is it?"

"I don't know." I couldn't let on that I knew Black Rider. There could be a ransom out for his arrest, or something like that.

Fanny huffed. "We don't have time for this." She scooted to the window and peered out. "Henry, move on," she ordered the driver.

Black Rider approached the carriage and said, "Milady."

I ducked my head and played with a ruffle of my dress. I could not, would not, make eye contact with him. If he didn't recognize me, the stepsisters would never know he and I had met.

"Please pardon me for delaying your journey," he said. As he came nearer, he must've seen Rose and me, because he added, "Ladies, what a treat to greet all of you on this road this morning."

Fanny spoke up. "Please, let us pass."

"I would love nothing more than to let you fine ladies pass, but I'm afraid that is not possible at the moment."

"Why?" Fanny exclaimed. "Let us pass!" At her shout, three more men slithered from the forest like snakes to surround our carriage.

This is bad, this is really bad.

"What is the meaning of this?" she asked.

I could feel Black Rider's eyes on me as he poked his head inside our carriage. "You will be on your way as soon as we take care of a small matter of business with your driver."

"What need do you have with our driver?" she asked.

Black Rider did not answer. Was he waiting for me to look at him?

Don't look up, don't look up, I told myself. I continued to focus on the stitching of my dress, as if it was the most astonishing thing in the world.

"Are you the ladies from Sherwood Manor?" Black Rider asked suddenly.

Crap! Double crap! He knew. The only way he would've been able to identify three random females on a well-populated road was if he recognized me.

"Yes, we are," Fanny replied. "And you should know that your action will not be tolerated. My mother will have you reported."

His laugh was low and alluring. "I'm sure she will."

He was quiet again, waiting. Why wouldn't he just leave?

"How much longer will we be detained?" Fanny asked.

"Not much longer." He stepped away from the carriage, walked to the front of the carriage, and spoke to the driver.

"This is criminal," Fanny complained.

Rose finally spoke. "What are we going to do?"

"If we get out of this—" Fanny was interrupted by a cry from Rose. *"When* we get out of this," Fanny continued, "it has to be reported. I don't care what Black Rider has done or says he's done, he does not frighten me. This is unlawful—holding women hostage like savages."

I was curious. "What has Black Rider done?"

"Nothing any other bandit hasn't done," Fanny said.

My mind reeled. What kind of criminal was Black Rider? What if he really was the bad kind? But didn't he save me from that awful chubby man named Isaac and deliver me back to Sherwood Manor? But what if he had an ulterior motive? What if he was visiting Sherwood Manor to visit one of his associates? What if one of the employees at Sherwood Manor worked for him and was hoarding valuables? What if . . .?

I looked out the window—just barely, out of the corner of my eye. Black Rider stared right back and winked.

This time when I cursed in my mind, it wasn't the nice word.

He came back to the window. "I need one of you ladies to step out of the carriage with me for a moment."

Fanny gasped. "We will do no such thing."

"I am only in need of a witness," he explained. "Someone impartial to the situation at hand."

Fanny folded her arms to show her defiance. Rose just squirmed in her place.

"You." Even with my eyes cast down, I knew Black Rider was talking to me. "Come with me," he ordered.

Did I have a choice? I looked at Fanny for guidance. Obviously not caring about my fate, she shrugged her shoulders.

"Please come," Black Rider said. "We will only be a moment."

I looked at him at last, which I knew would be a mistake. With the top of his face still masked by a black cloth, his eyes smiled at me with such intensity that it was hard to breathe, let alone get out of the carriage.

Once I was out, he grabbed my elbow and moved me toward the front of the carriage. "You are looking well, Miss Brinlee."

He remembered my name, I gushed silently. *Wait, Brinlee, he's the bad guy. Don't lose focus.* "Thank you," I muttered.

"You look much different than you did the last time we met," he teased. "You didn't have to clean up just for me."

And there it was—the male-chauvinist-pig attitude. Did it exist in every era? Did it ever *not* exist?

When we neared the front of the carriage, Black Rider did not stop to continue his talk with the driver but led me toward the trees.

"Where are you taking me?" I began to feel frightened.

"Just far enough so we can be private."

Far enough so no one can see you kill me?

"Here." He stopped behind a large tree. "This will have to do."

I looked around nervously. There wasn't a large enough clearing to dig a grave, so maybe he wasn't planning on killing me. Yet.

"Miss Brinlee, what do you know about Sherwood Manor?"

"What do you mean?"

"You told me you were a guest. Are you a frequent guest? Are you well acquainted with the household?"

"I don't understand. I thought you said you needed me to be a witness or something."

"Well, no. I just needed a reason to question you alone without anyone growing suspicious."

"Is there reason to be suspicious of Sherwood Manor?" I asked.

He ran his fingers through his hair. "No . . . I don't know. There's just a tangled mess of men and deceit that's leading to the corruption of the kingdom. More than we had originally guessed."

"You mean like that guy you were chasing yesterday."

Black Rider nodded. "We're locating more connections every day."

I thought about this. "So, you're just questioning our driver to see if he knows anything?"

"Yes."

"Does he?"

"He says he doesn't."

"Well, I haven't been at Sherwood Manor long enough to know anything, so I won't be much help either." I was sure Lady Catherine had some evil plan up her sleeve—I just didn't know what yet.

"You've already helped me." Black Rider grinned, tucking a stray strand of hair behind my ear. "You've let me enjoy myself by gazing upon your great beauty."

I rolled my eyes. *Really? That's his pickup line?* "All right, fun's over. Take me back to my carriage."

He laughed. "See? You always make me smile."

I turned and began to walk toward the carriage. I would never get used to someone else laughing at my expense.

"Wait," he said as he joined me. "Please don't take offense."

"I didn't," I mumbled.

"I was only enjoying the moment."

"I'm glad you enjoyed it."

"You are angry."

"Just annoyed."

"Please forgive me," he said softly.

We walked the rest of the way in silence. I shrugged his arm off as he grabbed for my elbow. When I stepped into the carriage, I still did not give him the satisfaction of my attention.

"We are done, miladies," he said to all of us. "Please have a safe journey."

Neither Fanny nor Rose responded. And of course, neither did I. My mind already had me in enough trouble. How could I even be slightly attracted to that man? And then let him flirt with me like I was some hussy? Who did he think I was?

"Thank you for your time, Miss Brinlee," he dared say to me.

I glared in his direction. His soft expression almost had me fooled, but I knew better. I continued my hard stare until our carriage began to move and I no longer had to look at his beautiful face.

"What did he want?" Rose whispered to me.

"I don't know." I exhaled, finally relaxing now that he was out of my sight.

"Was he completely awful?" she asked.

"Completely." *Completely breathtaking.*

Chapter 6

A Memory of My Father: Dancing in the Kitchen

My few memories of my father were foggy and sketchy, and not all of them made sense. Sometimes I'd be alone, and sometimes my sister would be there too. Sometimes there was another girl. Why would there be a third child in my memory?

In this memory, I was twirling in the kitchen, holding onto my father's finger while he spun me around. My mother was there, laughing and smiling. I was laughing and smiling too. And then my father held my hands and had me step on his feet while we danced across the floor. He called me his princess.

I think my fixation with being a princess began much earlier than I'd remembered. I think it started because of my father.

I never realized it until now.

The Kingdom of Fenmore Falls

As our carriage rounded a bend, Fenmore Falls' castle finally came into view. On top of a hill, the white stone palace stretched tall into the sky. The arched windows sparkled, making the place look magical, just like in the stories.

"Only in a fairy tale," I breathed.

"What did you say, Miss Brinlee?" Fanny asked.

"Oh, I was just admiring the castle."

"What do you think of our kingdom's palace?" she questioned.

"It's incredible. I've never seen anything like it."

"What have you heard of our royal family?"

"Only that your prince has just returned from a trip overseas." I didn't tell them what I knew of the prince's ship being captured by pirates, since Katie had advised me to keep quiet on the rumor.

"The prince's ship was captured by pirates," Rose explained.

I raised my eyebrows in feigned surprise. "What happened?"

"Prince Patrick Channing was injured in the attack."

Ahhh, Patrick Channing. What a wonderful name for a prince.

"But thankfully he was able to escape and return home to Fenmore Falls," Rose added.

"Thankfully," I agreed.

Seeming annoyed with the chitchat, Fanny said, "There is no fact in the gossip, Rose, and you know it."

"Just think of it." Rose dreamily sighed. "Our prince fighting against ruthless pirates."

I smiled at her dramatics.

"Honestly, Rose," Fanny snarled.

"In celebration of the prince's safe return, Fenmore Falls is having three balls," Rose said happily.

"Three?"

She nodded. "There will be a dance at the castle in the evening of each Friday for three weeks."

I reflected on the different Cinderella stories. Some versions spoke of three balls, giving the prince three chances to see Cinderella.

"Can anyone attend the balls?" I asked.

Fanny snickered. "Anyone who is suitable may attend."

I frowned. "What does that mean?"

"Anyone who can present himself or herself as civilized may attend any event held at the castle," Fanny answered.

"Any event?"

"Yes. There should be stricter guidelines, if you ask me."

"So, the only requirement is to look and play the part of a gentlewoman?" I asked.

"As long as they wear a mask, since it's a masquerade."

How interesting—a masquerade. This meant that all citizens, including servants, were invited to the ball if the conditions were met.

"They say the balls will serve two purposes," Rose put in. "In addition to celebrating Prince Patrick's return, the balls were planned for his betrothal announcement. He has been asked to marry for peace among the citizens of our neighboring country, but he has until the third ball to select a bride of his own choosing, if he wants."

"And then he'll choose Gabriella." I didn't realize I was saying my thought out loud until it came out of my mouth.

Fanny laughed boisterously. "How foolish would that be? Cinderella marry the prince?"

Rose looked confused, but she smiled.

I summoned my greatest strength to keep my mouth shut and not lash out at Fanny. There would be a time and a place to challenge her, and now was not the time. I would have to pick my battles carefully in this strange world.

Fanny chuckled. "And yet Cinderella is not here, is she? Even if she qualified to come to the ball, she's not even here to fulfill your prediction, Miss Brinlee."

My chest ached at the truth in Fanny's words. Without the real Cinderella, what would happen to the story? Realizing what Gabriella's absence meant to the most loved fairy tale in history, I foresaw catastrophe.

This is getting way too complicated, I thought. I needed to find a way home and bring Gabriella back—and now.

Our carriage reached the heart of town, and my gloom disappeared as I looked at the buildings and walkways. People stopped to see who was arriving in such a fine vehicle. I mimicked the stepsisters' reactions and faintly grinned and nodded at our brief superstar status.

As we rode along on the street, I was fully immersed in the mode and fashion of this outdated world. For example, men tipped their three-cornered hats or lifted their walking sticks as a gesture of greeting. Most of the high-class women wore full, hooped skirts and were accompanied by a helper who carried their supplies.

Little girls and boys wore white dresses with sashes at their waists. Boys over about three years of age wore suits with long trousers rather than knee breeches, a fashion visibly not in favor with adult men. This transition from skirts to pants seemed to be a step toward becoming a "little man."

A toddler caught my eye as he ran across the road with a padded cap on his head. "What is that little boy wearing on his head?" I asked Rose.

"Have you never seen a pudding cap, Miss Brinlee?" she asked.

I shook my head. "No, I have not."

"It protects a child's head if he or she falls," she explained.

Interesting, I thought. The pudding cap was an early version of the crash helmet.

I watched a woman striding slowly along the walk near the merchant store. Two servant girls followed closely behind, one carrying packages and the other restraining a lively youngster by strings attached to the shoulders of the child's garment.

I was unable to restrain my laughter as I watched the small child pull the servant girl forward until she bumped forcefully into the high-class woman in front.

"Honestly, Miss Brinlee," Fanny chastised me. "Do not laugh so loudly in a public area."

"Sorry." I covered my smile.

"When in company, do not put your hands to any part of the body," Fanny added.

Seriously?! I sat carefully with my hands in my lap, trying to look the part of the perfect gentlewoman. I did not drum my fingers or cough, sneeze, sigh, or yawn. I did not roll my eyes or puff up my cheeks, because when I did, Fanny said it made me look like a fish. All in all, I tried to conform to the silly rules of etiquette in their society.

The driver drove our carriage along the street, passing many unmarked buildings. I desperately wanted to ask what everything was, but I didn't want Fanny to yell at me again. So I kept my questions to myself.

Thankfully, Rose began guiding the tour. "That is Williamburn's Tavern." She pointed to a redbrick structure. "Most gatherings of Fenmore Falls, besides the events at the castle, are held there."

"Are you going to dictate our entire trip?" Fanny asked.

"Miss Brinlee is new to Fenmore Falls, Fanny."

Fanny straightened in her seat and turned her head away, clearly provoked.

Rose continued, ignoring Fanny. "Across the street is Malee Tavern." I followed her gaze to see a white building made of wood. "And that is Wilson's coffeehouse down the street." Again, I followed her lead and looked beyond the immediate shops to another white building, this one smaller than the first.

I listened intently as Rose told me about the rest of the buildings in Fenmore Falls. She pointed out a wheelwright building, a weaver shop, and a cooper store. There was a courthouse, a parish church, and even some shops for professions I recognized—a silversmith, tailor, shoemaker, wig maker, gunsmith, and brick maker.

I even saw the armory magazine—the one with the missing key that Black Rider traded for. Rose gave an account of how the king had the house built of brick to protect the kingdom's arms and munitions. The magazine was next to a public gaol, a type of prison. And a tall octagonal tower was erected to safeguard shot, powder, flints, tents, tools, swords, pikes, and flintlocks. The buildings were clean and the kingdom was lovely, but nothing compared to the castle that shined like a beacon on the hill. From every place in the city, it was visible, a magnificent reminder of the city's strength.

"So the royal name is Channing?" I asked. I liked how similar it sounded to "charming"—like Prince Charming.

"Yes," Rose answered. "'Chan' means 'snow,' so Fenmore Falls royal symbol is a snowflake."

"Never mind the Channing, bring on the Charming," I quietly uttered.

"Hmm?" Rose said.

Oops. "Just thinking out loud—terrible habit."

So, Channing was the surname of Fenmore Falls' prince. If the prince was anything like the Prince Charming in my Cinderella books, I couldn't wait to meet him.

We finally pulled up to our destination—the milliner's shop. My legs ached from the long ride, and I was grateful to exit the coach. As we entered the shop I instantly felt the humming of the crowded space. Happy chatter from a roomful of women, all with the same motive of ordering a new dress for the ball, sounded through the small room.

"Don't these peasants have anything better to do?" Fanny griped before heading to the counter.

Three workers were hard at work, each taking orders, measuring customers, and stitching dresses. Fanny walked right up to one of them—an older, plump woman who was sewing, with two needles held in between her teeth—and said, "Miss Margaret, we are here to select new fabric."

The woman pulled the thread through her last stitch and slowly removed the needles from her mouth. "All of Fenmore Falls is requesting new fabric for the ball, Miss Fanny," she said, still looking downward.

"Yes, but does all of Fenmore Falls have the wealth of my family?" Fanny challenged.

Miss Margaret's eyes fluttered upward. "No, not everyone."

"Precisely. Now, we would like to see your newest fabric."

"Our newest material is what you see on the shelves."

Fanny marched over and began to rummage through the fabrics on the shelves. She shoved a couple of girls along the way. *Watch out, future Bridezilla in the making.*

Meanwhile, I walked alone and looked at the rest of the shop. It looked like the milliner sewed and sold not only gowns but also masquerade dresses, cloaks, mantles, hats, hoods, caps, gloves, petticoats, hoops, and riding costumes. Jewelry, hosiery, shoes, and other accessories were offered as well. The displays were stunning.

"I am disappointed in your selection, Miss Margaret," I heard Fanny say to the worker. "Don't you have anything else?"

The woman shook her head. "Our last shipment was delivered two days ago. The next isn't due for another week."

Fanny rummaged through the pile she had made on the counter. She tugged on a green piece of cloth. "This one will have to do."

"Fine choice, Miss Fanny." Miss Margaret took the soft fabric from Fanny, along with a light blue textile chosen by Rose. "I'll get started on these right away."

From studying the Cinderella story, I knew fabric was the largest cost for a dressmaker. For that reason, fabric was not sold to customers. Instead, the dressmaker cut, fit, and sewed the dress in the store.

"The gowns will be ready by Thursday," Miss Margaret said.

"That will be fine," Fanny replied. "We'll return on Thursday morning for the fitting."

"What about you, miss?"

I didn't realize Miss Margaret was speaking to me until Fanny answered, "Miss Brinlee will not need your services today. She is not a citizen of Fenmore Falls."

"Thank you anyway, Miss Margaret. Your work is amazing," I said.

"You're welcome, Miss Brinlee."

I nodded and moved to follow Fanny and Rose out the door. But suddenly I felt a hand at my elbow. Miss Margaret was at my side. "You're not like them."

"Excuse me?"

Wait, does she know something?

"You're different—in a good way." She leaned closer and whispered, "People like them don't show appreciation like you."

"Um, thank you." How sad that it was unusual for people to thank others for their hard work.

"Don't conform to their standards," she said.

"I won't."

She patted my arm. "Good."

"Hurry, Miss Brinlee," Fanny said from outside the door. "Our carriage is waiting."

"Thank you again, Miss Margaret. Your work really is amazing," I said.

The old lady gave me a warm smile as I left.

I met Fanny and Rose outside. They stood talking to a girl who looked like her corset was a few inches too tight.

"Miss Fanny, Miss Rose, what brings you to town?" the girl asked.

"Miss Gretchen, I'm so glad to see you." Fanny smiled, but I knew she was faking it.

The blond beauty half smiled and then looked at me. "Who is this?"

"This is Cinderella's friend, Miss Ashlee . . . I mean Brinlee." Fanny snickered.

Oh, Fanny, you're hilarious.

She and her equally evil friend Gretchen shared a quiet laugh.

"Well, Fanny," I began, "I'd choose my nickname any day over yours rather than having to constantly be reminded that my name was the *butt* end of a joke."

Immediately the chuckling stopped, and Fanny's face turned red with embarrassment and anger.

I curtsied in her friend's direction. "It was nice to meet you, Miss Gretchen." With that, I turned and climbed into our carriage.

Rose followed, and then Fanny. Suffice it to say, we rode back to Sherwood Manor in silence. Every bump and jolt of the journey in silence. It was a long two hours.

Where was Black Rider to break up the monotony when you needed him?

Chapter 7

Cinderella, or *The Little Glass Slipper*
France, 1889

Once there was a gentleman who married, for his second wife, the proudest and most haughty woman that was ever seen. She had, by a former husband, two daughters of her own, who were, indeed, exactly like her in all things. He had likewise, by another wife, a young daughter, but of unparalleled goodness and sweetness of temper, which she took from her mother, who was the best creature in the world.

No sooner were the ceremonies of the wedding over but the stepmother began to show herself in her true colors. She could not bear the good qualities of this pretty girl, and the less because they made her own daughters appear the more odious. She employed her in the meanest work of the house. She scoured the dishes, tables, etc., and cleaned madam's chamber, and those of misses, her daughters. She slept in a sorry garret, on a wretched straw bed, while her sisters slept in fine rooms, with floors all inlaid, on beds of the very newest fashion, and where they had looking glasses so large that they could see themselves at their full length from head to foot.

Day 3

The next morning, pain shot like fire from my back to my neck. Every time I moved, I was reminded of the carriage ride the day before.

"Good morning, Miss Brinlee," Katie said as she entered my room.

I lay motionless on the bed, afraid to move my sore limbs.

"Did you sleep well?"

"Yes, I'm just a little sore."

"Nothing that a warm bath won't fix."

Mmm, that sounds nice.

Servants brought in a tub and pails of warm water for my bath. I washed the grime from my hair and soaked until the water got cold. After Katie helped me dress, I realized my tired muscles did feel better. And when she tightened my corset, it helped support my stiff body and prevented me from moving too much.

"Was the castle beautiful?" she asked dreamily as she brushed through my damp hair.

"Have you never seen the castle?" When I returned from my trip the night before, and all morning, I'd talked on and on about the beauty of the castle, but I'd never paused to wonder if Katie had been there.

"No, I have never left Sherwood Manor."

Sad, just sad, I thought. Even I, from my little town in Idaho, had traveled the great distance of the United States because of my mom's career. How would it be to only know your home and nowhere else?

"I can only imagine how it would be to dance in the palace," Katie said.

"Why don't you go?"

"It would be impossible."

"Anybody who is able can go to the ball."

"'Able' is the key word," Katie said. "I do not have a dress, and I do not have a way to get to the ball. Therefore, I am not *able* to go."

I'll just have to do something about that, I thought, recognizing my first mission in this strange fairy-tale land. Call me her fairy godmother, but I was going to make sure Katie went to the ball.

A tall woman met us as we entered the dining room for breakfast. With beady eyes, she looked down her pointy nose and asked, "Is this Miss Brinlee?"

"Yes," Katie said.

The woman folded her bony arms across her chest. Her gray-streaked dark hair was tightly pulled into a bun under her cap. "The food has already been returned to the kitchen."

"That's all right," I said, "I'm not hungry."

"Nonsense," Katie replied. "You haven't eaten since your arrival home yesterday afternoon."

The tall woman kept her firm posture but said, "Katie, you may take Miss Brinlee to the kitchen and see if there is anything left to eat."

"Thank you," both Katie and I said as the older lady strode off.

"That's Miss Brenda, the headwoman," Katie explained. "She's been here longer than anyone else. She's actually a very kind woman, but she doesn't like people to notice."

"I have a lot to learn about this place," I said.

Katie linked her arm through mine. "Don't worry, I'll teach you everything you need to know."

As we entered the kitchen, my gaze fell on the magical door where I'd entered this place. It looked like nothing more than a decorative design on the wall. In fact, it almost blended in completely. I had done everything I could think of to open the door. Besides endlessly banging my fists on it, I had also tried to pry it open with the fireplace poker. Strangely, there was no seam around the door—not even a crack to show where it opened. Besides the doorknob, there was nothing to prove it was a door—nothing but my being here.

"Would you like me to warm up the food for you, Miss Brinlee?" Katie asked.

Motivated by my roaring stomach, I sat on a wooden chair to look at the breakfast leftovers on the table. There was a plate of round biscuits, each about two inches in diameter. "What are these?"

"Have you never had pancake puffs?"

Uh, no. You see, I live on a little planet where we have fast-food restaurants that cook frozen pancakes in magic microwaves. I shook my head at Katie.

"The lack of your understanding amazes me, Miss Brinlee. Pancake puffs are like a pancake but more light and fluffy, similar to a popover. Hence the name pancake puffs. A more proper term would be æbleskivers."

I picked up one of the puffs. "Are they hard to make?"

"Not really, once you get the hang of it. They're cooked in special copper pans with hammered indentations in the bottom."

I bit into the puff. "Not bad." I ate three more before I said, "I'd love to meet your mother and sister."

Katie's face lit up. "My mother is going to love you. She is the kindest woman you will ever meet." Katie grabbed both of my hands. "You will love her, Miss Brinlee."

"I'm sure I will." If Katie's mother was anything like her daughter, I was guaranteed to love her.

"And my sister, Amanda, has been so anxious to meet you." Katie looked over her shoulder in the direction of the hallway. "She's around here somewhere—probably dusting the entrance room."

"How many people live in Sherwood Manor?"

"Besides Lady Sherwood and her two daughters, three servants live within the walls of the manor—Henry, the coachman, and Miss Brenda, whom you met this morning, and William, the headman."

"You don't live here?"

"No, I live with my sister and mother in a cottage behind the garden. A few others, the groundskeepers and stablemen, dwell in the cottages near the stables."

When I finished eating, I helped Katie wash the dishes, ignoring her insistence that it was below my station.

After we were done, she asked me, "What would you like me to show you first—the locked and haunted rooms of Sherwood Manor, or the sanctuary of the gardens?"

"The gardens—definitely the gardens."

My newfound friend grabbed my hand and led me outside to the lush green garden. We wandered along a stone path that bordered a small herb patch, where I smelled basil, rosemary, sage, and thyme. I was surprised to see the herbs blooming just as beautifully as the flowers nearby.

I heard squawking and noticed chickens roaming freely just beyond the small path. A dog circled the chickens.

"Miss Brinlee, meet Fred, our hen dog," Katie said. "He thinks his job is to keep watch over the chickens."

I watched the playful dog trying to herd the hens, like a sheep dog with its lambs. Katie slid her hand to the side of her mouth and whispered, "I think he takes joy in taking charge of an animal smaller than himself."

I giggled, enjoying Katie's companionship. I knew from the first moment I met her that we would be fast friends. She was almost like a sister. At that, I remembered my sister and stopped in my tracks. *What am I doing here?*

In that moment the dog, Fred, bounded over, jumped up, and put his paws on my skirts.

"Wow, he likes you," Katie said. "He's never that friendly with strangers."

"He must recognize the smell of Gabriella's clothes."

"Even so, he doesn't seem the list bit concerned that you're a visitor, Miss Brinlee."

I squatted near the dog to scratch behind his ears. As he nuzzled my hand, my heart instantly warmed toward the small, shaggy gray mutt. He licked my hand, making me laugh.

"Katie, there you are," said an unfamiliar voice.

I stood up and was presented with a slightly shorter version of Katie. "I've been looking everywhere for you," she said.

"Amanda, this is Miss Gabby's friend, Miss Brinlee," Katie said.

Amanda curtsied. "I'm pleased to meet you, Miss Brinlee."

I curtsied in return. The gesture seemed easier than it had when I wore sweats and a T-shirt. "I'm pleased to meet you too."

"I was showing Miss Brinlee the gardens," Katie explained. "Do you want to join us?"

Amanda planted herself on my other side, sandwiching me between the two sisters. "Where shall we go first?"

Fred pawed at my leg. I waved my hand toward him, hoping he would go back to his chickens.

Amanda laughed. "It looks like Fred has found a new friend."

"That's what I said," Katie put in.

I giggled at the dog. "He's a cute little guy."

Amanda said, "Just wait until he's begging you for food under the servant's table."

"Miss Gabriella was Fred's favorite, since she was the only one who would satisfy his begging," Katie added.

With Fred at our feet, we continued along the path. As we chatted, I realized Amanda was like her sister in every wonderful way. She was two years younger than Katie, just as my sister and I were two years apart.

"Good morning, ladies," a handsome boy said as he walked out of the stable, leading a young horse. His eyes focused on Katie, and she instantly blushed. A smile crept across her face as she shyly lowered her gaze to the ground.

When Katie wouldn't answer and Amanda simply giggled, I decided it was up to me to address the young man. "Good morning."

The stable boy tipped his hat on his wavy brown hair and grinned, showing the whitest of smiles against his tan skin. It was no wonder Katie had acted so shy—this boy was handsome.

I didn't know what else to say, and with Katie and Amanda mute, he placed his hat back on his head and continued on his way, the horse following.

"K, who was that?" I asked as I gawked alongside the open-mouthed sisters.

Amanda recovered her voice. "That's Krys. He was hired a year ago. Katie has never had the courage to say even a word to him."

"Hush now, Amanda, or he'll hear you," Katie whispered.

"Maybe he should hear me. Then you can stop whining to me about how cute he is and how you wish you could talk to him."

"Hush, Amanda," Katie pleaded.

I smiled, not at Katie's discomfort but because I had just witnessed what might be the beginning of her storybook romance.

"Let's go this way." Katie pulled my hand in the direction opposite from where Krys had gone.

Amanda, Katie, and I cut through some bushes and walked away from Sherwood Manor until we were on the gravel path on the edge of the property. Through the trees of the forest that bordered the path, I saw a cliff, probably less than a hundred yards away. Rolling hillsides mingled with mountains of stone, and I stood for a moment, inhaling the beauty of the earth and the freshness of the air.

Scattered about were the colors of early summer. Lavender grew on either side of the path, and daylilies and hollyhocks flanked the green shrubs along the short stone walls. Before me was one of the most beautiful displays of nature I had ever seen, courtesy of the skilled groundskeepers of Sherwood Manor.

As I turned to look at the manor itself, the sun caught the glass of a large window, and I had the eerie impression I was being watched. I shuddered.

Sherwood Manor was built in an L-shape, with a three-story main portion, and a four-story tower on the other side. We continued our tour of the property, and I forced myself to look away from the ominous building.

"This place is amazing," I said.

"Is it different than where you are from?" Katie asked.

"There is beauty where I come from, but not like this. This place is a masterpiece." *It's almost not real.*

"Come. If you love it out here, you'll love it inside."

We entered the manor through the front entrance and stepped into an enormous, long hall. My jaw dropped as I took in the expanse of the room. I was simply awestruck. Beautifully carved beams stretched across the ceiling, and a stage filled one end of the hall. Every sound resonated through the space in the open room. My shoes clinked and echoed against the stone floor. Even my breath seemed louder.

I heard footsteps from the opposite side of the room, and my heart paused as I saw William—Ponytail Man—walk toward us. His gaze seemed to hold me motionless.

"What is the meaning of this?" he fairly shouted.

"We only meant to introduce Miss Brinlee to Sherwood Manor, Sir William," Katie said.

Turning from his stare, I glanced toward the stage at the far end of the room. "Katie and Amanda were nice enough to show me around as I had asked."

William let out a puff of air. I dared look at him again and was surprised by his softened expression. As the corner of his mouth lifted into a smile, my heart nearly stopped. His strikingly handsome face with its square jaw was bewitching.

"Welcome to Sherwood Manor, Miss Brinlee," he said calmly.

I was unable to resist. In the entrance hall of Sherwood Manor in a faraway land, I smiled at Ponytail Man—a very fine male specimen of the late eighteenth-century.

As William continued to stare, I nervously cleared my throat. "Thank you . . . Sir William, was it?"

"I'm afraid we have not been properly introduced." He offered his hand. "I am William, the headman of Sherwood Manor."

He kissed the back of my hand. For reasons I couldn't identify, I was unnerved by him. Nevertheless, I dipped into a slight curtsy with all the grace I could muster.

"I apologize for my rudeness at our first encounter, Miss Brinlee." He finally let go of my hand. "I did not know who you were, and your clothes gave me no indication."

That makes two of us who were confused. "That's all right."

"Well, I must take my leave now." William bowed his head. "I hope you enjoy your stay here, and please let me know if I can be of any assistance." Then he turned and exited the room as promptly as he had entered.

"He fancies you, Miss Brinlee," Amanda whispered.

"You've already won the affection of two men—Sir William and Fred," Katie teased.

"How will I ever choose?" I sighed. "Do I pick Fred, who will love me as long as I give him food scraps, or the beautiful headman who breathes fire when he speaks?"

I joined the sisters in their giggling, happy to have friends to help me endure this crazy place.

As we continued our tour of the manor, my mind kept coming back to Sir William and my eerie feelings about him. It was obvious he was hiding something, and I didn't want to stay in Fenmore Falls and find out what it was.

The sooner I get out of here, the better.

Chapter 8

Cinderella

Germany, 1812

*"What is that useless creature doing in the best room?"
asked the stepmother. "Away to the kitchen with her! And if she
wants to eat, then she must earn it. She can be our maid."*

*Her stepsisters took her dresses away from her and made
her wear an old gray skirt. "That is good enough for you!"
they said, making fun of her and leading her into the kitchen.
Then the poor child had to do the most difficult work. She had
to get up before sunrise, carry water, make the fire, cook, and
wash. To add to her misery, her stepsisters ridiculed her and
then scattered peas and lentils into the ashes, and she had to
spend the whole day sorting them out again. At night when
she was tired, there was no bed for her to sleep in, but she
had to lie down next to the hearth in the ashes. Because she
was always dirty with ashes and dust, they gave her the name
Cinderella.*

Day 4

Thanks to the grand tour the day before, I felt more comfortable
with Sherwood Manor. I began to fall into a rhythm and no longer

needed Katie or Amanda to show me where to go. But no matter what, I would never fall into a comfortable rhythm with wearing a corset. *How do these women do it, day after day?* I wondered.

Speaking of wondering, I spent a good part of the day thinking, *Will I ever make it back home to Idaho? How much longer will I be here?* The longer I stayed, the more I worried I might be destined to reside in Fenmore Falls forever.

On a positive note, going back in time had its advantages, such as being an expert of the ultimate social scene—a place back home we call high school, where popularity determines the pecking order. In Fenmore Falls I applied the same strategies—act is if you belong, never lose your sense of humor, accept that peer pressure is everywhere, ask for help when you need it, be yourself, and forget about perfection.

Like high school, Fenmore Falls tended to force people to fit into a mold. People born into wealth were considered cool, and the rest of the people were not. Underneath the labels, everyone was the same, but society didn't acknowledge it.

"Lady Catherine hosts a dinner party each Wednesday night," Katie told me that morning as she brushed my hair.

"Every week?" I said.

"Yes. The guests are rather elderly men of great wealth." She wrinkled her nose.

Here we go again with social ranking.

"There is talk that Lady Catherine is in earnest to find a suitor for Miss Gabriella before her nineteenth birthday," Katie said.

"Why nineteen?"

"That's when Miss Gabby will be free from Lady Catherine's guardianship and entitled to her father's wealth."

"Then why would Lady Catherine be so eager to find a suitor for Gabriella?"

"If Miss Gabby marries someone in favor with Lady Catherine, Lady Catherine will receive a generous sum of money," Katie said.

"What if Gabriella marries someone of her own choice?"

"If Miss Gabby marries before her nineteenth birthday without Lady Catherine's approval, the will would be void and Lady Catherine would receive none of Miss Gabby's wealth."

"When does she turn nineteen?"

"The 27th day of August."

That's in two months. Did Gabriella escape to my world in an effort to avoid a marriage arranged by her stepmother? If only Gabriella knew she would meet the prince and that inheriting her father's fortune wouldn't matter!

"When Gabriella marries the prince, everything will be all right," I said without thinking . . . again. *Why do I keep doing that?* Once I realized my stumble, I joked, "Since I'm intended for the lovable Fred, maybe Gabriella's destiny is to be whisked away by the handsome prince."

"And I will marry the mysterious knight of the road," Katie said.

Glad she bought my story, I asked, "Who is the knight of the road?"

Her grin widened. "There is a highwayman who roams the roads, protecting Fenmore Falls from criminals."

"You mean Black Rider?" Once again, my mind flooded with memories of the handsome masked man. He *was* mysterious, but not in an eerie way like Sir William.

"Yes, Black Rider," Katie replied. "Have you seen him?"

"Yes, he stopped our carriage when we went into town the day before yesterday."

"What did he want?" Katie placed her hand on my arm, excitement in her face.

I shrugged. "I'm not really sure. He said something about people trying to overturn the kingdom. He asked our driver some questions and then said we could go."

"Is he as handsome as everyone says he is?"

I felt my cheeks turn red. *Why am I blushing?* My sister, Cassidy, was the blusher, not me.

"The top of his face was hooded, but you could still see his eyes," I explained, "and they were dark and beautiful."

Katie sighed. "I bet he's handsome. Someone with beautiful eyes just has to be handsome."

Agreed.

Shaking the thoughts of the unobtainable and fictional knight of the road, I said, "You haven't showed me the locked and haunted rooms yet. You can't tempt me with such an idea and then not do it."

"Very well, Miss Brinlee." Katie beamed. "Your curiosity is as powerful as mine."

She placed the last pin in my hair and guided me out into the hallway. "There is much about Sherwood Manor that is unexplained, Miss Brinlee—many mysteries and secrets," she whispered.

Now we're talking. My arms tingled with goosebumps.

"For instance, no one besides Lady Catherine enters the fourth-floor tower," Katie continued. "She holds the only key. Some say the fourth tower is a shrine or vault of her stolen wealth. Others say she is a witch and needs a secret chamber for her potions and spells. There are a few who believe it is a crypt for her victims."

"What do you think?" I whispered back.

Katie paused. "Well, it was rumored that Lady Catherine had always admired the estate, and many people were not surprised when she set her sights on Miss Gabriella's father."

"Do you think Catherine had something to do with his death?"

When Katie nodded, chills ran down my spine.

"Miss Gabriella's father became ill only a week after the presumed nuptials were exchanged," Katie said.

"How awful."

"At Lady Catherine's request, Miss Gabriella's father was moved closer to town to be nearer Fenmore Falls' only apothecary, where he could receive medical treatment."

"What happened?"

Katie shrugged. "No one saw Miss Gabriella's father again, not even Miss Gabby."

"How can that be?"

"He died suddenly, and because of fear his disease might be contagious, his body was buried right away," Katie whispered as we walked down the hall.

"Gabriella never saw her father after he died?"

Katie's blond hair swished against her shoulders as she shook her head.

"It seems like someone is trying to hide something," I said.

Katie's eyes grew wide. "Now you understand why there are many secrets here at Sherwood Manor."

"Do you think Lady Catherine is in league with the people trying to overturn the kingdom?" I asked. "Is that why Black Rider was questioning our driver?"

"I don't know, but I wouldn't be surprised if it were so."

From down the hall, a voice said, "Katie, what are you about?"

We jumped at the sudden sound. From the opposite end of the hallway came a stout, redheaded man, his round belly protruding over his trousers. A chuckle escaped me as he wobbled over to us, wiping his nose with the back of his hand. As he came closer, I recognized him as Henry, the man who'd driven us to town a few days before.

"Katie, Lady Catherine needs your service and is angry with your tardiness," he said with a slur.

Katie bowed her head and curtsied. "Sorry, Sir Henry."

"Don't waste my time with a curtsy," the short, freckled man growled. "Make haste!"

Katie rushed down the hallway, glancing over her shoulder to wave at me. I waved back.

The short man narrowed his gaze to mine. "Good day, Miss Brinlee," he mumbled. Then, he turned abruptly and wandered away. I watched until he turned the corner.

It was times like this, standing alone in a possibly haunted manor with a possibly wicked stepmother, that I was miffed at my childhood friends for showing me all of those horror movies. Thoughts of Chucky sneaking up behind me, or pets rising from the dead, made my heart beat a loud bass inside my chest. Wait until my friends got a load of this story—"Brinlee Stuck in Time, Fighting off Evil Stepmothers."

Now that would make a good movie.

I spent the rest of the day in the kitchen, helping prepare for the dinner party the next day. Amanda and I cut and boiled celery, while Miss Brenda creamed butter, ground wheat, and got milk for a cream sauce. The main course would be a creamed-celery casserole topped with pecans and breadcrumbs.

The servants of the manor shuffled in and out of the cozy kitchen for their noon and evening meals. Much to my joy, I met Katie and Amanda's mother, Maryanne. She was as sweet as my nana but a bit more round and jolly, like Mrs. Santa Claus. My eyes brimmed with tears as I remembered my own home and my family, and I savored every bit of Maryanne's motherly attention.

Krys, the cute stable boy, entered the kitchen and was joined by two young men who introduced themselves as Jeremy and Ben. Neither was as striking as Krys nor as obviously smitten with Katie. While Krys was in the kitchen, his eyes frequently wandered to her. Once more, she blushed and shyly stared at her hands in her lap.

The only time the room was quiet was when Sir William entered. The other servants stopped talking as if deferring to his authority, and William didn't speak a word as he quickly placed some food on his plate. He nodded in my direction before he left.

With its friends and warm food, Sherwood Manor's kitchen reminded me of home. I felt my sister next to me through Katie and Amanda. Maryanne reminded me of Nana. With Fred sleeping at my feet, I almost forgot my crazy circumstances in the shadows of my nostalgic memories.

By the end of the evening, the tables were covered with vegetables and ingredients that were measured and ready for the next day. Even the coals for the fire were placed and set for the morning rush, when the majority of the work would have to be done. Cooking back then required more skill, as it was done over wood fires. Several times, I had watched Miss Brenda stoke the fire, judging the temperature by color and brightness before placing the food near the heat. I discovered that yellow heat was hotter than orange, and orange was hotter than red. I also noticed that when Miss Brenda took hot coals out of the fire, she always put more wood on it.

That night, all of us were tired. I was the last one in the kitchen, and I heard Fred clawing at the kitchen door to go outside. Wearily, I opened the door for him to exit and do his duty. When he returned, I said, "It's a good thing you're so cute or I would have locked you outside."

Just as the dog crossed the threshold, I noticed the mud splattered on his paws. "Stop," I commanded. I knew Lady Catherine would be furious if an animal brought muddy footprints into her house.

The cute mutt followed my order and halted. I lifted him and carried him over to the washbasin, where I cleaned and rinsed his paws with my apron. The mud complemented the food and ashes already on my clothes. I laughed, thinking I almost looked the part of the storybook Cinderella.

After I put Fred on the floor, I turned to the magic door next to the hearth. Tonight was my fourth night at Sherwood Manor, and I was no closer to finding my way home than I'd been that first night.

Perhaps there was a trick to opening the door. Maybe I was doing it wrong. I raised my fingers to the frame of the door and searched for a latch or button or anything that might be hidden. I crawled on the floor and looked beneath the door, hoping to find a lever. I remembered a scene in a movie where someone finds a piece of rope stretched across the floor, and when they lift it up it opens a secret passageway. But in my case, I found nothing. *Yep, I'm destined to stay here forever.*

Exasperated, I began to bang on the door with my fists. "I'm not supposed to be here!" I shouted. "I'm not Cinderella!" *I'm just a misplaced girl from Idaho.*

I pressed my palms against the wooden door. What if everything important failed to happen in this Cinderella story because I was here instead of Gabriella? How could there be a happily ever after without the real Cinderella riding off into the sunset with her prince?

"There is going to be a ball, Gabriella," I said to the magic door. "At the ball, you meet the prince." My forehead rested on the door. "You have to meet the prince, Gabby."

As before, there was no response.

"I'm not Cinderella," I pleaded. "You are."

I pushed myself away from the door and slowly turned to go to my bedroom. "This fairy tale is your territory, Gabby, not mine," I mumbled. "Fight your own battle."

Chapter 9

Nana's Bridge Club Friends, Every Thursday

Nana and her two friends had been together for as long as I could remember, even before my mother was born. They had shared life together, raising babies, building houses, and supporting husbands. And now they were soaring through life widowed, ignoring the fact that they were sad and alone.

Miss Wendy, now in her midsixties, had been an actress in her prime years, a golden-haired song lark. Her darling Victor had been gone for five years, but her blue eyes still sparkled as vibrantly as the heavens. At fifty-seven, Alice "Allie" Holt was the youngest of the three friends. Her husband, Lynn, had died only the previous winter. The feelings of her forlorn heart often showed on her face.

During one of their weekly bridge club visits, Miss Wendy asked me, "Where is your mother this summer?"

"She had a conference in New York last week, and I think she is now in Chicago taking a graduate class for the next month or so."

"I miss Abigail," Allie put in. "I haven't seen her for so long."

Miss Wendy said, "Don't forget that Miss Businesswoman, who doesn't like to visit us anymore and spends all of her summers working too much, doesn't like to be called Abigail anymore, or Abby, for that matter. She prefers Gail."

Allie wrinkled her nose, "I'll never call her Gail. I've always called her Abigail, and that's what I'm going to keep calling her."

"Well, either way, she prefers Gail. She's decided to grow up on us, and I guess her childhood nickname goes along with the change," Miss Wendy said sadly. "She's not our little princess anymore."

Day 5

I awoke to screaming. I opened my bedroom door and peeked into the long corridor just in time to see Amanda racing toward Lady Catherine's room.

"Amanda," I called as she sprinted by my door.

She stopped and put a hand to her heart, propping herself against the far wall. "Miss Brinlee, you startled me."

"I'm sorry. What's going on?"

"The animals are in the kitchen—they've eaten everything."

"What? What do you mean the animals are in the kitchen?"

"The chickens, the pigs—all of them—are in the kitchen eating the food for the dinner this afternoon." She started again for Lady Catherine's bedroom, where the screaming was coming from.

"I don't understand. Why are the animals in the kitchen?"

Over her shoulder, Amanda said, "The kitchen door was left open last night."

Realization hit me like a cold, hard snowball in the face. *It was me—I was the one who left the kitchen door open.*

I remembered unlocking the door the night before to let Fred out, but I didn't remember locking it after he came in again. I was too preoccupied with finding a way to open the magic door.

A wave of nausea hit me as I began to panic. Lady Catherine would probably kick me out of Sherwood Manor for this mistake. *Where will I go? What will I do?*

I twisted a strand of my hair between my fingers. I needed to explain to her what had happened. Somehow, I had to fix this.

Amanda exited Lady Catherine's bedroom and ran past me.

"What did she say?" I asked.

"She says everyone needs to meet in the kitchen right away."

My heart sank to my stomach.

"Katie will help you get dressed, Miss Brinlee," Amanda said, then hurried down the hallway.

I forced myself to speak. "Thanks."

Slowly, I stepped into my bedroom and shut the door. With my hands on my forehead, I slumped to the ground. *I'm doomed!*

Soon, Katie came into the room. Seeing me on the floor, she asked, "Are you all right, Miss Brinlee?"

"No." *No, I'm not all right. I'm far from being all right.*

"What is the matter, Miss Brinlee?" She sat on the floor next to me.

I turned my head to face her. "Katie, I was the one who left the kitchen door open. I let Fred out to go to the bathroom last night and forgot to close the door when he came back in."

Tears loomed behind my eyes as I waited for her reply, but she just sat there. "Say something," I said finally.

Katie took my hand. "It's going to be all right, Miss Brinlee."

"How is it going to be all right?"

"Trust me—it's going to be all right."

"Lady Catherine will kick me out. She didn't want me here in the first place, and now she has reason to kick me out."

"Do you trust me?" Katie asked.

"Of course I trust you," I said without hesitation.

"Then believe me when I say that everything will be all right."

I wasn't sure how trusting her would make everything all right, but so far Katie had proven herself dependable and honorable. "Okay," I said.

She helped me stand. "We must hurry and get you dressed because I also need to help Miss Fanny and Miss Rose."

"I'm sorry, Katie. You don't need to help me."

"Do you think you can tie your corset laces by yourself?"

Cursed corset! "Nope, haven't learned that trick yet."

"Then help me by being quiet so I can get you dressed as fast as possible," she said with a smile.

"Deal."

Without another word, she finished dressing me and quickly brushed my hair. Then she left to help the stepsisters.

Alone, I pondered my fate. In the worst-case scenario, Lady Catherine would send me to jail to serve time for the lost food and supplies. In the best-case scenario, she would hire the animals to serve in the kitchen. Maybe Fenmore Falls had magical, talking pigs and chickens like the mice in Disney's movie version of *Cinderella.* I'd like a couple of animal friends named Jaq and Gus.

Stranger things have happened, right?

After a few deep, cleansing breaths, I finally made my way to the kitchen. When I walked into the room, my best-case scenario—the one with helpful, talking animals—was blown to smithereens. It looked like a tornado had gone through the room. Food was splattered everywhere. Amanda was picking up food and broken pieces of bowls that had been strewn across the floor. All of the food preparation from the night before had been for nothing. In addition, the smell in the small room was bad . . . animal-poop bad.

"Look at this mess!" Miss Brenda sat in her chair, obviously in a daze. "Milady will have my head for this!"

Amanda spoke out from her spot on the floor. "She will not have your head, Miss Brenda. She will understand that it was a mistake."

"I will be held accountable for this disaster," Miss Brenda complained.

Katie entered the door behind me and announced, "Lady Catherine, Miss Fanny, and Miss Rose are coming."

Miss Brenda stood from her chair and straightened her apron. "I have given thirty long years of service to this house. She can't fire me."

With her usual arrogance, Lady Catherine entered the room and glared at the mess. "How did this happen?"

"I am sorry, Milady," Miss Brenda said. "The animals must have forced the loose door open."

Lady Catherine walked over to the door and pushed it open and closed. "It does not appear to be loose. I believe someone left the door open."

Unable to ignore the guilt gnawing at me, I took a nervous step forward, ready to admit my mistake. My suicide attempt was stopped when Katie touched my shoulder and pulled me back.

"It was me, milady," she said. "I left the door open."

No!

I stared at my friend and shook my head. She tenderly squeezed my hand. As I looked into her pleading eyes, I sensed the value of her sacrifice. This is what she'd meant when she'd asked me to trust her. This was her plan all along. *I hope she knows what she's doing!*

"Katie, you left the door open?" Lady Catherine asked with bewilderment.

Seeming to gather her courage, Katie stood a little straighter. "Yes, milady, I must have forgotten to lock the door after I let the dog outside last night."

Lady Catherine walked toward her. "Why did you not say a word of this before?"

"I'm sorry, milady."

Lady Catherine stood glowering at Katie. "That dog has caused more problems than it is worth. I have the common sense to get rid of it."

I felt even sicker now. Everyone, including Fred, would be punished for my stupidity. It seemed everything I did in this world was wrong. In my old world back home, all I ever did was dream about the loveliness of this world, but now I was messing everything up—and hurting good people.

I want to go home, I silently begged, looking at the magic door.

"Katie, I'm disappointed in you," Lady Catherine said. "As a result of your mistake, the entire staff will pay for the food out of their wages."

"You're a real jerk!" I blurted out. I couldn't help it.

She narrowed her eyes at me.

"Sorry," I said. "You don't know what that means."

Lady Catherine pointed a finger at me. "I understand the intent of your speech well enough."

She took an imposing step closer to me. I took a step back.

"Now, understand mine," she said, still pointing her finger. "Do not forget about my previous warning. The activities of this house are none of your concern. Your unruly actions will not be tolerated. One more outburst from you will result in the loss of another week's salary for all of the servants."

I clamped my mouth shut. Threatening me was one thing, but threatening innocent servants was another.

Lady Catherine turned to Miss Brenda. "The dinner party for today will remain as scheduled. Will another trip to town be needed, or will you be able to prepare the meal with the food remaining in the pantry?"

"I think we'll be all right if I change the menu a little," Miss Brenda answered.

"Very well," Lady Catherine said. "See that it is done."

Miss Brenda bowed her head and curtsied. "Yes, milady."

"As for the rest of you, the priority above every other chore will be preparing the meal for this afternoon. Is that understood?"

Katie and Amanda curtsied. "Yes, milady."

Lady Catherine lifted her skirts and moved back to stand by her two daughters, who were silent spectators. Lady Catherine gave one last reproach, "Let this be a warning to all of you. I will not tolerate foolishness in my household. Next time, the consequence will be termination."

Still lifting her skirts, she exited the room. Rose trailed close behind her mother, and Fanny turned up her nose before following.

The quiet peace was short lived when Miss Brenda practically shouted at Katie, "You and your family are useless! We will all suffer the consequence of your mistake."

"Leave her alone!" I said, feeling tears in my eyes again.

This is all going so very wrong.

Miss Brenda shook her thin, pointed head. "I don't have time for this. What's done is done. We will have to work quickly to fix this." She looked directly at me. "Without any further interruptions."

"Oh, right. I'll get out of your way."

"Katie, fetch a chicken for cleaning," Miss Brenda ordered.

I followed Katie outside. "Katie, I'm so, so sorry."

"It's all right," she said softly, not looking at me.

"Katie, your family is not useless!"

When she turned, I saw the tears on her face. "Thank you, Miss Brinlee."

I embraced the trembling girl. "I shouldn't have let you take the blame for me."

Katie wiped at her tears. "No, it was necessary. Lady Catherine would have been even angrier at you."

"But now all of the servants will suffer because of my mistake. I can't believe she would take away everyone's wages."

Katie looked toward the horse stables. I knew she was thinking of Krys. "Yes, it is an outcome that will affect everyone, including those who weren't even involved."

"Katie, I'm so sorry. Is there anything I can do?"

She smiled weakly. "Could you be the one to tell Krys that his earnings for the week will be gone because of me?"

I swallowed the lump in my throat. "If you want me to tell him, I will."

Katie inhaled deeply. "No, I should be the one to tell him."

"Let me explain to him what happened and how you helped me," I said.

"No, he needs to believe what everyone else believes. Lady Catherine cannot discover that my confession was false."

"Are you sure?"

"Yes." Katie paused. "I need to do it."

She walked toward the horse stable.

This isn't fair! I screamed inside my head.

The tears began to trickle down my face. I couldn't endure watching Katie walk toward the end of her love story, especially since it was my fault. So, I did what I always did best when I was faced with a trial—I turned and ran.

I followed the path around the house and then hurried down the road. Unlike the first time I ran away, when I was conveniently wearing my sweatpants and slippers, I now wore a corset and long dress. I got as far as the end of the gravel path when I felt faint.

As I stopped to catch my breath, I remembered the pond and its inviting waters. With a new objective, I headed in that direction.

Soon, I slowed to a jog. But the corset around my chest seemed to tighten with each desperate inhale, and my lungs began to burn. I simply couldn't draw a deep breath. Starting to panic, I leaned against a tree near the pond. "I'm going to faint," I said, stating the obvious. This was what happened when someone was about to faint—lightheadedness, shortness of breath, hallucinations. *Yes, thinking I'm in Cinderella's world MUST be a hallucination.*

I needed to loosen my corset so I could breathe. My fingers fumbled with the ties of my dress. I desperately ripped off the apron and neckerchief, and then the dress. Finally, with most of my clothing on the ground, I reached back and yanked on the strings to release the corset. When the terrible thing went loose, I took great gulps of air. I leaned back against the tree, inhaling the fresh air. My head still buzzed, but my vision soon grew steady.

Why am I here? I thought. Everything about my situation was getting worse. How was I supposed to make it through another day when I kept messing everything up?

After several more deep breaths, I slipped off my stockings and shoes. Then I unfastened my petticoats and let them fall to the ground next to my dress. What I needed was to feel like myself.

So, with my attire piled on the ground and dressed in only my white nightgown, I walked to the pond. I sat down next to it and let my feet slip beneath the cool surface.

Ah, that's nice, I thought with a sigh. I leaned back and rested on the grass. I closed my eyes. *It's going to be okay, it's going to be okay,* I repeated in my mind.

Suddenly, I felt someone watching me. I opened my eyes and slowly sat up. There, standing next to my tree, was a man—a tall, dark, masked man.

Black Rider.

Chapter 10

Boyfriend Number Two: Kade Tyler

Kade was handsome—a blond, blue-eyed hunk. I initially crushed on his best friend, Rodney, but after my friend hooked up with him, I went for Kade. We were actually a good match, with our similar interests and friends. Meaning, his friend liked my friend, and mine liked his. I was only fifteen and not officially allowed to date, but Kade and I always hung out with Rodney and my friend at parties and school dances. The four of us got along perfectly. Kade would hold my hand, and I would giggle like a schoolgirl—which I was.

I'd like to say Kade was my first kiss, but we never kissed. We never really spent time alone, since his best friend and mine were always around. I don't think Kade and I ever existed as just Kade and me. So, when my friend dumped Rodney for a senior guy on the basketball team, it was a given that my relationship with Kade was over. We never spoke again.

Encounter at the Pond

Black Rider's arms were folded across his massive chest, his half-buttoned shirt revealing his bronze skin. "Good morning, Miss Brinlee. Did a gypsy steal your clothes?"

Heat flooded my cheeks. I clutched the neck of my nightgown and promptly stood up.

"Don't get up on my account." Humor played on his face.

"Um . . . I need to go back to the house." I looked at the ground to avoid his beautiful eyes.

"You just got here," he said. "Why do you need to get back already?"

Still staring at the grass under my bare feet, I said, "They'll be expecting me."

"What's the real reason you need to go, Miss Brinlee?"

The sound of my name on his voice made my stomach flutter like hummingbird wings.

Stop it, Brinlee!

"Is it because of me?" he asked.

I raised my head to glance at him. His eyes were the darkest brown, shaded by thick, black lashes, and a lock of his chin-length hair had fallen across his mask.

My hand itched to push the mask away. *It's a pity to hide such a pretty face.*

I forced myself to pay attention to the conversation. "Just because I've met you a couple of times does not mean you know me," I said. "You don't know anything about me."

"I know you well enough to know I make you uncomfortable."

"Don't flatter yourself," I mumbled.

Black Rider's deep chuckle caused my stomach to drop. "You're not like anyone I've ever met," he said.

"What do you mean by that?"

"Where do I begin? Let's see . . . your choice of dress, or lack thereof—"

"Hey!" I interrupted.

"Don't get me wrong—your lack of clothing interests me. It's just that I've seen you twice now dressed in anything but proper attire."

He had a point. The first time we met I was wearing pants, running unchaperoned in the woods, and now I was dressed even more scandalously in my shift that resembled my nana's tattered old nightgown. And I was still unchaperoned.

"You seem like an animal trapped in a cage, waiting to be freed," he said.

I was impressed but played along. "So, what was it then? Was it the way I threw my clothes on the ground without hesitating, or the way I dipped my feet in the water as if I hadn't a care in the world—assuming, of course, that I was alone? Without spectators. Without someone spying on me. Which of those things did you notice?" *Cough, cough.*

Black Rider's eyes twinkled. "It was more of the latter, I suppose. You seemed to be in your element when you were next to the pond. It was as if a peace suddenly came over you."

He straightened, no longer leaning against the tree. When he spoke again, I was drawn to his lovely mouth. "Girls around here are only in their element when they are confined indoors and in pretty dresses. You contradict the norm."

"I don't know if I should take that as a compliment or not."

His lips lifted into a full grin. "Take it as a compliment. It's refreshing to see something different."

I blushed again. "I really should go."

Black Rider took a step closer but stumbled. He grasped the tree and leaned over as if in serious pain.

"Are you all right?" I asked.

Without thinking, I approached him and leaned over to grasp his forearm. He let out a groan and jerked his arm away. Shocked, I tried to step back and nearly fell, but his hand reached out for mine. The warmth of his touch sent shivers up my arm.

"Don't go," he said so quietly I almost didn't hear him.

I loved the way my hand felt in his and was happy when he didn't let go.

As his labored breathing continued, I blurted, "What is your name?"

He slowly straightened and stood. "I still can't tell you that."

"Well, you've got to give me something. You know my name, but I have nothing on you."

"My job is my identity," he said. "No one can know who I am."

"I'm not from here," I reminded him. "I know no one. Therefore, I will not know you."

At his silence, I assumed he was tempted to tell me his name. But when he reached his free hand behind his head and untied the cloth from his face, I could not have been more surprised. And believe me, I had never been more pleased in all my life.

This man, with his high cheekbones, chocolate-colored eyes, and stubble growing across his chin, was nothing like the boys I had dated before. This man was all grown up—an adult male specimen.

My eyes examined every feature of his beautiful face. There was a small scar just below his right eyebrow, but the imperfection only added to his masculine beauty.

His square jaw twitched as he watched my reaction. "No one can know who I am," he said.

I nodded, unable to speak.

"My name is Dennan."

Dennan! What an unusual, wonderful name, I swooned silently.

"Do I have your word that you won't tell anyone who I am?"

I let out a feeble yes.

"You look stunned." He tilted his head.

I tried to shake off my dazed stare. "Just shocked. I guess I thought you were hiding something gruesome under that mask."

He smiled, and I noticed a small dimple in his left cheek. "Is this not gruesome enough for you?"

Hardly! "I just figured you had a larger scar than the one above your eye." My hand involuntarily reached up to touch his eyebrow.

Have you ever had one of those out-of-body experiences when you watched your body do something you had no control over? Like when you're on happy gas at the dentist's office and you watch your hand float in the sky and feel your body spinning? Well, this was one of those experiences.

Taking control of my body, I retracted my fingers from Dennan's face. Then I pulled my other hand out of his grip and took a step backward.

The next moment happened so fast. My foot landed on a small rock and I lost my balance. With lightning-quick reflexes, Dennan grabbed me by my waist to stop my fall. I heard him groan and felt his body tense, but he didn't release me until I was standing upright.

"Sorry," I said.

He crouched down again, this time favoring his forearm—the same one he used to save me from my graceful fall.

"I'm so sorry," I muttered. I couldn't believe I'd injured Fenmore Falls' highwayman. *Chalk it up to my clumsiness.*

"Don't be sorry," Dennan finally said. "It wasn't you."

I gently placed my fingers on his shoulder. "Is it bad? Can I help?"

He looked up through his dark lashes. "It is nothing," he said as he straightened, but I could tell he was faking it.

"Let me look at your wound." I reached out for his arm.

"It's fine." He moved it out of my reach. "It's just a little sore."

"Whatever. Let me see it." I grabbed his hand, and this time he didn't object.

I pulled up his sleeve. *Oh. My. Goodness.* The entire inside of his arm was filled with splinters. No wonder he flinched every time something touched his arm.

"What happened?" I asked.

He gasped as I turned his arm around to find more splinters on the underside. "I was climbing a tree."

"How did you get splinters from climbing a tree?"

"Well, I fell out of the tree?"

Frowning, I cocked my head. "How did you do that?"

"Someone was following me, and I tried to lose his trail by climbing a tree. The man examined my track longer than I had anticipated, and by the time he left, my legs were numb from holding onto the tree. I had no choice but to slide down."

"Do you have splinters on the other arm too?"

When Dennan didn't respond, I knew the answer.

"How were you going to get these out?" I asked.

"One at a time."

"Funny." I couldn't hold back a smile. "You're going to need someone to help you."

I attempted to remove one of the splinters with the fingernails of my thumb and finger, but the tiny piece of wood only seemed to dive deeper into his skin.

"I'm sorry," I said as he fidgeted from the pain. "Let me go back and get something to help get those splinters out." I wondered if Sherwood Manor had any tweezers. Then, I remembered something my nana used when my sister and I got splinters on the farm. It was a nasty-smelling mixture of herbs and roots that loosened the skin.

"I just need to get some elder root and Jamestown weed. They will lift the splinters away from your skin," I said. "I'm sure Sherwood Manor will have some in their herb garden."

"Miss Brinlee, I'll be fine."

Would I ever get used to hearing him say my name? "Don't be silly. You'll never get these out on your own."

"You really don't need to help me."

"I want to," I said.

Dennan's eyes showed his gratitude. I wondered if his plan had been to just wait until the splinters worked their way out or until the infection spread.

"It will only take me a few minutes," I said.

He placed his fingers on my hand as I touched his injured arm. Sparks shot through my arm and into my chest.

"Thank you," he said. He bowed before releasing my hand.

Wondering if he could hear the pounding of my heart, I folded my arms across my chest. "I'll hurry as fast as I can." I turned to walk toward my pile of clothes.

I could hear his footsteps as he followed me. Eager to fetch the supplies I needed to remove the splinters, I wasted no time in slipping into my corset and pulling it up to my waist. However, I soon realized I would not be able to tighten the corset on my own, with the ties in the back. Higher-class women showed off their wealth and only wore clothing that required the aid of a servant or housemaid.

Plan B: Maybe I could just wear the dress without the corset. Nobody would notice. Right?

"May I assist you?" Dennan stepped close behind me.

"I can do it myself."

"Are you sure? It looks to me like you need some help."

"I'll just wear the dress without the corset."

"You and I both know that if you were caught in this fashion, your social standing along with your virtue would be in question. Besides, I'm letting you help me, remember?"

Argh, he's right. I can't return looking like this. I had already caused enough havoc at Sherwood Manor. Returning practically naked wasn't going to help my cause.

Plan C: Wait until nightfall to sneak back into the manor. *Yeah, it's only 8:00 or 9:00 in the morning. I'd have to wait like what, ten hours? Um, no.*

"Fine, but no funny business." I tried to act annoyed, but secretly I knew I would enjoy Dennan's assistance.

He furrowed his brow at the modern saying. "No funny business—I promise." He chuckled.

I took a deep breath and turned around. His strong hands brushed against my sides while he grabbed the strings to my corset. He pulled hard on the strings, and as the corset tightened, I envisioned myself in a prison with walls of leather and bars of whalebone.

"Thank you for helping me."

"Don't talk," he said. "You'll put me off."

"I'm sorry." I took another deep breath and remembered almost fainting earlier. I held my breath as long as I could while the stays grew snugger, and then I let the air out with a gasp and panted.

"I think that's tight enough," Dennan said.

I wondered how he'd gotten so proficient at corset tying. Even though I had worn this awful thing for three days, I didn't have the slightest idea how to lace it up and tie it.

"There, that should do it," he said after he finished tying the laces. His hands rested on my waist.

I stepped away from his touch. When I turned to face him, I realized once more how remarkably handsome he was. "Thanks," I said nervously.

"You and I have more in common than you may think."

"Like what?" I questioned, starting to put on the rest of my clothes.

"We both oppose being suitably dressed every living moment of the day."

I looked at his messy hair and at his open shirt that showcased his chest—examples of his abandonment of societal norms. Dennan's grin deepened, accentuating his dimple.

My, oh my.

I turned my head and concentrated on fastening the stomacher to my dress. I slipped on my stockings and reached underneath my gown to put on my shoes. Finally, I tied my kerchief into place.

Smoothing the waist of my dress, I said, "The key word is 'comfortably,' not 'suitably.' It's easy to dress suitably. The worst part is being *uncomfortably* dressed every living moment of the day. Especially in countless layers of clothing according to so-called rules."

"Here, here," Dennan said.

Knowing that wearing a corset was really a small sacrifice for living out my fantasy, I sighed. "I have to confess to the beauty of it all, though."

"How do you say?"

I twirled once in the grass. "There's magic in the way courtesy is respected, as if everyone you meet is worthy of your attention."

He chuckled through a wide grin.

"For example—" I lifted my skirt slightly and bowed in a deep curtsy "—a greeting is considered essential. Gentlemen and ladies greet each other with great esteem."

Dennan bowed in return.

"Moreover, you live in a kingdom, with a castle and a prince," I exclaimed. "What could be more charming and wonderful than a prince?"

The highwayman's good humor lessened at the mention of the prince, but his lightheartedness quickly returned. "Oh, you're one of those girls who swoons over the prince. You may be more alike them than I thought."

"Who can blame me?" I lifted my shoulders.

After a few moments of silence, Dennan rubbed the toe of his shoe in the grass and looked behind one shoulder. "I'll wait for you on the other side of those trees."

I was grateful for the change of subject. "I'll hurry."

"I'll watch out for you to make sure no more gypsies come to steal your clothes."

"You're hilarious."

He took my hand, causing my heart to flutter. He leaned over and placed a kiss on the top of my hand. His soft lips left my skin tingling. When he released my fingers, I watched myself slowly pull my arm back and let it hang next to my body.

In that moment, everything seemed to stand still. A warmth crawled up the inside of my chest. Before Dennan's lips touched me, it was as if I lived in a cell made of skin, with my feelings sealed inside. But now I felt the barrier breaking. How could a simple kiss on the hand have such a powerful effect on my soul?

My life would be altered forever, absolutely and completely. No longer would I dream only of Prince Charming. My dreams would now include Dennan—the stranger who'd stolen my heart.

Chapter 11

My First Kiss: Jeff Mitchell

I was sixteen, and it was the usual boy/girl party. The girls sat on the couch and giggled, while the boys stayed in the kitchen eating candy and having a burping contest. Did guys really think that was impressive to girls? Note to teenage boys: girls don't like that stuff!

After spin the bottle—the most infamous boy/girl game of all—was announced, I gathered in a circle with the other teenagers and watched the bottle spin. And when my name was called out along with the name of one of the cutest football players at our school, Jeff Mitchell, my nervousness morphed into full-fledged fright.

Jeff was a good sport, though. I followed him into the designated closet, with onlookers chanting our names. He knew I was scared to death, so he kissed me on my cheek.

I know it wasn't a real kiss, but I can tell you that I've never had a kiss since then that measured up to the magic of that first one.

Return to the Pond

I grabbed everything from Sherwood Manor I thought I might need, and then hurried back to the pond. None of the servants at the manor paid any attention to me, since they were busy preparing dinner.

Finding Dennan sitting in the spot where I'd dipped my feet in the pond, I asked one of the many questions I'd thought of while trekking to the house and back. "So, why was someone chasing you so close to Sherwood Manor? Are you just a creep who's on a stakeout?" I still didn't know who he was, and I figured his charming charade was probably just that—a charade.

He slowly lifted his head "Are you now passing judgment on me?"

"Well, if the shoe fits, wear it."

He really didn't seem like a criminal, but my time alone had intensified my worry.

He opened his mouth, feigning shock. "I can't believe it. Are you pronouncing me a scoundrel?"

"You are a stranger to me," I said. "I find you in the woods, your clothes in shambles, with unkempt hair and no inhibition toward a woman. Of course the evidence leads me to wonder if you are a criminal in hiding."

"For your information, I am in the woods for good reason. I must protect my identity." His voice rose in defense as he stood.

"I know, I know. Your job is your identity."

"My access to clothes and other essentials is limited."

"I know. I get it." I backed up when he stepped closer.

Dennan drew in a breath. "I apologize if I have given you any discomfort."

Now I just felt bad. Why did I have to go all ballistic on him? He had given me no reason to feel uncomfortable.

"I'm sorry, Sir Dennan. I just had a flash of fright."

"I thought we were well past the point of formalities." He grinned. "Call me Dennan."

I returned the grin. Shaking off the awkwardness of my accusations, I lifted the herbs I held in my hand. "Give me a minute to mash these into a paste, and then we'll get those splinters out."

I knelt in the grass and concentrated on mixing the ingredients in the bowl I'd brought from the kitchen. I hoped I grabbed the right herbs and root. It was hard to tell, since so many herbs looked alike.

"So, where are you from, Brinlee?" He was standing right next to me, so close that shivers crawled down my back.

I considered what I should tell this handsome yet risky man. The truth was unbelievable, and anything close to the truth would sound outrageous. "I come from a land far, far away," I said finally.

"Where?"

"Very far away."

"What's the name?"

"You wouldn't know it."

"Are you purposely avoiding answering the question?"

"Yes." *Get a clue.*

He went silent.

I finished mixing the foul-smelling herbs. "All right, I think it's ready."

Dennan knelt next to me, but took special care with one of his legs. I didn't ask and didn't want to know if he had splinters on his thigh too. If so, he'd have to get them out himself.

I carefully rolled up his sleeve. His arm was huge—muscularly robust. His veins stood out above his tight muscles. I gulped down my exhilaration and dipped my fingers into the paste, then slathered it onto his skin. He flinched slightly but put on a brave face.

"My nana usually cooks this mixture in a frying pan, so I hope it has the same effect unheated." I sighed at the thought of my grandmother.

"You miss her, don't you?" It was more of a statement than a question.

"I miss her terribly."

"You talked before of your sister," Dennan said. "Who else belongs to your family?"

At first, I couldn't recall mentioning Cass, but then I realized I'd spewed out the info in frustration when I first met Dennan and we rode his horse together.

"It's usually just my nana and my sister. My mother travels a lot."

"Where is your father?"

The question was innocent, but I instantly tensed. "I don't know. He left when I was three."

"Why did he leave?"

I shrugged. "I've spent my life trying to answer that question."

Dennan didn't push any further, for which I was very grateful. I quickly covered all of the visible splinters with the paste. Then, I bent my head and pulled his arm closer for inspection. The knuckles of his outstretched hand bumped into my chest.

"I'm sorry."

I looked at his widened eyes, searching his expression for any sign of regret or embarrassment. All I saw was uncertainty, reservation, and something akin to desire.

"No, I'm sorry," I said. "Did that hurt?"

"No, you're not hurting me."

I lowered my head and blew on his arm. He jumped but held his arm still. Keeping my focus on the herb mixture drying on his arm, I continued to blow for a few more minutes.

"I'm going to peel it off now," I warned.

I pulled at the goop caked on his arm. I gathered it into my hand and piled it onto a rock to reuse on his other arm. It looked like the elder root had done its job and had drawn the splinters to the surface of the skin so I could easily grab them. I began the process of extracting each one. I hadn't found any tweezers at Sherwood Manor, so I pinched each splinter between my fingernail and thumbnail.

"Did you know that you bite the tip of your tongue when you concentrate?" Dennan asked suddenly after a long silence.

I startled at the sound of his voice. I immediately retracted my tongue, which I'd unconsciously caught between my teeth.

"I find it very charming." He shifted his position in the grass.

Ignoring him, I placed my hand under his elbow and turned his arm to the side to see if I had missed any splinters. This time when his fingers bumped into my corset, I pretended not to notice and continued to scan his arm.

Satisfied, I dropped his arm and grabbed for the other one. When I spread the mixture onto his skin, I sadly realized the advantage of frying the elder root and making the mixture more pliable. I had a hard time spreading the goop and had to knead it over his sore arm, making him flinch.

"How about you? Do you have any brothers or sisters?" I asked.

"No. It's just my mother, my father, and my grandmother, but I don't see them much," he said. I peered up in time to see him glance towards the outlying trees. "They don't approve of what I do."

I blew on the mixture drying on his arm. "What? Doesn't your mother support your tree-climbing profession?" I teased.

Dennan chuckled. "Well, the casualties are one reason for their disapproval."

"I don't blame them. Splinters are the number-one cause of death these days." *That's funny, Brinlee.* Why couldn't I be this funny in any of my high school classes? People would love me.

On cue, Dennan laughed.

See? Living in this era brings out the best in me.

"Splinters are the least of my parents' worries right now." He flattened his other hand against his thigh.

Seriously, what was wrong with his leg?

"Any luck finding out who is trying to destroy the kingdom?" I asked. "Are you still suspicious of anyone in Sherwood Manor?"

"No, my leads have all run dry. I feel like I'm running around in circles."

"And up trees," I muttered.

"Brinlee, I love that you always make me smile."

"I'm glad."

During our conversation, I'd already removed the herb mixture and pulled out about half of the splinters. I continued to pinch and pull until all that was left was red, swollen skin.

"Finished," I announced.

Dennan jumped up and quickly reached out to assist me.

"Thank you." I put my hand in his.

"It is I who should thank you." His thumb caressed the side of my hand. "You run in men's pants, bathe in a pond, and brew magic potions. If you are not a witch then you must be a fairy—a beautiful fairy from a land very far away."

My face turned red again. "I probably should be going now."

"You're right." Dennan frowned. "I've taken up enough of your time today."

It's the best time I've had in this crazy nightmare, I thought.

"Until we meet again, Miss Brinlee." He lifted my hand and bowed.

"I thought we were past the formalities, Sir Dennan."

He smiled. "You're right." He stepped closer and abruptly leaned in and gave me a kiss on the check. "Until we meet again, Brinlee," he whispered next to my cheek.

I'm melting, I'm melting. Yes, I often quote *The Wizard of Oz.*

I do believe in spooks. I do! I do! I do!

See what I mean? The movie is contagious. Once I get going, I can't stop.

How about this one: *Not having fear isn't brave, it's foolhardy. Any real hero knows fear. The difference is a hero masters his fear.*

And you've got to love this one: *As for you, my galvanized friend, you want a heart. You don't know how lucky you are not to have one. Hearts will never be practical until they can be unbreakable.*

That's what was running through my mind as my eyes fluttered open (I didn't remember closing them) and looked into the smoldering eyes of the beautiful knight of the road. Why couldn't hearts be made unbreakable? I could tell this heartbreak was going to be a doozy, requiring a full weekend of limitless chocolate, gummy bears, and plenty of pillows to throw at the TV while I watched sappy movies.

"I hope I see you again, Brinlee." Dennan dropped my hand.

I sure hoped there would be an again. My heart fluttered at the prospect.

I stepped backward, desperately trying to stabilize my pulse. "Thank you, Sir Dennan . . . I mean Dennan." I took another step. "Um, I'll see you later. Maybe down the road, or in the next town, or tomorrow, or never. Like whatever." Another step. "Um, yeah, I'll see you later." Another step. "Um, bye." I waved.

Yeah, I actually waved goodbye. Let's see, weird girl flailing her hand, looking like a complete idiot in an era where no one, especially girls, waved. Can we say "weirdo"?

That was my signal to turn and walk quickly away. I clamped my mouth shut so I wouldn't blurt out any other obnoxious farewell, then gripped my folded arms to punish them for their embarrassing display.

Yes, my heart would need a full weekend of chocolate, gummy bears, pillows, and probably a loaded can of Fresca to get over Dennan.

Chapter 12

Conkiajgharuna, the Little Rag Girl
Country of Georgia, 1894

One holiday the stepmother took her daughter, and they went to church. She placed a trough in front of Little Rag Girl, spread a large measure of millet in the courtyard, and said, "Before we come home from church, fill this trough with tears and gather up this millet, so that not one grain is left." Then they went to church.

Little Rag Girl sat down and began to weep. While she was crying, a neighbor came in a said, "Why are you in tears? What is the matter?" The little girl told her tale. The woman brought all the brood hens and chickens, and they picked up every grain of millet. Then she put a lump of salt in the trough and poured water over it. "There, child," said she, "there are your tears! Now go and enjoy yourself."

That Afternoon

When I made it back to Sherwood Manor, Katie was still hard at work in the kitchen. "Can I help with anything?" I asked her.

"I'm all right in here. See if Amanda needs help in the dining room." Katie was cutting vegetables at the table and didn't look up.

As I left the room, I couldn't help but skip down the hallway. Everything seemed a little cheerier when I thought of Dennan.

Amazingly, I could still feel his lips pressed to my cheek. I held my palm to my face, savoring the sensation.

Looking out a window, I noticed a carriage in front of the manor. Strangely, Sir William sat in the driver's seat instead of the usual chauffeur. Even more peculiarly, Lady Catherine climbed into the carriage alone. William slapped the reins on the horses' backs and drove the carriage away from the house. *What is that about?*

I caught up to Amanda in the dining room and asked, "Does Lady Catherine typically leave Sherwood Manor alone with Sir William?"

Still shining a piece of silver, Amanda raised her head. "Milady leaves every day at noon with Sir William."

"Every day?"

Amanda nodded. "She leaves every day at noon and is gone for no longer than an hour." Amanda tucked a loose blond strand of hair behind her ear. "Milady trusts only Sir William as her escort."

"That's odd."

"I guess it would seem unusual to a visitor, but ever since Lady Catherine moved into Sherwood Manor, it has been her habit."

"Where do you think she goes?"

"No one knows for sure." Amanda grinned slyly. "I think she ventures out each day to restock her supply of tonics and potions."

"You are as bad as your sister." I giggled. "You two would have Lady Catherine pegged as the Wicked Witch of the West."

Amanda laughed so hard she snorted, making us both laugh even more. "Your amusement is refreshing, Miss Brinlee," she was finally able to say when she regained her breath.

"I'm glad to be of service."

She returned her focus to the silverware. "Dinner is in just a few short hours, and there is still so much to be done."

"Let me help."

"No, miss. This is no work for a gentlewoman."

"Now, Amanda, we both know I'm not a gentlewoman. I only pretend to be one. Besides, the work will be finished faster with an extra pair of hands."

"I will not request your assistance, but if you wish to give it, I will not prevent you from doing so."

"Deal."

I moved to the opposite side of the table and attempted to shine a silver fork.

Long, silent moments passed as I thought about Dennan—the brilliance of his dark eyes and the thrill of his touch. But where did he come from? Who was he? Even though my heart fluttered at the very idea of his handsome face and roguish attitude, I felt uneasy about his vague answers to my questions.

I didn't tell Amanda about him. Maybe I wanted to keep the secret to myself, or maybe I was afraid no one would believe me and assume I had made the whole thing up.

After Amanda and I worked for an hour in the formal dining room, the rumbling of Lady Catherine's carriage signaled her return. I stepped near the window and watched her descend from the vehicle and step quietly into the manor. Sir William led the horses and carriage to the stables. I decided to tell Dennan about Lady Catherine's strange disappearance, just in case she had something to do with the plot to destroy the kingdom.

After Amanda and I finished in the dining room, I met Katie in my bedroom so she could help me get ready for dinner.

"How did Krys react when you talked to him?" I asked.

"He assured me that it was only the consequence of Lady Catherine's bitter temper and not any fault of mine."

"I'm sorry."

I looked at Katie in the mirror. She stood behind me, pinning up my curls. Tears trickled down her cheeks.

I stood and turned so I could wrap my arms around my dear friend. "This never should have happened," I said, sobbing with her. "I never wanted you to take the fall for me."

She tried to straighten and pull away from me. "I'm just tired. Everything will be better once this dinner party is over."

I grabbed her hand. "Thanks for being my friend, Katie."

Tears escaped her eyes again. "It is I who should thank you, Miss Brinlee. You and Miss Gabriella have treated me better than any servant could ever wish to be treated."

I felt a tinge of pride at Katie's pronouncement. Gabriella—Cinderella—was the essence of unselfishness and kindness in my fairy-tale dreams. Being compared to her was way cool.

"Now let's get you ready for this dinner party." Katie turned me around to finish my hair.

I needed to find a way to get out of there. My presence was messing up everything.

When it was announced that the dinner guests had arrived, I descended the staircase in my beautiful, dark green dress. My elegant skirts whispered around me as if telling secrets, carrying me along as I wandered through a dream come true.

Just outside the dining room, Sir William unexpectedly stepped into my pathway. "You look beautiful, Miss Brinlee." He looked me up and down as if he'd eat me alive.

"Thank you, Sir William." I tried to step away from him.

"Call me William, remember?"

I heard the murmur of voices in the dining room. "Do you need something? Lady Catherine is expecting me."

He grinned. "I'm looking forward to being alone with you."

"Maybe another time." I took a step toward the door.

"How about after dinner tonight?"

"Tonight?" I was unable to hide my surprise.

"Meet me in the gardens after dinner, and I'll escort you down to the shore just beyond the cliff. I want to show you the colors of the setting sun reflected upon the waters."

I was intrigued with the idea of visiting the shore at sunset, even with William.

"It's a date." I smiled. "I'll meet you in the gardens after dinner."

He held his hands firmly at his sides and bowed. "Thank you, Miss Brinlee."

I curtsied and moved around him to enter the dining room.

Lady Catherine stood next to her chair at the head of the table. "Gentlemen," she said, "Miss Brinlee has at last decided to grace us with her charm."

Rose and Fanny stood next to their mother and three gray-haired men.

"I apologize for my late arrival, milady." I curtsied with my head bowed.

As I stood, I looked at Gabriella's elderly suitors—or leeches, as I preferred to call them. One sported a white moustache, another was tall and lean, and each gripped his vest with one hand and leaned on a walking stick with the other. Just as I had suspected, the men weren't appealing or interesting. They were just old.

Lady Catherine spoke. "Let's take our places at the table."

We waited for her to take her seat, and then everyone else sat. Rose glanced at me and pointed to the chair next to hers, and I quickly sat in it.

Once we were all settled, ruffles and all, dinner was served. The first course was steamed apples sprinkled with nutmeg. In the second course, not a speck of the chicken was wasted, with the bird's heart and brain presented on a silver platter. It was way different than eating McDonald's chicken nuggets in your car.

The delicious food almost made up for the tediousness of the meal, but not so much. Everyone lingered on each mouthful, chewing as slowly as humanly possible. Time seemed to crawl.

I tried to remember everything I'd been taught. I sat quietly, ate little, didn't shift my position, and paid attention to the conversation— the little there was. I spoke only once, when Lord Trentville, the tall gentleman, asked if I had enjoyed my stay at Sherwood Manor. I told him it had been lovely.

The dessert course was the highlight of the evening, served a full hour after the feast began. All in all, the event was tedious, quite unlike the enchanting meal I'd dreamed of. The whole thing made me miss mealtime back at home with Nana and my sister. We loved breakfast food and often ate it for dinner as well. We'd make pancakes, smear bagels with cream cheese, squeeze our own orange juice, and giggle over how much we could eat. Sometimes Nana's friends Allie and Miss Wendy joined us, and when they did, it was a blast.

But there was no merriment at the dinner table at Sherwood Manor. At the end of the meal, I glanced up at the serious faces looming over empty serving dishes. It was like everyone was trying to win the quiet game.

I hate that game! When I was a kid and we went on a long ride in the car, my mother always suggested that my sister and I play it. It didn't help that Cass always won, because then I'd feel compelled to try again and again and again, until finally I won and my mother beamed at her cleverness in keeping us quiet for a while.

Yes, here I was at the feast, feeling like I was stuck in a car ride enduring the quiet game, where no one spoke and it seemed to last forever. Would this evening ever end?

I rested my hands in my lap and quietly studied each bachelor at the table. I quivered at the thought of Gabriella being forced to wed and then kiss one of the wrinkly old men.

Obviously, Lady Catherine had planned this dinner so she could court wealthy prospective suitors for Gabriella. If she failed to wed Gabriella to any of them, Lady Catherine would be left penniless once her stepdaughter inherited the estate. Lady Catherine's only hope was to remain in control of Gabriella's money by making a bargain with a man who was only interested in marrying a young, beautiful girl and didn't need Gabriella's wealth.

When Lady Catherine stood to thank her guests for attending the dinner, I was beyond thrilled it was over. She excused Gabriella's absence and assured the suitors that the young woman would be there next time.

As soon as the men exited the room, I asked if I might leave too. Lady Catherine and Fanny gave me disapproving glares, but I didn't care. I had given enough of my time to propriety, and I couldn't get away fast enough.

I rushed to the kitchen, where I found the staff gathered around the table, eating a simple meal of hominy, a corn soup flavored with vegetables and salt-cured pork. All eyes looked up when I entered the room. Miss Brenda grunted, and Sir Henry, the portly man I'd met the day before, snorted from his chair in the corner of the room.

"So, how was it?" Katie asked.

I sat on a vacant chair. "The food or the entertainment?"

Amanda chuckled in the middle of a mouthful of food, then wiped her mouth and said, "We already know the food was good. Miss Brenda's cooking is flawless."

"You can say that with certainty," Miss Brenda piped in.

I grinned at her humility.

"So, how was it—the entertainment?" Amanda asked.

I decided to play with my audience. "Lord Trentville was actually very enjoyable."

Amanda's eyes went wide. "Really?"

Sir Henry coughed. "Those three ancient men couldn't interest a fly if it sat on their nose."

"Sir Henry's right," I admitted. "The three bachelors were probably the most dried up, boring men I have ever met."

Katie shook her head. "Lady Catherine only invites rich men as suitors for Miss Gabby, and they're usually old enough to be her grandfather. It's disgusting, if you ask me."

"Completely," I said.

"Who knows? Maybe Brinlee will have the opportunity to explore Lord Trentville's more enjoyable side at the ball." Amanda giggled.

"You're funny," I said.

Sir Henry sniffled noisily and wiped his nose on his sleeve. He got up and approached the table to stand directly behind Katie. "Are you attending the ball?" he asked her.

Katie sat still as if already aware of his intentions. I, on the other hand, was surprised and couldn't help being appalled by the redheaded man's beer belly.

"No, I will not be able to go," Katie answered.

"Surely Lady Catherine will allow you to go if your duties are finished," he said.

"I am not suitable to attend."

Sir Henry seemed to consider Katie's answer. "Very well. I will bid you ladies good evening." He tipped his head and left the room.

Once he was out of earshot, I exclaimed loudly, "What was that all about?"

"Henry has favored Katie for months," Amanda said. "Even though Katie shows him no interest, he is very persistent."

Miss Brenda, who often ignored our conversations, declared, "In that case, Katie, it's a good thing you are not suitable for the ball."

We giggled at the offhand comment. Who would have known the stiff Miss Brenda had a sense of humor?

"What are your plans for the rest of the evening?" Katie asked me, reminding me of my hasty promise to Sir William.

"I almost forgot," I said.

"Forgot what?"

"Sir William invited me to watch the sunset down by the ocean tonight." I stood. "I was supposed to meet him in the gardens after dinner."

"How romantic!" Amanda said.

"Yes, that sounds fun," Katie added.

"It will be fun," I said. *But I'd rather be watching the sunset with Dennan.*

"I think Sir William is hiding a tender heart inside his cold exterior," Katie said.

Amanda sighed. "And he's so handsome."

"Maybe he'll ask you to the ball," Katie said.

I didn't want to go to the ball with Sir William. I wanted to go with Dennan. In fact, I would've been happy to just see him again, maybe even touch him again to make sure he was real.

This is crazy! I had only just met the guy, and I couldn't stop thinking about him.

"Tell us everything when you get back," Amanda said, bringing me back to the present.

I took a deep breath, shaking Dennan from my mind. "Wish me luck."

"Good luck," Amanda and Katie replied cheerfully in unison.

Before exiting the room, I glanced at the magic door next to the hearth. *Gabriella, if I don't return home soon, I don't know how much more my heart can take.*

Chapter 13

Current Boyfriend: Shane Harper

I often wondered how this fabulously attractive older guy was interested in me, since he had graduated from high school and I was still seventeen. Shane and I met that summer at a movie theater near Grandma's house. During the show, he kept looking at me across the room. I mean, most of the time it was too dark to see each other, but when I'd glance over at him, he was always looking my way with a flirtatious grin. When the movie ended, he asked for my number. As they say, the rest was history. We kept in close contact through emails and texts, and when I visited my grandma we hung out a lot.

One night, Shane cupped my cheek in his hand, obviously planning to kiss me. From the fire in his eyes, I knew this would be different from the playful kisses he had planted on me in the past. This kiss was destined to be passionate—possibly even blissful.

Finally! I thought. I had waited so long for a passion-filled kiss. I'd never experienced a fairy-tale kiss—the kiss dreams are made of.

I watched as Shane's head bent toward mine. The pivotal moment was upon me. His kiss was soft and sweet, but as his lips lingered, my spirit felt numb and my heart did not soar. This definitely wasn't the kiss I'd always dreamed about.

I turned my head, ending it.

Still Day 5—That Night

Living in a fairy-tale land was stressful (who knew?), and I tried to calm myself while I walked through the gardens. My heart took courage as I gazed at nature's brilliant rainbow of colors. My fingers brushed against the delicate flowers, and I admired each plant as it swayed gently at my touch. Soon, my selfish worries seemed distant and insignificant. There was no pressure about finding a way back home, following the standards of this world, or dealing with Lady Catherine and the stepsisters.

Leaning my head back, I stopped, closed my eyes, and inhaled deeply. The delicate, heady fragrances of the blossoms filled me with a tranquility nothing could disturb . . . well, almost nothing. As if on cue, I heard the crunch of pebbles and looked up to see William marching toward me, his polished black shoes making the offensive noise.

"There you are," he said. "I worried I wouldn't be able to find you when I didn't indicate an exact meeting place."

"Well, here I am." I held out my hands.

Once he stood directly before me, he bowed. "Miss Brinlee, will you do me the pleasure of accompanying me down to the water's edge?"

I was delighted with his sophisticated invitation. My uncertainty about Sir William had clearly been foolish. This man—this gorgeous man from the storybook of my dreams—was escorting me to a romantic seaside setting. How could I be uncertain about that?

I curtsied. "I would love to."

William offered his elbow. Feeling almost giddy, I slipped my hand into the crook of his arm

Thanks to Dennan, the day had been long and emotionally taxing. Now, I reminded myself that he was a stranger whom I knew absolutely nothing about. I would not tax my mind by thinking about him further. Instead, I would treat myself to a once-in-a-lifetime experience of walking along the stunning coastline of a mythical fairy-tale land with a beautiful headman named William.

Dennan? Dennan who?

I strengthened my hold on William's arm. "You have no idea how excited I am to see the seashore."

He placed his hand on mine. "I'm glad."

He guided me across the gardens to a path leading down to the edge of the cliff. He was chivalrous and kind, assisting me in navigating the steep, rocky trail. If it wasn't for the annoying layers of clothing I wore, I would have made it without a hiccup of difficulty. Instead, my petticoats wrapped around my legs and I was constantly lifting my skirts away from my feet.

Once we reached the sandy shore and gazed at the horizon, I knew the trek coming down the cliff with my tangled mess of skirts was worth it. The colors on the rippling waters were spectacular. I couldn't remember ever seeing a more magnificent picture.

"It's beautiful, isn't it?" William said quietly.

"It's amazing!"

Vivid colors spread across the sky and reflected on the water. Far away on the horizon, the sun appeared to rest on the edge of the world before it dipped slowly away.

"Let's sit over here," William said. When I didn't respond, he touched my shoulder.

"Yes," I finally replied, "let's sit."

We leaned against a large rock and watched the sun's reflection playing on the waves. The color shifted to a rich orange and then a dark pink. Each new color spilled onto the water in breathtaking splendor.

After the sea sparkled blue and then light purple, William broke the silence. "We should head up the cliff before it gets too dark to proceed safely."

I nodded and allowed him to help me stand. I didn't want to leave, but he was right. I took one last look at the sunset and then followed him to the cliff. He pulled me by the hand while I used my other hand to hold onto my cumbersome skirts, and we made it up the cliff easier than I'd imagined.

When we got back to Sherwood Manor, it was dark.

"Thank you, William," I said as we stood just outside the manor near the kitchen door. "I had a really good time."

Could I curtsy my appreciation, or would he expect a kiss? What was the norm on first dates in the late eighteenth century?

"Thank you for accompanying me," he said courteously.

"I'm sorry we didn't talk more. I guess I was overcome by the beautiful sunset."

"It's all right." He stepped closer, reaching for my hand. "I'm not one to overstrain with needless talk."

Whoa, boy. Back up!

My heart did not flutter but rather quivered with his implication. Had I been wrong not to worry about this guy?

Suddenly, I felt William's lips on mine. I stood awkwardly, with my eyes open. I wanted to pull away, but I didn't know the proper way to refuse him. After all, this was partly my fault, since I had accepted his courting.

I stepped away abruptly. I was tempted to wipe William's saliva from my lips, but I stopped myself. "Good evening." I smiled politely. "The sunset was beautiful."

He nodded and said, "Good evening," then turned and retreated around the corner of the house.

I leaned my back against the door and pressed my hand to my forehead. *I'm such an idiot!*

Everything was turning out to be a complete mess. And to add to my lifelong romantic problems, William's kiss had obviously meant nothing to me. I was as much of a hopeless romantic here in Fenmore Falls as I was back home in Idaho. I decided I wasn't destined to find my Prince Charming, let alone true love. What I needed was a good night's sleep and to wake up from this horrible nightmare.

I stood outside for a few more minutes, not ready to face anyone or answer any questions about my date. If I waited long enough, everyone would be in bed.

I only closed my tired eyes for a second, but when I opened them a tall figure emerged from the shadows. As he rapidly moved closer, I was shocked to discover it was Dennan.

"What are you doing here?" I asked.

He didn't say a word but continued his determined approach until he stood in front of me. He looked the same as earlier—shirt unbuttoned, dark hair in boyish disarray, black cloth covering his face, eyes piercing with emotion.

My heart raced. "Dennan?"

He was frowning. "How could you let him kiss you like that?" he almost growled.

"Excuse me?"

Dennan stepped close—so close I could feel his chest rise with his measured breathing. "Why did you let him kiss you?"

I was completely flustered. First of all, what was Dennan doing here at Sherwood Manor? And secondly, why was he so angry? I looked at the side of the house where William had retreated and then to the stables. Had Dennan been noticed by anyone else at the estate?

"You shouldn't have let him kiss you."

"I don't think that is any of your business!"

Dennan clamped his mouth shut.

"I don't understand why you care," I said angrily.

"I don't care. It's just that if you let someone kiss you, he should kiss you decently." Dennan shook his head. "You shouldn't let him slobber all over you like that."

"He hardly slobbered all over me," I lied. "And I still don't see what business it is of yours."

"I just expected more from you." His eyes narrowed.

"Who do you think you are, Sir Dennan?" My voice cracked with emotion. "You, all high and mighty, creep up to me in the dark of night, eavesdrop on a private conversation, and feel like you can give me advice just because we spent a couple of hours together by the pond?"

He inhaled slowly. "I'm sorry. I shouldn't have come."

It had been a long day, and I felt the sting of tears behind my eyes. "Why did you come, Dennan?"

He leaned forward until I could feel his breath on my face. "I was just passing by."

A tear trickled from the corner of my eye. "Why are you here?"

His expression softened and he lowered his gaze. "I saw you at the ocean and wanted to make sure you made it home without harm."

I was flattered. "I assure you that my safety was not in question. William would have protected me from danger."

"It was the potential danger from your companion that I was referring to."

"What? And you think that you would be a safer companion? You're Black Rider, the knight of the road, and you dwell in the forest, waiting to rob your next wealthy victim."

"I shouldn't have come," Dennan said gruffly. "Good evening, Miss Brinlee." He turned and began to walk away.

As I watched him go, my heart ached for him to stay. And since I possess the most untimely talent of not thinking before I speak, I blurted out, "I assume you know the decent way?"

Did I really just say that? I held my hands up to my cheeks as they began to burn. *Maybe he didn't hear me.*

Wrong!

Dennan slowly turned, raising an eyebrow. "The decent way of doing what?" He walked back to me.

I couldn't figure out how to erase what I'd said, so I went with it. "You said that if I let someone kiss me, he should be worthy of kissing me in a decent way." When Dennan stopped in front of me, I looked up into his brown eyes and asked, "How are you so sure William didn't kiss me in a decent way?"

Dennan leaned close so his mouth was next to my ear. His breath sent goosebumps down my neck and my arm. "His kiss didn't leave you breathless like you are when I am close to you," he whispered.

I exhaled the breath I didn't realize I was holding. *Oh, he is smooth.* But he was right. I felt nothing with William, while Dennan made me feel things I'd never felt before.

"Come with me." He grasped my hand and pulled me away from the kitchen door.

"Where are we going?"

"Do you trust me?"

Surprisingly, I did. "Yes . . . I think so."

He led me around the corner and down a path leading away from the manor. I kept up with his hurried pace until he stopped abruptly behind some trees. I bumped into his back.

"Oops, sorry."

Using the hand he wasn't holding, I pushed myself away from his back. All I could feel was muscle. *Is he made of steel?*

He turned around, and my hand sort of traveled across his arm to his chest. *It just happened . . . I swear.* Again, one of those out-of-body experiences. But I'm not going to say I was saddened by the convenient position.

I could feel him waiting for me to look up at him. Instead, I stared at his shirt, or should I say I was hypnotized by his chiseled chest. *Oh my!*

"Brinlee?" he asked.

I still did not meet his eyes. He was too close.

He placed a finger under my chin and forced me to raise my eyes. His gaze bore into my soul.

"I followed you tonight because I had to see you again." He lowered his eyes, looking embarrassed.

Touched by his honesty, I reached behind his head to untie the cloth that hid most of his face. Once the mask fell away, I rested my hand against his cheek, feeling the rough whiskers on my palm.

His eyes met mine. "I can't stop thinking about you," he said.

"I've been thinking about you too."

Dennan turned his mouth into my palm and gently placed a kiss in the center of my hand. My body trembled.

"Will you allow me to demonstrate how you should be kissed?" He placed his free hand at the hollow of my neck. "Then maybe you'll pay closer heed to whom you allow to kiss you."

Knowing my inexperience with passionate kisses, I looked away shyly.

Dennan gently grasped my chin and directed my gaze back to his. "Are you afraid of me?"

"No," I said a little too quickly.

"I will never hurt you."

"I know."

His hand returned to my throat, his fingertips playing at the back of my neck. I was sure he could feel my speeding pulse under his hand.

"Now let me illustrate the difference between a kiss" —he pulled my head closer to his— "and a decent kiss."

With his lips hovering above mine, he asked, "You didn't enjoy his kiss at all, did you?"

"No," I breathed, then closed my eyes as Dennan's mouth finally descended on mine.

At first his kiss was gentle, as if he was testing the waters. Then his lips were more demanding. His hand moved to the back of my head, and he pulled me closer. I slid my hand up his chest to his neck and threaded my fingers through his long hair.

I gasped out a breath. *Is this really happening?*

"I couldn't stop thinking about kissing you," he whispered, pressing his lips just below my ear.

How was this kiss different from any other? What made kissing Dennan so special? My burning heart shot out the answer: I was falling in love for the first time.

Did I just say the L-word? Was it possible to love someone so soon?

Dennan playfully kissed the corners of my mouth, and when I couldn't take it any longer, I took his face between my trembling hands and forced his lips back to mine. A sigh escaped him as he pulled me firmly against his powerful body. My fingers were lost again in the softness of his hair.

In that moment, nothing else mattered in the world—nothing but Dennan. It was my first thoroughly impassioned kiss. It was the kiss I had been waiting for, the kiss that made my heart soar.

Suddenly, I realized I would never again experience such a kiss. I pulled away, knowing that the longer I kissed Dennan, the more I'd know what I was missing when I returned home. In hindsight, it was probably better to never have felt what it was like to be kissed decently by the most handsome man in the world.

"I'm sorry." I moved my hands from the back of his neck and placed them squarely on his chest, pushing him to create distance between us.

He held my face in his hands. "You have no need to be sorry." His eyes were filled with concern. "It is I who should apologize to you."

I shook my head between his strong hands. "Don't apologize for what happened," I said. "If you do, it would be like it never happened."

He stood quietly, still holding my face between his hands. Lost again in his penetrating stare, I studied the green specks in his brown eyes.

Why now? Why did I have to find the perfect guy in a make-believe world? "I should go." I lowered my eyes to hide my tears.

Dennan kissed the top of my head. "You're right. I promised you that I would never put you in danger, and right now the best way for me to do that is to leave."

He stepped away from me, leaving me feeling oddly cold.

Don't go, I begged silently.

"That's how you should let someone kiss you," he said as he turned to go. "Good evening, Miss Brinlee."

I watched as he walked away in the moonlight.

And thanks to you, Cinderella, Miss Gabby, magic door, or whoever is to blame for this mix-up, if I wasn't a psychological mess before, I can guarantee a whopping diagnosis when I get home.

Chapter 14

The Wonderful Birch
Russia, 1890

Now it happened that a great festival was to be held at the palace, and the king had commanded that all the people should be invited, and that this proclamation should be made:

Come, people all!
Poor and wretched, one and all!
Blind and crippled though ye be,
Mount your steeds or come by sea.

And so they drove into the king's feast all the outcasts, and the maimed, and the halt, and the blind. In the good man's house, too, preparations were made to go to the palace. The witch said to the man, "Go you on in front, old man, with our youngest; I will give the elder girl work to keep her from being dull in our absence."

Days 6 and 7

The following day came and went with no incident. That included no word from Dennan, whom I had nicknamed the Heart Assassin.

I'd almost given up on opening the magic door. I was stuck in this demented world forever.

For-ev-er! For-ev-er! Yes, I also liked to quote the movie *The Sandlot.*

I tried to hide my sadness, but as Katie assisted me with my corset that morning, she asked, "Is something troubling you, Miss Brinlee?"

"I'm just a little homesick."

She accepted my explanation, even though I saw a flash of doubt in her eyes.

Fanny and Rose traveled to town that day to inspect their gowns at the milliner's. While they were gone, I took a walk and ventured out to the cliffs.

I let my thoughts dwell on Dennan for a moment. I closed my eyes and wrapped my arms around myself as I relived our enchanting moment from the previous night. My heart pounded at the ecstasy of feeling his lips on mine, yet my chest ached because I would never have that pleasure again. Why did I ever let him kiss me?

For the rest of the day, I attempted to push all thoughts of him aside by helping the servants around Sherwood Manor. I probably worked more in Fenmore Falls in a dress than I ever did at Nana's farm in Idaho in pants. I worked hard and fell on my bed exhausted that night. In the morning, I would beat at the magic door again, pleading for Gabriella to free me from this place.

I woke Friday morning, my seventh day in Fenmore Falls, with the ache in my heart only a murmuring echo. Everything was eclipsed by my throbbing hands, blistered from spending several hours the day before untangling knotted ropes in the stable.

I was more grateful than ever to have Katie to help me dress. With my injured hands, I was unable to even lift my clothes off the floor. She also wrapped my hands in linen to protect them.

That morning at breakfast in the dining room, Fanny asked, "Are you going to attend the ball this evening, Miss Brinlee?"

"I don't have the right clothes to wear."

"Doesn't Cinderella own something you can borrow?" Fanny snickered.

"Now, Fanny," Lady Catherine said, but it was clear she delighted in her daughter's cruel comment. "I am certain that we, as Miss Brinlee's hosts, can provide her with an appropriate gown so she may attend one of Fenmore Falls' most significant events."

"I don't think there's a dress with sleeves long enough to cover her bandaged hands," Fanny managed to say between giggles.

I stood. "May I be excused?"

I exited the room, leaving my untouched food on my plate. When I reached the hall, I allowed the tears to fall down my cheeks. *What am I supposed to learn from this insane place?*

Footsteps approached from down the hall. I quickly wiped the tears from my face.

Thankfully, only Katie rounded the corner. As she approached, she did not seem to notice my blubbering or my teary eyes.

"Has Lady Catherine finished her food?" she asked.

"Um . . . no. Not yet."

"She told me to be here as soon as breakfast was finished."

"Busy day?"

Katie nodded. "She has requested my assistance for the entire day. After breakfast, I am to inspect the women's costumes and trimmings to see if I need to make any necessary alterations for tonight's ball. Then, stockings will need to be ironed, corsets tightened, dresses pinned, hair curled, and faces primped."

Suddenly, I longed to join in the merriment and to waltz with Prince Charming at the ball. But even if I'd had an appropriate dress, I had failed to act like a gentlewoman, so I could not go. Sadly, there were no such events in my reality world in Idaho, and I was unable go to a ball here in the fictional world of Fenmore Falls. Being Cinderella and dancing at the ball with Prince Charming just wasn't in the cards for me.

"Oh, there's so much to do," Katie fretted.

I rested my hand on her shoulder. "I'll help you."

"Thank you, but you should be attending the ball too."

"No, my place is to stay here and help you. Besides, in my dreams, I have a perfect picture of what it would be like, and I don't want the truth to ruin it."

Katie smiled. "In your dream, are all the princes tall and handsome, while all the other women in attendance are horridly unattractive?"

I laughed. "Yes. There would be no wicked stepmothers and no stepsisters, and the true Cinderella would win Prince Charming's heart."

Katie held a hand to her mouth, restraining her giggles. "You live in a storybook world, Miss Brinlee."

More than you know.

"The world seems more magical when you see it as a fairy tale," I said. "But the real magic is when someone wins your heart."

"That sounds wonderful."

"I'm sure you've already won Krys's heart."

Katie's cheeks went pink. "He only sees me as a dimwitted child."

"He does not. I've seen the way he looks at you."

She scrunched her eyebrows. "What do you mean?"

"He watches you when you're in the same room, and he stares when you're leaving a room, just so he can watch you a little longer without you noticing."

Now Katie's cheeks were scarlet. "He does not."

"Yes, he does."

"I don't believe it." She shook her head.

"You better believe it, and you better take action before Henry continues to express his affection and gives Krys the wrong idea."

Katie stuck out her tongue. "Henry is a portly mound of cheese."

I laughed at her description of the revolting man. She was a quiet girl but had quite a quirky sense of humor, especially for this era.

"Just be a bit friendlier towards Krys the next time you see him," I suggested. "And when you're walking out of a room, peek over your shoulder. When you see him staring at you, you'll know I'm not lying."

"Do you really think he fancies me?" Her eyes held all the hope of a young girl in love.

"Yes, I do."

"Have you ever been in love, Miss Brinlee?"

Katie's question shouldn't have caught me off guard, and it irritated me that I immediately thought of Dennan, the man who hadn't returned since he kissed me and used me.

Had I ever been in love? No. And I wasn't in love with Dennan, either. I was smitten by his good looks, and I would never forget the way he kissed me, but it wasn't love.

Why am I even deliberating over this issue?

"No," I replied finally, "but I know what love is supposed to feel like. I've lived my whole life searching for that perfect love—the kind that's written about in storybooks."

"I'll have to read some of those storybooks you're always talking about."

I smiled to myself, thinking that Katie was smack dab in the middle of a story right now.

"Katie!" Lady Catherine's shout from the dining room shattered the peace in the air.

And just like that, my relaxing conversation with Katie ended, and our busy morning began. The two of us obeyed every command of the ladies of the house. By the time they climbed into the carriage, with Sir William as escort and Sir Henry as chauffeur, the three women looked stunning.

After they left for the ball, Katie and I had to clean up. The bedrooms looked like war zones instead of gentlewomen's private abodes. Katie and I scrubbed until everything shined.

Finally, long after the sun had set, I sat at the kitchen table, exhausted. It was probably an hour past midnight, but my mind was too worked up to let me sleep. I was alone—except for the dog Fred, who slept at my feet.

I sat with my chin propped in one of my hands, imagining how it would have been to go to the ball and meet Prince Charming. My eyes brimmed with tears. Too tired to try to control my emotions, I hung my head and watched the tears drop to my dirty apron.

Come on, Brinlee, stop being such a baby. I held my head up. *Happy face,* I commanded silently.

I wiped my face. I wasn't going to cry anymore, and I wasn't going to lose any more sleep over something I couldn't control. Tomorrow was another day—not today or yesterday, but a new day.

I stood and opened the kitchen door. Lady Catherine and her daughters would soon return from the ball, and I needed energy to face their pompous attitudes again. A short walk and some fresh air would do the trick.

The darkness outside enveloped me with peace. The moon lent just enough light so I could see to meander through the gardens. Eventually, I ended up at the edge of the cliff, looking out across the sparkling water. The moon's glowing outline reached from the water's edge and dove across the sea's ripples into the deep horizon.

Lost in the beauty, I raised my left hand as if placing it on the shoulder of a dance partner, then positioned my other hand in the air to grasp my imaginary partner's hand. I twirled in the grass as if I was being spun in a waltz, and envisioned myself dancing with the prince at the castle.

I closed my eyes to picture the moment more clearly. Just like all of the books and movies about Cinderella, there was an orchestra playing music, a king and queen sitting on their thrones, dance partners floating across the floor, and a handsome prince holding me and guiding me across the room.

When my imaginary dance ended, I curtsied and spoke to my imaginary prince, "Thank you, Your Highness."

Over the sound of the waves softly colliding with the sandy beach, I heard a stick crack a few yards behind me. I turned and was astonished when none other than Dennan stood behind me.

Chapter 15

Cinderella
Germany, 1812

She kneeled down in the ashes next to the hearth and was about to begin her work when two white pigeons flew in through the window. They lit on the hearth next to the lentils. Nodding their heads, they said, "Cinderella, do you want us to help you sort the lentils?"

"Yes," she answered. "The bad ones go into your crop, the good ones go into the pot."

And peck, peck, peck, peck, they started at once, eating up the bad ones and leaving the good ones lying. In only a quarter of an hour there was not a single bad lentil among the good ones, and she brushed them all into the pot.

Then the pigeons said to her, "Cinderella, if you would like to see your sisters dancing with the prince, just climb up to the pigeon roost." She followed them and climbed to the top rung of the ladder to the pigeon roost. There she could see into the hall, and she saw her sisters dancing with the prince. Everything glistened by the glow of a thousand lights. After she had seen enough, she climbed back down. With a heavy heart she lay down in the ashes and fell asleep.

The Shock of Seeing Him

By the faint light of the moon, I could see Dennan smiling in amusement. "Please don't stop," he said. He wasn't wearing his mask, and his hair was combed back. He wore a different set of clothes, including a dark vest. Of course, his shirt was halfway unbuttoned in true rogue style.

I barely held back my tears of frustration. "Go away, Dennan."

"I missed you," he said with a grin.

"Ha! I haven't seen a sign of you for two days, and now you have the nerve to say you missed me? You're probably going to say you couldn't stop thinking about me. Oh wait, you already used that one."

He walked toward me in hurried strides. I tried to step away, but he grabbed my arm. I flinched at the familiar thrill that shot through my body.

"I'm sorry, Brinlee," he said, sounding so sincere. "I had some business to take care of."

Some business to take care of? Did he mean highwayman business? Realizing that might be the case, I pushed aside my anger and disappointment. After all, everyone had to work, right?

We stood so close I had to lean my head back to look at Dennan's face. "I thought I'd never see you again."

His grin returned. "It sounds like you missed me too."

"I didn't say that. I'm just saying I was disappointed you didn't have the good manners to visit me after our last encounter."

"Encounter? Is that what you call it?" He smirked. "In that case, would you demonstrate to me what an encounter is? Because I might have forgotten."

I lowered my eyes self-consciously.

"It's true that I can't stop thinking about you," he said softly. "Even though I was away, my heart and mind stayed here with you."

Is he saying what I think he's saying?

Dennan grabbed my hands and brought them up to his lips. Too late, I remembered my blistered hands and tried to pull them away, embarrassed at how rough they must feel. But he firmly held my hands in place.

"I'm sorry," I said. "I've been working and have a lot of blisters on my hands."

"They're hard-working hands," he replied.

"Exactly. They're not the hands of a gentlewoman."

He kissed my knuckles, and with the attention his mouth paid to my hands, my lips grew jealous.

"Did I ever tell you I don't like soft, gentlewomen's hands?" Dennan asked. "They're not practical." He intertwined his fingers with mine. "Your hands show your ambition for life."

His deep voice brought my gaze back to his face. Any woman would swoon over his dark eyes, his strong jaw, and his perfect lips.

"I would compare you to an autumn's breeze," he said in a formal tone.

I smiled. "Is that something Shakespeare said?"

"I have to admit I've never been interested in rhymes or poems before—they always struck me as too fancy and feminine." Dennan moved his hand to touch my cheek. "Poets write about their blinded love and deepest longings, some attainable and others not." He caressed my bottom lip with his thumb. "Well—" his smile grew serious "—now I know how they feel."

My heart paused in its wild beating as I waited for him to continue. His gaze drifted to the ground.

He's nervous. Sweet! I leaned in, closing the gap between us.

His arms slid around my waist and held me against his chest. "I've been a lovesick fool since I met you."

Even if my self-doubt wanted to disbelieve him, the sincerity of his gaze showed me he was telling the truth. And with how he had consumed my thoughts, I could relate to what he was saying.

"Your beauty whispers as the wind in the trees," he said with a wink.

"Okay, you can stop now." I wasn't used to men reciting poems to me.

"Your eyes, your hands." He raised my hand and placed it on his chest above his heart. "Your lips." He focused his gaze on my lips. His breath was warm and enticing as his mouth lingered close to mine.

Kiss me already! I wanted to shout.

Thankfully, before I fainted, he took my face in his hands and said, "I'm going to kiss you now."

I closed my eyes and braced myself as his mouth captured mine.

Why do we close our eyes when we kiss? Why do we close our eyes when we pray? I would wonder later. Because the most wonderful and powerful things in life are unseen and are felt only with our hearts. Just like the enchantment I felt while kissing Dennan.

But back to the kiss. Everything around me vanished, and I relished in the magic of being in his arms. His hands soon moved from my face to my hair. As he tangled his fingers in my curls, goosebumps erupted along my skin.

I touched his face and could feel the muscles in his cheeks work as he kissed me. His face was smooth, not covered with rough whiskers as before. I ran my hands over the contours of his face. I loved the way he smelled—the wonderful, manly scent that was only him. It was the smell of someone who rode free, the smell of wind and trees and dirt.

Dennan's lips parted from mine. "I know exactly how those poets felt, because I'm feelings words I've never felt before." He kissed me softly and pulled back. "Look what you've done to me."

"Me? What have I done?"

"I'm wearing my heart on my sleeve, and it's entirely your fault." He sneaked another quick kiss. "You've cast a magic spell on me."

There was that witch reference again. "I'm not a witch, Dennan, and if you think I've cast a spell on you, you're wrong. I'm only a girl who is stuck in the wrong place in the wrong time and is trying to find her way home."

"That's not what I meant," he said with worry in his eyes. "I know you're not a witch. But I can't understand how you have possessed my mind so completely."

"I bet you say that to all the girls."

"That's just it. You're not like the other girls."

"I know I'm different. It's because I don't belong here."

"Well, I'm glad you're different."

He placed a lingering kiss on my forehead, causing me to lose my train of thought.

"Why didn't you go to the ball tonight?" he asked suddenly.

I shrugged my shoulders. "It's complicated."

"Did you not want to go?"

Of course I wanted to go. "I stayed home to help the servants."

"You didn't answer the question." He leaned back to look at my face. "Did you want to go?"

"I didn't have an appropriate dress to wear."

"Brinlee," he said in a low tone as if scolding a young child. "Did you want to go to the ball?"

"Yes," I finally admitted.

"What would you have said to the prince if you danced with him?"

"What?"

"You told me earlier how wonderful it would be to meet the prince, so I figured that's who you were pretending to dance with."

Wow, this guy is perceptive. I looked away, feeling guilty about my infatuation with the prince.

"Explain to me the fascination," Dennan said. "Why would you dream of a spoiled, pampered prince when you could have a brave, strong man—like me?" He puffed out his chest. "Wouldn't you want someone who could defend you with his fists instead of his nobleness?"

I giggled at the comparison. "The prince is not a spoiled, pampered coward."

"How do you know?"

Dennan's question had merit. How did I know the prince of Fenmore Falls was the brave and fearless Prince Charming of my dreams?

"Because he recently returned from fighting pirates." There, that would defend the valiant prince.

Dennan chuckled. "How do you know he didn't return home and spread rumors of the supposed battle?"

"Because he wouldn't do that—the prince is better than that." *I hope.*

"You think highly of your prince, don't you?" he asked seriously.

"I've thought of him my entire life," I admitted.

There was no getting around it. I could lie to Dennan and tell him I never wanted to meet the prince, but Prince Charming was as big a part of my dreams as the Cinderella story had always been. Dennan could take it or leave it—my whole crazy package.

"What would you have said to the prince if you had danced with him?" he asked again, this time with a touch of sadness.

"I would curtsy first." I dipped into a bow. "Then, I would say, 'It's an honor to meet you, Your Highness.'"

"That's what you would say?" Dennan raised an eyebrow. "That's what you would say to the prince of your dreams, 'It's an honor to meet you'?"

"Well, what would you want me to say? Would you want me to say, 'I just noticed you look a lot like my next boyfriend'?"

It took Dennan a few seconds, but once he understood my cheesy pickup line, he laughed boisterously. I loved the way he leaned his head back, I loved the sound of his voice, and I loved the dimple in his left cheek. If possible, his boyish enthusiasm made him even more attractive.

I remembered another pickup line. "How about I say, 'Are your legs tired, because you've been running through my mind all day long?'"

Dennan laughed even louder at that one. "See what I mean? You always make me smile."

I remembered another pickup line, this one from personal experience. I was at a dance when a guy came up to me and said,

"Do you mind if I hang out here until it's safe back where I farted?" He really said that. Can you believe it? Even more unbelievable is that the guy ended up being a good friend later on. No romantic feelings were felt though, obviously. I decided not to share that story with Dennan.

"I've got one," he said, surprising me. "You should say, 'I've never had a dream come true until the day I met you.'"

"Ah. I like that one."

Dennan stroked my cheek with his hand. "You're the woman of my dreams, Brinlee."

The sound of his voice made everything disappear—the trees, the gardens of Sherwood Manor, the ocean. We were in our own world.

"I know I'll never measure up to your prince," he said, "but will you dance with me?"

"Now? Here?"

He gave me a crooked grin. "Yes, right now. What better place than in the light of the lovers' moon?" He looked up into the sky.

I gazed into the heavens as well. It was definitely a magic night—a night dreams were made of.

Dennan slid his right hand to my waist and placed his left hand in the air. "May I have this dance?" he asked as he dipped his head.

For a rogue of the forest, he cleaned up nicely. He could probably even pass as a courtier. I curtsied. "I'd love to."

Once I placed my hands in position, Dennan began to lead me in a waltz. He executed the dance smoothly, and I basked in the feeling of floating on a cloud.

"How do you know how to dance so well?" I asked.

He shrugged. "It's something I learned on the road."

"Really? They teach this at gypsy school?"

"No." He turned me around in a slow spin. When I moved close again, he bent down and whispered against my ear. "My mother taught me when I was younger."

Remind me to thank his mother, 'cause this boy can dance.

He spun me around again, but this time when we were close again, his mouth captured mine suddenly and insistently. I felt the sweetness through the back of my head and down my back. We still turned as if we were dancing, but I was hardly aware of my feet moving. The world was in motion. I was in paradise.

He abruptly removed his lips from mine and said, "You should go to the next ball."

Like a fish yanked out of a stream, I was swiftly brought back to the present. "Come again?"

"You should go to the ball and dance with the prince."

Wait, I think I missed something. "What are you talking about?"

"I'm no substitute for what your heart truly wants."

I placed a palm against Dennan's cheek. "I wouldn't be here if I didn't want to be with you."

He took my hands and raised it to his lips. He kissed my fingers. "You need to go the ball. Your heart will never be open to anything else unless you know what's out there."

I knew he was getting ready to say goodbye. "You can't just leave again." I sounded like a whiny puppy, but I couldn't help it. I was tired.

He squeezed my hands. "I'll come back."

"When?"

"I need to take care of a few things, but I'll be back."

The tears behind my eyes began to overflow upon my cheeks.

"I'll come back." Dennan brushed at my tears.

"Promise?"

"I promise." He gathered me into an embrace.

My tears fell onto the front of his shirt. I slid my hands under his arms and wrapped my arms around his back.

"I promise to come back if you promise you'll go to the ball." His chin rested on the top of my head.

"I don't have anything to wear." I sniffled.

"Will you promise to go if I find you something to wear?"

I looked up. "You're not going to steal me a dress to wear to the ball, are you?"

"I'm not going to thieve you a dress." His dimple showed as he gave me a reassuring smile. "Meet me Thursday of next week, and I will give you the dress."

"Thursday?" I exclaimed. "Not until Thursday?" My tears continued their steady stream down my cheeks.

"You're tired. You need to get some rest."

I couldn't argue. My body wanted to collapse to the ground.

"You need to rest so you can continue to dance in your dreams." He smoothed my hair. "I'm glad I got to see you dance like nobody's watching."

I gave a small sigh. Could this guy be any more perfect?

"Always dance like nobody's watching, and sing like nobody's listening," he said. When I looked up at him, he added, "And love like you've never been hurt." He kissed me once, gently.

All at once I opened my eyes. "Dennan?"

"Yes?" he said against my mouth.

"I have a favor to ask you."

"Anything."

"My friends Katie and Amanda are servants here at Sherwood Manor, and they are also in need of dresses for the ball . . ."

"And you want me to steal—" he quirked his eyebrow "—I mean find gowns for them also?"

"If it's not too much trouble."

"I think I'll be able to meet your request."

"Thank you, Dennan." I gave him a peck on the cheek.

"Anything for you, milady." He bowed.

"I'm glad you came back."

"I would come back every day if I could."

At that, he turned and disappeared in the darkness.

Chapter 16

Another Song from My Favorite Movie

These lyrics are from the soundtrack to *The Slipper and the Rose*. Quite fitting, huh?

> *Though this lovely night was only a fantasy*
> *And I know tonight is all there will ever be*
> *Dancing in his arms forever*
> *My heart will never be free!*
> *Dreaming of the night he danced with me*

("He Danced with Me/She Danced with Me," Image Entertainment, 1976)

Back to the Manor

After Dennan left, I walked back to Sherwood Manor, humming the melody to this beautiful, addictive song. I was weary beyond measure, but I walked in a waltz rhythm along the path near the gardens. *One, two, three. One, two, three.*

As I got closer to the manor, I saw a light in the fourth floor of the tower—the forbidden tower. A chill ran down my back. Only Lady Catherine had a key to the tower, and who knows what she was doing there.

A shadow in the shape of a woman moved on the curtains of the tower window. Then the light went out and the tower was dark.

You're dreaming, I told myself. *You're tired and need some sleep.*

Suddenly, a ghostly voice said, "Brinlee?"

I jumped and turned to see William walking toward me. I cried out and pressed a hand to my pounding heart.

"I'm sorry if I startled you. I was returning the horses to the stable and heard noises. I came out to check."

"When did everyone get back from the ball?"

"We just returned a few moments ago." His blond hair was slicked back, his jacket straight and orderly.

"Was it lovely?" I asked.

William smiled, his perfectly white teeth gleaming in the moonlight. "I guess you could say it was lovely. At least that is what the ladies say."

I was unable to prevent a yawn from escaping my mouth, but managed to ask, "Was the prince there?"

William ignored my question. "Why are you outside at such a late hour?"

"I couldn't sleep, so I came out for some fresh air."

He cocked his head to one side. "Did you notice anything unusual on the grounds?"

"No." Despite myself, I glanced up at the mysterious forbidden tower.

"Be careful of where you decide to meddle, Miss Brinlee," he said in a sinister tone. "The tower is none of your concern, and you would be smart to leave it alone."

Nodding, I thought, *What have I gotten myself into?* When I walked through the attic door of my bedroom into a kingdom called Fenmore Falls, I certainly hadn't imagined how dangerous a Cinderella story could be.

William smiled woodenly. "You should retire to your bed. Would you like me to escort you to your chambers?"

"No," I nearly shouted. Wanting to get as far away from him as possible, I brushed past him and hurried toward the kitchen door. *Walk,* I commanded my legs. *Just walk.*

As I reached for the door handle, he asked, "Who was he?"

Fear washed over me. Had William seen me with Dennan? If Dennan was truly the knight of the road, would his identity be compromised because he hadn't worn his mask?

I didn't turn to face William. Instead, I stared straight at the door. "I don't know who you're talking about."

He stepped close behind me. "I saw you." His hand was suddenly on my shoulder. "I saw the way you let him hold you." William's hand slid down my arm. "Who knows what might happen to a woman when she finds herself alone at night."

I wanted to scream. If this guy didn't watch it, I'd do some Karate Kid on him.

He moved my hair away from my neck and pressed his lips against my ear. "Good night, Brinlee. If you need anything, I'll be more than willing to gratify your desires."

Finally breaking away, I pulled open the door, raced inside, and flew up the stairs. In the safety of my bedroom, I locked the door and stripped off my clothes. I wanted to rid myself of the filth I felt all over my body at being touched by William. I would have taken a bath if I could've gone to the kitchen and heated several pails of water without waking half of the household.

I slipped into a fresh nightgown and collapsed onto the bed. Despite the events of the evening, I quickly and thankfully faded into a deep sleep.

Chapter 17

Pepelyouga
Serbia, 1917

Next morning the woman roughly ordered the maiden to spin a still larger bag of hemp, and as the girl, thanks to her mother, spun and wound it all, her stepmother, on the following day, gave her twice the quantity to spin. Nevertheless, the girl brought home at night even that unusually large quantity well spun, and her stepmother concluded that the poor girl was not spinning alone, but that other maidens, her friends, were giving her help. Therefore she, next morning, sent her own daughter to spy upon the poor girl and to report what she saw. The girl soon noticed that the cow helped the poor orphan by chewing the hemp, while she drew the thread and wound it on a top, and she ran back home and informed her mother of what she had seen. Upon this, the stepmother insisted that her husband should order that particular cow to be slaughtered. Her husband at first hesitated, but as his wife urged him more and more, he finally decided to do as she wished.

Day 8

I woke to sunlight streaming through my open window. My dreams had been filled with Dennan, and I practically glowed with happiness. It was as if I was walking on rays of sunshine.

So this is love, I mentally sang. No, this was better than love. This was what I had been waiting for my whole life.

But this isn't real, I reminded myself. *I'm trapped in a fairy-tale world!* The William situation also intercepted my cheerfulness. I squeezed my eyes shut, now wishing I could go back to sleep.

"Miss Brinlee?" Katie said from just outside my bedroom door.

"Come in."

She opened the door with a smile. "The entire household has slept late today."

"I'm not the only one who overslept?"

"Miss Fanny and Miss Rose are still asleep in their beds."

"I stayed up way too late." I pressed my palm against my tender head, feeling a headache coming on.

"Sir William told Lady Catherine this morning that he met you in the gardens last night," Katie reported.

I sat up straight in bed. "What did he say?"

"He said you couldn't sleep and needed some fresh air."

"Did he say anything else?" I remembered him ordering me to stay away from the tower. Had he relayed his suspicions to Lady Catherine?

Katie shook her head. "No, nothing else."

Why was the tower such a secret? What was Lady Catherine hiding in there? Was she involved in the evil conspiracy to overthrow the kingdom? Is that why Dennan was often near Sherwood Manor?

Hmm, that's something to think about.

"What were you doing outside all alone, Miss Brinlee?" Katie asked.

"I wasn't alone."

If I couldn't tell a friend, whom could I tell?

I patted the bed next to me for Katie to sit. "You can't tell anybody, but I met somebody."

She leaped onto the soft bed and gathered a pillow into her arms. "Tell me everything."

I told her the whole story, starting from when I first met Dennan, to our dance the night before.

"He's bringing a dress for you too," I told her after explaining how Dennan had promised he would get me a dress for the ball.

"No. I couldn't possibly go to the ball."

"For heaven's sake, why not?"

"It wouldn't be proper."

"But whoever is suitable may attend. With our new dresses, there is no reason for us to miss the ball."

Katie lowered her head.

"I thought you would be excited," I said.

"I am excited. It's just that I don't want to go to the ball if Sir Henry is my escort."

"Henry? Why would Henry be your escort?" I wrinkled my nose in disgust.

"Do you remember when he asked me if I was going to the ball?"

"But he only asked if you were going. He didn't actually ask you to be his date, did he?"

"Well . . . no." She smiled.

"Now you can go to the ball with Krys."

Instantly, the color drained from Katie's face.

"Relax, Katie. It was only a suggestion."

"I couldn't possibly imagine going to the ball with Krys."

"You never know," I said with a wink, "maybe he'll gather up the courage to ask you."

Katie looked anxious, but a faint pink began to return to her cheeks. "He will not ask me."

We'll see about that, thought my scheming mind.

Later that night—sooner than I had expected—I got the chance to help Katie on the path to having her dreams come true.

As the servants socialized in the kitchen, the discussion shifted to the upcoming second ball at the castle.

"I wish I could go to the ball," Amanda said as she leaned her chin on her palm, her elbow resting on the table.

"You and Katie are going to the ball with me," I said, completely forgetting who else was in the room. I hadn't told Amanda about the dresses yet, and once I realized Henry sat in his usual place in the corner, it was too late.

He stood up and loomed near the table. "Are you attending the ball on Friday night, Katie?" he asked.

She looked at me with panic in her eyes. I raced to think of a way to save her from being stuck at the ball with Henry. Going with him as her date was not in my fairy-godmother plan for her. Going with Krys was.

I had no choice but to do something dreadfully awful. "Sir Henry." I looked at the freckle-faced servant. "I wanted to ask you a question."

It wasn't necessarily his looks that spawned my distaste. It was the way he conducted himself, like the way he scratched his crotch in front of us . . . like right now, in front of all of us. *Who does that?* He was simply repulsive.

I swallowed hard, forcing down the bile in my throat. "Would you escort me to the ball, Sir Henry?"

Yep, I said it. That really was me.

Henry looked as surprised at my words as I was. "Yes, Miss Brinlee." He puffed up his chest. "I would love to do the honor of escorting you to the ball."

"Thank you."

He walked back to his chair and continued to sloppily eat his dinner.

What have I done? I thought. *This better work.*

Chapter 18

A Love Letter from My Dad to My Mom

I found this letter in a box under my mom's bed.

My dearest Abby (no one called her that anymore—it was always Abigail or Gail),

I miss you already. I'm hoping this trip will be shorter than the last. I think I've found a buyer for my mother's house. If everything goes well, I'll be home before you know it.

In the mean time, keep my mother's locket forever around your neck and close to your heart. I replaced my father's picture with mine so you can remember what I look like . . . in case you ever forget.

I'll be home soon. Kiss the girls for me.
Love always,
Jack

I spent countless hours gazing at the portrait in that locket to remind me of what my father looked like. Since I was only three years old when he left, my brain often had a hard time remembering.

Day 9

The following morning, the nicer of the two evil stepsisters, Rose, joined me in my bedroom. She was actually pleasant company when her older sister wasn't nearby.

"I'm thrilled you will be attending the ball," Rose said.

It surprised me how fast the news had spread that I was going to the ball with Henry. "I'm excited too," I said. *Except that I'll have to dance with Henry.*

Rose twisted a lock of her auburn hair. "The castle is incredible."

"What does the prince look like?" I asked.

"Prince Patrick is magnificent."

I let out a sigh. "I bet he is."

"I nearly fainted when he entered the ballroom."

"Did you dance with him?"

"No." Rose shook her head. "He didn't dance much—mostly watched." She leaned in closer with a sly smile on her face. "There's word that the prince has invited company to Friday night's ball."

"Company? What company?"

"Fanny's friend, Miss Gretchen, says that King Edwin's daughter, Camilla, arrived in Fenmore Falls yesterday."

"A princess?" my voice squeaked.

This is not good. Without Gabriella here to be Prince Patrick's Cinderella, would he marry this princess Camilla?

"Yes. Princess Camilla is the only child of King Edwin."

"Have you seen her?"

"No, but many people speak of her beauty," Rose said.

"Well, she's a princess. She must be beautiful."

"She has long yellow hair." Rose touched her own hair.

Of course she does. I bet it's soft like silk, too.

"She's also very gracious. She oversees the orphanages in her kingdom and ensures that the children are properly educated."

Lovely. She sounded perfect.

"It looks like we have some competition, don't we?" I said.

Rose snickered. "Yes, we do."

Days 10 Through 12

The upcoming ball was discussed excitedly at Sherwood Manor over the next few days. As the event approached, I worried I wouldn't be able to convince the shy Krys to ask Katie to the dance. I wouldn't be her fairy godmother if I didn't make some magic happen—and soon. I had planned to hint that he should ask Katie to the dance, but ancient boys were about as quick to understand women's hints as modern boys were. Therefore, I knew I needed to just tell Krys point-blank.

On Wednesday afternoon, I headed out to talk to him. He was walking toward the stables, and I called out his name.

The young man stopped in his path and looked at me. "Miss Brinlee?"

It wasn't hard to see why Katie was infatuated with Krys. He was handsome, and though he was still young, the muscles in his arms bulged against his tight work shirt.

He ran his fingers through his wavy brown hair as he strode toward me. "Can I help you, Miss Brinlee?"

"Yes . . ." I paused. "I guess there's no great way to say this, so I'm just going to say it."

He raised an eyebrow.

"You need to ask Katie to the ball," I blurted.

Krys's face went beet red. I reveled in his obvious attraction to my dear friend.

"I can't do that," he mumbled.

"Why not?"

"She would never go to the ball with me. I'm a lowly stable boy." He shifted his gaze to the ground.

"Do you not know of Katie's interest in you?"

"You flatter me, Miss Brinlee." He looked up through his eyelashes.

"I speak the truth, Krys."

He ran his fingers through his hair again. "Do you really think she would go to the ball with me if I asked her?"

"It would be her dream come true." I hope I didn't scare him off, but time was running out. "I'm sorry to be so blunt with you."

"Thank you, Miss Brinlee. I'll think about what you said."

He tipped his head and walked back to the stables.

That went better than I expected. Hopefully there would be a big smile on Katie's face the next time I saw her. I wondered if I should act surprised or admit to my involvement.

After I retired to my bedroom late that Wednesday night, I heard a quiet knock on the door.

"Miss Brinlee?" Amanda said.

"Come in."

She opened the door and stepped in. "A letter for you."

A letter? Who would send me a letter? My heart leapt. *Dennan!* I reached for the folded paper. "Who delivered it?"

Amanda shrugged. "I don't know. Henry answered the door. Well, good night, Miss Brinlee." She left my bedroom.

My fingers trembled as I opened the letter. It read, *I miss you . . . until tomorrow.*

That was all. No signature or address. But my pounding heart knew who had written the note. Once I got over the shock of Dennan being so near—after all, he must've dropped off the note—I peered out my window in search of him. He was nowhere to be seen. I would have to wait.

Until tomorrow.

Chapter 19

Katie Woodencloak
Norway, 1888

So when the sermon was over, and the king's daughter was to go out of the church, the prince had got a firkin of pitch poured out in the porch, that he might come and help her over it; but she didn't care a bit—she just put her foot right down into the midst of the pitch, and jumped across it; but then one of her golden shoes stuck fast in it, and as she got on her horse, up came the prince running out of the church, and asked whence she came.

"I'm from Combland," said Katie. But when the prince wanted to reach her the gold shoe, she said:

Bright before and dark behind,
Clouds come rolling on the wind;
That this prince may never see
Where my good steed goes with me.

Day 13

By late afternoon, clouds were dark and threatening rain. When I eagerly stepped outside that evening to meet Dennan, it began to sprinkle. But even if it decided to pour, nothing would have stopped me from seeing him.

"Where are you going?" William spoke from behind me.

He must have seen me leave the manor and followed me. What a weirdo.

"I wanted to come outside and smell the fresh rain," I said calmly.

This guy had given me the creeps all week. He was always watching me and trying to catch me alone. I didn't like the way he looked at me, just as he was doing now, studying every square inch of me.

"You wouldn't be meeting someone tonight, would you?" he asked.

"No, I came outside for a walk and to take a break from the household chores."

"Do you need an escort?"

"Thank you, William, but I wish to be alone." I curtsied and walked away before he could investigate any further.

When I peeked over my shoulder, I was glad to see him going back to the manor.

I walked through the gardens, letting the rain caress my cheeks. Night had begun to descend, like a dark blanket falling around me. I thought I heard a horse in the distance, but I could see nothing but the outline of the trees against the dark blue sky.

Worry and doubt pressed heavily on my mind. What if Dennan had a change of heart and decided not to meet me? I didn't even know where we were supposed to meet or what time.

I gasped as a hand covered my mouth and a powerful arm wrapped around my waist. "You must be cautious when traveling alone, miss."

I was breathless with delight at the sound of Dennan's voice. I turned to face my captor and stepped directly into his arms.

"You came," I exclaimed.

"Of course I came." He leaned forward and kissed my cheek. He wasn't wearing his mask, and his whiskers brushed against my skin. "Why wouldn't I?"

His strong hands moved to my face, and his fingers slipped into the softness of my hair. "I've come to steal another kiss from you."

"How can you steal a kiss from me when I give them to you freely?"

He grinned, showing his dimple. "When I found you damaged by the kiss of that servant boy more than a week ago, did I not steal a kiss from you?"

"That kiss was willingly given, and you know it," I said. "Besides, you have done nothing improper where I am concerned. That proves you are not a thief."

I watched as Dennan licked his lips and stared at my mouth.

"How do you know I will not take liberties tonight?" he asked.

"You may be a rogue, but you are not a villain. You are a gentleman."

"No gentleman's kiss ever gratified any rogue." And then his lips captured mine in a driven kiss.

I sighed as he gathered me into his arms. I felt my body go weak as he kissed me. If I'd managed to think anything right then, it would've been *Seriously, this is amazing!*

Abruptly, he ended the kiss. "I want to show you something."

Slightly dazed, I allowed him to lead me toward his horse. Dennan mounted the beautiful beast and held out his hand for me. I put my foot on his in the stirrup and leaned on his thigh for support as I climbed up to sit behind him in the leather saddle. He winced in pain, and I remembered his injured leg.

"Sorry!"

"Hold on tight."

I wrapped my arms tightly around him, and in the next moment the horse broke into a mad gallop through the rain. I leaned against Dennan's back, breathing in the scent of him—the smell I would remember forever.

"Here." He slowed his horse to a canter.

I looked to where he pointed on the rocky hillside through some thick bushes. "What am I supposed to be looking at?" I asked.

Dennan hopped off the horse and held his hands out for me. "I'll show you."

I placed my hands on his wide shoulders, and his hands went to my waist. When my feet hit the ground, I loved the way he let his hands linger for a moment. I looked up into his dark eyes. Our gazes locked, and my heart purred.

Wow, I've got it bad for this boy.

He broke the trance and turned to guide me toward the hillside. I shook off the spell and followed him across the grass. Soon, he pushed back some bushes to expose a cave.

Am I missing something? He wants to show me a cave?

"This is a cave." I didn't know what else to say.

"It's a great place to disappear for a while."

"Do you come here often?" I was trying to figure out why this cave was so special, as opposed to all the other dark, dreary caves.

I heard a rustling sound in the cave.

"What was that?" I stepped closer to Dennan, afraid a large animal would dash out of the cave at any second.

He put his arms around me and pulled me close. "Many animals live in this cave. It's probably just a bat."

"A bat?" I squealed.

Dennan laughed. "Be glad it's only a bat. The true cave dwellers live far inside the cave, where the light never touches."

I trembled at the thought of what might live in the cave

He tucked me closer into the comfort of his chest. "I missed you," he said.

"You've been on my mind every day," I admitted.

He kissed the top of my head.

"I feel so safe in your arms, as if no one could ever hurt me." With him, everything seemed simpler. Life wasn't complicated with evil stepmothers, servants' lost wages, magic doors, or even the scary William. Life was just beautiful.

"Why would you think someone is going to hurt you?" Concern was evident in Dennan's voice.

"Oh, it's nothing," I lied.

"What is it?" He leaned back to look at my face.

I inhaled deeply. "It's the guy you saw me with the other night—Sir William." I saw anger in Dennan's eyes before I continued. "He's been overly attentive lately."

"And?" Dennan urged.

"He makes me uncomfortable. He follows me everywhere, and he watches me."

"Has he made improper advancements towards you?" Dennan almost growled.

"No, not really. He's only suggested it."

"You must stay away from him, Brinlee." Dennan grabbed my upper arms. "He truly may mean you harm."

"There's something else."

"What?" Dennan's eyes sparked with fury.

I looked over his shoulder, anywhere but at his face. "It's not really someone else I'm afraid of. Well, I'm afraid of her, but not in the same way I'm afraid of William. It's more like I'm afraid she'll cast a spell on me and turn me into a toad. But that would be silly, because why would she turn me into a toad? What use is a toad?"

"Brinlee!" Dennan's shout interrupted my rambling.

"It's Lady Catherine. She's very mean and a devious, shady person. I think she's up to something."

Dennan frowned. "What is it that causes you suspicion?"

"Well, first of all, she leaves the house with William every day at noon, and when she returns, she goes to the tower on the fourth floor of the manor. Catherine is the only one who has a key to the tower. She'll be up there for hours—I even saw a light on in the window late one night."

"But why do you believe she is up to something devious?"

"The same night I saw the light in the tower window, William frightened me and told me to be wary of where I decided to meddle. He said the tower was none of my concern and to leave it alone."

"You should take his advice. I don't want you hurt." Dennan tucked a strand of hair behind my ear.

At that moment, I knew. I knew I loved this man who had such concern for my safety, who had come to me in this fabricated world. I knew I loved him and would never love anyone else this way.

I looked up into his eyes and gave into the urge to tenderly run my finger across the scar in his eyebrow. His eyes closed at the gentle touch.

"Did it hurt?" I asked.

"I didn't even feel it until I noticed the blood."

"What happened?"

"Someday I'll tell you," he answered.

I didn't push him further, but I wondered what had left such a mark. Was it a result of his dangerous occupation, or just a scar from a mischievous childhood?

The sound of an approaching rider brought me to attention. My fists tightly gripped onto Dennan's shirt.

"It's all right, Brinlee." He moved to my side. "I want you to meet someone."

I didn't know what to expect, but I would've never guessed the person on the horse would be a plump older woman.

"Did you get lost, Grandma?" Dennan walked over and helped her off her horse.

"No, I took the scenic route." Her voice made me homesick for my own grandma. It was the sound of bedtime stories and bedtime songs. The sound of comfort and peace. The sound that made you recollect your entire childhood in one gentle sweep.

Dennan helped his grandmother off her horse and then placed her hand in the crook of his arm to lead her toward me. "Brinlee, I present to you my grandmother."

"I'm pleased to meet you." I curtsied.

I was becoming quite an expert in curtseying.

The woman winked at me and looked at her grandson. "She's stunning, my boy."

"Yes, she is," Dennan said softly.

I blushed at the compliment.

"Hush or you'll give her the wrong impression of who you really are," she reprimanded with a twinkle in her eye.

"It's the right impression I want to give." Dennan smiled his dimple smile.

She swatted his arm. Even though she reminded me of my own grandma, the title was the only similarity. My grandmother was sixty years old, where Dennan's looked at least eighty. She had long, beautiful gray hair, braided and hanging past her waist. I was impressed that she could wear her hair so long at her age. Most grandmothers I knew chopped off their hair and had a stylist fix it every Monday.

"I hope Dennan has been a gentleman and not like the unruly boy who presently stands next to me."

I shook my head. "No, he has been very kind."

"Grandma, why do you doubt me? You've taught me how to treat a lady, and I use that knowledge to charm every girl I see."

He left his grandmother's side and walked up to me. He brushed his knuckles against my cheek, then whispered so only I could hear, "Especially if I find one alone in the woods—without her clothes."

I couldn't help but smile.

"Dennan, help me get the packages before the rain becomes something worse. I can feel it in my bones that tonight will be a long, wet night." Dennan's grandmother was standing next to her horse, opening the large leather bags attached to the back of her saddle.

Dennan caressed my cheek one more time and then followed his grandma to her horse. They returned carrying three packages.

"My dear," she began, "Dennan tells me that you are in need of a gown for the ball."

"Yes . . ." I drew out the word, unsure where this was going.

"I asked my grandmother to bring you a dress," Dennan said excitedly. "She's one of the best milliners in town."

"A dress? For me?" I gaped at Dennan and then his grandma.

She held out a package. "It was one of my daughter's dresses when she was about your age. It should fit perfectly."

"You brought me a dress?" I asked in awe.

"Didn't I promise to bring you a dress?" Dennan said gently.

"Yes, you did."

"Well, open it then."

I opened the package and pulled away the delicate paper that covered the contents. I couldn't speak as I gazed at the most gorgeous red fabric I had ever seen. It was the color of burning embers, and the red of a velvet rose. I touched the gown to find the soft material was like nothing I'd felt before.

"It's beautiful," I breathed.

"I'm glad you like it," the kind woman said.

"I love it."

"There's more." Dennan presented a small package he had been hiding behind his back. I watched as his rough, tan fingers fumbled over the knot holding the paper together. He dropped the twine to the ground and gently unfolded the paper to reveal a mask, teardrop earrings, and a necklace of small red crystals with a large pearl pendant.

"Dennan," I gasped.

He moved the jewelry closer for me to inspect. "This set belongs with the dress in your arms. The jewelry was made in the same hue."

My fingers reached out to touch the necklace.

"You'll look like a princess," Dennan's grandmother said.

I'm not a princess, but I could pretend to be one for one night.

"Thank you." I said, looking straight at Dennan. I hoped he could see the sincerity in my eyes. There was no way he could know he was fulfilling my deepest wish: to attend Cinderella's ball.

My eyes burning with grateful tears, I walked over to his grandma and threw my arms around her. "Thank you so much."

She returned the hug and patted my back. "You're welcome, my dear."

She was like my personal fairy godmother. She was grandmother to the most handsome highwayman ever, and she sewed dresses like a fairy. Definitely my kind of fairy godmother.

"My grandson also said you needed two other dresses for the ball." She released me and picked up the two other packages.

"Yes, for two friends of mine."

She handed me the packages. "Then I hope the three of you have a delightful time at the ball."

"We will."

I am going to the ball! I am really going to the ball. Whoopee!

"I like this girl." She pressed her finger against Dennan's chest. "You better not mess this up."

"I like her too, Grandma." He rubbed his chest where her finger had jabbed.

"It's getting late," she said. "I should be heading home."

"I'll escort you home, Grandma."

Wait, no.

"Honey, you don't need to take me home," she said.

Right. You don't need to take your old, defenseless grandma home through the cold, scary forest. Ha ha. I'm so kind.

"Follow me to take Brinlee back, and then I can take you home. Sherwood Manor isn't too far."

Fine, take your stinking grandma home. I'll just die another night without your love.

"You are always so good to me." She lovingly patted his cheek.

Yes, he's good. I'll admit it. He's perfect.

After Dennan helped her mount her horse, and he and I were seated on his, we rode back to the manor. His grandmother followed close behind. Thankfully the rain had stopped.

"Thank you for finding me a dress for the ball, Dennan," I said.

"Am I not as good a man as the prince?"

His question was completely unexpected, and I didn't know how to respond. After several seconds of silence, he said, "I understand."

"No, Dennan." I placed my hand on his shoulder. "You are the most amazing man I have ever met."

"I would ask for a chance to win your heart."

Done. "Nothing will change after tomorrow night."

Was it true? Did I really think nothing would change after the ball?

Dennan halted his horse and spoke to his grandmother, who had stopped next to us. "Stay hidden behind these trees while I take Brinlee a little closer to her home. I'll be right back."

"Thank you again." I reached my hand out to the sweet lady. "It was so nice to meet you."

"Likewise, my dear." She squeezed my hand.

I waved goodbye and returned my hands to Dennan's waist. In my last few minutes of savoring the feel of him next to me, I didn't say half of the things I wanted to say. I didn't know how to say many of them, or if I should even say them, so I simply held onto him as I held onto every wonderful memory of him.

When we were near the entrance to the manor, he jumped off his horse and turned to help me down. As soon as my feet landed on the ground, he slid his hand behind my head. "Grant me one more kiss to win your heart before you find yourself in the arms of the prince tomorrow night and swept away from me forever."

I stood on my toes and pressed my lips to Dennan's. He grinned mischievously just before our lips met in another blissful reunion. I sighed and reveled in the perfection of the moment. I wanted to remember every feeling and every sensation, to capture them inside my soul.

"I need to take my grandmother home," Dennan said breathlessly against my lips.

Not wanting the night to end, I pressed my lips against his again. He met my passion with fervor only for a moment before resting his hands on my shoulders and pushing me an arm's length away.

"I really need to leave . . . now." He exhaled. "Before the gentleman in me completely disappears."

My cheeks grew hot at his meaning.

He ran his fingers through his hair, unconsciously making me want him to stay even more. "Brinlee, you are the most beautiful woman in the world."

"I'm sure I look lovely after riding through the rain." I touched my damp, ruffled hair.

Dennan stroked a curl behind my ear. "You look more beautiful than ever, if that's even possible."

I shyly lowered my lashes.

He kissed the top of my head. "Have fun at the ball tomorrow night."

It was unfair and cruel that I would meet the man of my dreams in a fantasy.

Dennan walked back to his horse and retrieved the packages from his saddle. He placed them in my arms. "I'll be here waiting for you when you get back."

I wanted to say "I love you," but I was too afraid. I watched him climb onto his horse, but I still couldn't say it. I had never told a boy I loved him.

"Good night, Brinlee."

I still didn't say anything, and he rode off into the darkness. I watched him until horse and rider blended into the black of night.

I love you.

Chapter 20

Cinderella
Germany, 1812

Peck, peck, peck, peck, it went as fast as if twelve hands were at work. When they were finished, the pigeons said, "Cinderella, would you like to go dancing at the ball?"

"Oh, my goodness," she said, "how could I go in these dirty clothes?"

"Just go to the little tree on your mother's grave, shake it, and wish yourself some beautiful clothes. But come back before midnight."

So Cinderella went and shook the little tree, and said:

Shake yourself, shake yourself, little tree.
Throw some nice clothing down to me!

She had scarcely spoken these words when a splendid silver dress fell down before her. With it were pearls, silk stockings with silver decorations, silver slippers, and everything else that she needed. Cinderella carried it all home. After she had washed herself and put on the beautiful clothing, she was as beautiful as a rose washed in dew.

She went to the front door, and there was a carriage with six black horses all decorated with feathers, and servants dressed in blue and silver. They helped her into the carriage, and away they galloped to the king's castle.

Day 14—The Night of the Ball

I was nervous as I sat in the carriage next to Amanda and Katie on our way to the castle.

Lady Catherine rode in a separate carriage with her daughters. "I will not appear at the castle with those commoners," Fanny had declared that morning.

Thankfully, I was assigned to travel with the "commoners," which I much preferred to sitting in Lady Catherine's carriage with Fanny's unbelievable arrogance.

Henry, my date (eew . . . . I still couldn't get used to the idea), drove Lady Catherine's carriage, while Krys, who had finally gathered the nerves to ask Katie to the ball that morning, drove our carriage.

"How does social rank work at the castle?" I asked Katie. With everyone invited to the ball, I was curious.

"There is no discrimination at the castle. At some events in town, people are separated by status, but not at the castle. The royal family discourages division, which is part of the reason for the masquerade."

"Then why do they allow it to be done everywhere else?"

"The high-born think it is necessary for servants to work for their place in society, where the wealthy class's place in society is decided solely by their lineage and inheritance."

"That's just wrong," I said.

"That's how it is."

"Well, at least you can take a break from social ranking at the castle."

"Yes, but I've never dreamed of visiting the castle," Katie replied. "This is the first time it hasn't mattered who I am. I don't know if I'll be able to pretend I'm something I'm not."

I grabbed Katie's hand. "Dreams and wishes gladden every heart—it is the infinite power of hope. It's good to dream once in awhile." Life lesson #101 from my grandmother.

"At least we can dance in our dreams in beautiful gowns," Amanda said, smoothing her hands over her emerald green dress.

"Yes, this never would have been possible without you." Katie looked at her own dress, which was a dazzling light yellow.

"Don't thank me," I said. *Thank the man I've fallen in love with.*

"We know you are as much to thank for thinking of us, Miss Brinlee."

I was humbled by their words. If being rich meant the absence of the kindness these two sisters showed, I didn't want one penny.

As we rode along, I looked down at my radiant dress. It was only because of Dennan and his grandmother that my friends and I were able to go to the ball. At the thought of him, my skin tingled as if he was touching me now. I could feel his hands circle my waist as the fabric of the dress snuggled close to my skin. His breath crawled against my neck right where the seam of the wide collar rested on my shoulders. Katie had arranged my loose curls on the top of my head, and I broke out in goosebumps with Dennan's imaginary breath on my bare skin.

I patted my warm cheeks, and then toyed with my necklace. It was tied with a simple black ribbon behind my neck, and the red pearl pendant hung at the hollow of my throat. Just as Dennan's grandma had predicted, I felt like a princess.

In a way, I felt disloyal to Dennan—and to myself. Didn't he ask for a chance to win my heart? Why was I throwing it away for an encounter with Prince Charming, who, I had to keep in mind, was not even real?

But Dennan was also an illusion, a figment of my dreams. Sitting in this gorgeous red dress in a creaking carriage, driving through the quaint town of Fenmore Falls to the picturesque castle—none of it was real.

"Are you nervous?" Katie asked.

"Yes." Nervous and a little on edge. *I'm officially going crazy.*

Amanda peered out the window. "We're almost there."

I gazed out at the spires of the castle, shining like beacons on the hill. With its tall towers and windows, it reminded me of Rapunzel's fortress. It was the embodiment of every storybook castle.

When Krys pulled our carriage to a stop in front of the castle's marble steps, we sat in awe at the majesty before us. The evening sky cradled the great rock walls, and the castle merged with the backdrop, preventing me from viewing the tops of the towers.

Before Krys opened the door, Amanda, Katie and I put on our masks. He assisted each of us in descending from the carriage.

"Miss Brinlee, are you ready?" Sir Henry stepped in front of me and held out his elbow.

I looked to my side, where Krys was offering his elbow to Katie. I took a deep breath and accepted Sir Henry's.

"Thank you," I said. This night would work out fine if it meant Katie got to be with Krys.

We followed Lady Catherine, who was escorted by William, up the steps and into the castle. Two uniformed men met us at the doors and led us through the massive foyer and into the crowded ballroom. Apparently, everyone from town had shown up at the ball. The men, some in powdered wigs, appeared regal in their waistcoats, vests, and hats, while the women looked polished in their gowns and jewels.

"There's Princess Camilla, King Edwin's daughter," Rose said quietly. I hadn't noticed her come up next to me until she spoke.

I looked to where she indicated. There, near the stage, stood the most gorgeous blond-haired model I had ever seen. The young woman stood tall and regal, with her hair pulled back and wisps of curls delicately framing the porcelain skin not hidden by her mask. Her pleated dress was pink and adorned with lace. Most arresting was how composed and confident she seemed. She was beautiful, just like a *real* princess.

There's no contest. She's beautiful.

"Ladies and gentleman," a loud voice suddenly announced.

The orchestra ceased playing, and a hush fell over the crowd.

"May I introduce Your Highness, the king and queen, and their son, Prince Channing."

I choked down the excitement that raced to my throat.

This is it! I'm going to meet Prince Charming!

Rose grabbed my elbow and nudged me closer to the stage. All of the eligible women in the room were crunched together like sardines in our hooped skirts.

"King Nathaniel Channing of Fenmore Falls," the voice announced from the sidelines.

A tall man with broad shoulders and olive skin walked onto the platform while the crowd applauded. The king didn't wear a wig, as I had pictured in my collection of Cinderella stories, and he didn't wear a robe as an emblem of his power. Amazingly, he didn't even wear a crown. He raised his mask to greet the crowd. With his rough whiskers and kind expression, the handsome King Channing looked like a normal man.

"Queen Danielle Channing," the voice announced.

The queen entered and stood next to her husband. Her long blond hair hung freely over her shoulders, and her smile sparkled with exuberance. She held onto the king's arm, while he looked at his beautiful, ageless wife.

The boisterous voice made a third introduction. "Prince Patrick Channing."

At the mention of his name, my breath stopped. *Here we go!*

I peered between the row of heads in front of me at the young man walking onto the platform to join his parents. Like them, he had raised his mask to greet the audience. I couldn't get a good look at him because of all the other girls who stood on their tiptoes, but I could tell he had his father's dark, rugged features. Suddenly, I knew something was familiar about the prince. When he looked straight at me, I realized in shock that I had seen him before.

I had seen him many times before. I had *kissed* him many times before!

It was Dennan.

I felt dizzy and tried not to faint. He stepped off the stage and began to make his way through the crowd toward me. I didn't move. I couldn't move. My brain had stopped working.

Before I knew it, he was standing before me, looking at me—watching me, obviously waiting for my reaction.

Looking into this man's face as I had many times before—not into the faceless prince of my childhood dreams but into the features of the man I had recently grown to love—my heart raced. This was the man I had met at the pond, the man who waltzed with me in the moonlight, the man who had stolen my heart. I was looking into the face of Dennan.

Dennan is Prince Channing!

The room closed in around me, and everything went foggy.

Do not faint, Brinlee!

Chapter 21

No Story to Tell

I'm not going to distract you from this story. Who wants to read about what happened in my life that led to this moment? Who wants to read about how my mother actually burned my copy of *Jane Eyre* because she felt I wasn't living in reality? In fact, she felt compelled to demonstrate how fast a dream can be destroyed just like my book—just like *her* dream of love. No, I'm not going to tell you about that. It's much more fun to talk about the story and to forget about reality.

Moving On

No, I didn't faint. But I was close. I was in love with Prince Charming—well, technically, Prince Channing. Perhaps that's what was supposed to happen. I was like an understudy. Gabriella, the star, had failed to show up, and I had to go on and do the show. The show must go on, right?

Who am I kidding? Dennan is Prince Charming. Cinderella's Prince Charming, not mine. I'm not supposed to be here! I need to get away from him. I need to go home.

"Hello," he said with a tentative smile.

Whispers began to circle the room—I'm sure everyone wondered whom the prince was talking to. Nervously, I toyed with my necklace, avoiding Dennan's questioning gaze. Looking anywhere but at him, I glanced at the beautiful queen and saw recognition in her eyes.

That's when it dawned on me. Dennan's grandmother is the queen's mother. *I'm wearing the queen's necklace!*

Didn't she say this was her daughter's dress, too? *I'm wearing the queen's necklace and her dress!*

I forced my trembling legs to take a step back, but Dennan reached out and grabbed my arm. "Where are you going?" His familiar, calloused thumb brushed against my arm. "Aren't you going to say it's an honor to meet me, or something like that?"

I placed my hand over my mouth to cover my gasp. I was so embarrassed I thought my cheeks would burst into flames. I couldn't believe I'd discussed probable pick-up lines for the prince—with the prince! Most of all, I couldn't believe Dennan hadn't told me who he really was.

"I've been dreaming about that blush all day." His eyes smiled.

The orchestra resumed playing, and the crowd began to disperse to the sidelines. Having lost all control of my senses, I just stood there. Yep, that was me—the strange girl standing in the middle of the ballroom, drooling over the prince. Bonus points for popularity.

Dennan looked at me, his eyebrows creased. "Are you okay?"

Just peachy.

"Don't go anywhere. I have to dance the first dance with my mother. After that, you're not leaving my side." He gave my arm a gentle squeeze and then turned to assist the queen, who was stepping down from the stage.

Finally able to move my legs, I quickly walked back to one of the far walls and pushed myself behind a group of chatty girls. This was not a time to be seen but a time to blend.

I was not alone for long. Rose approached me with wide eyes.

"What just happened?" she asked.

I didn't answer.

Soon, I was swarmed by girls asking me where and how I'd met the prince. I wasn't prepared to answer their questions. It worked out nicely, since they all excitedly guessed the answers and chatted with each other about what they thought had happened.

Henry's voice interrupted the voices of the mob of girls surrounding me. "Dance with me," he commanded.

For the first time since I'd met him, I appreciated his bossiness. "Thank you, Sir Henry," I replied pleasantly.

A genuine smile spread across his chubby cheeks. I threaded my hand into the crook of his arm and followed him onto the dance floor, where only a handful of brave couples had joined the queen and her son in the opening dance of the evening. I assumed the dance position and tried to smile warmly as Henry led me in a shaky waltz.

What am I doing here? Why didn't I just stay at the manor? I was no better than any of the other flamboyant girls in the room who were waiting for an opportunity to fall in love with the prince. In all honesty, I don't think I really could have left this fantasy world without seeing Prince Charming. Why had my desire to meet him overpowered my longing to find a way home?

I looked toward the castle doors. Maybe if I left now, things would return to normal. It seemed like I always ran away when things got hard in life. Just like my dad did. *Wow, did I just have a major emotional breakthrough? I'll have to think about that later.*

I formulated an escape route. Once the song ended, rather than allowing Henry to escort me back to the sidelines, I would turn and make a beeline for the doors.

When the orchestra signaled the end of the song, I turned and began to walk hastily toward the doors. I felt a hand grasp my arm and whipped around, expecting Henry. I found Dennan instead.

"Where are you going?" he demanded.

I clenched my jaw. "I was dancing with my date."

"Not anymore." As he kept hold of my arm, I felt him tremble. "I don't feel like sharing you."

He slid his arm around my waist, then led me through the crowd and out through the nearest doors toward the balcony where we could be alone.

"Why are you running away?" he asked once we were outside. There was no use in lying about it. "You're the prince."

"Are you disappointed?" There was a touch of sadness in his voice.

"No, I'm not disappointed." In fact, learning that Dennan was Prince Charming was the icing on the sweetest cake of my fantasy. It just wasn't meant to be my cake. I sighed. "Why did you say your name was Dennan?"

"My name is Dennan—Patrick Dennan Channing," he answered. "I was named after my parents—Danielle and Nathaniel. I use Patrick when I am merely known as the prince."

"What do you mean when you are *known* as the prince?"

"Everything I told you before about my frustration with etiquette and protocol is true," he explained. "I loathe how most people only think of me as the prince. To my friends and family, I am Dennan."

"You are the prince of Fenmore Falls. No matter how far you run away from it, you will always be the prince."

"I do not want to be the prince," he confided.

I looked up into his unsettled face. "What do you mean?"

He did not answer, which only made me more frustrated. My fragile emotions were finally breaking through, and I could feel them pressing behind my eyes. I was angry. I was angry because he lied, but also because I didn't foresee it.

I couldn't hide the tears that trickled down my cheeks. Dennan raised his hand to stroke my cheek, but I pushed his hand away.

"Look at all the possibilities you have as prince to inspire and help your people." I focused on his issue instead of mine. "Have you ever heard the phrase 'I give not because I have not, but if I had I would give'? I mean, aren't we all beggars? Don't we all depend on God for everything we have? You must be diligent in your responsibility to help others."

Dennan placed his hand over my mouth to quiet my speech, which was more like a sermon. "Yes, you're right. That's why I dress as Black Rider, to help those I couldn't help as the prince."

I calmed a little, realizing my nervousness had caused me to lecture the prince of Fenmore Falls. Sometimes I didn't know who controlled my mouth. My stupid mouth!

Dennan moved his hand to my neck and caressed it tenderly. He tilted my chin to the side and leaned so his mouth was next to my ear. "It's a nice change to have you the one wearing a mask." Goosebumps rippled up my neck as his breath drifted across my skin.

Just then, my memories grasped onto something that had bothered me since the first time I met him. I took a step back to look at him. "Your injury on your leg is from the pirates, isn't it?"

Now it all made sense. Gabriella had told me the prince's ship had been captured and rummaged by pirates. Dennan had told me the injury on his thigh was an old wound, but it always seemed to bother him—which meant it was serious.

"Were you acting as Black Rider when the pirates attacked?" I asked.

"Shh." Again, he covered my mouth with his hand, then looked over his shoulder as if to see if anyone heard.

"What happened?" I mumbled through his fingers.

"You have to keep quiet." He lowered his hand. "Nobody knows I'm Black Rider."

"Not even your parents?"

"They know. Like I told you before, they object and forbid my expeditions."

"Did one of the pirates hurt your leg?"

He nodded. "Captain John of the pirate ship *Passed Angel.*"

"How did you become Black Rider?"

With a bright smile, he began. "I was almost sixteen when I first discovered the cave I showed you last night. I used it whenever I wanted to run away from my royal responsibilities. Soon, my escape evolved into something greater. I was tired of sitting and waiting. I didn't want to be the prince, so I made myself into what I felt was the opposite—the bold, heroic Black Rider." Dennan paused and asked abruptly, "Are you sure you want to hear all of this?"

"Yes, yes," I said. "I want to know everything."

"I've never told anyone before."

I smiled, honored that I would be trusted with his secret.

His story continued. "I gathered some men to help me, and we've been upholding the law ever since. Three months ago there was word of a conspiracy against the kingdom. Our sources led us to investigate vessels in the shipping path near Fenmore Falls for spies.

"As far as anyone knew, including my parents, the purpose of my sea voyages was to form alliances with neighboring kingdoms. In truth, I was inspecting ships and questioning sources who might have knowledge of who was traitorous to the kingdom.

"When we were narrowing in on one of our suspects, our ship was captured by pirates. I would've lost my life if my first mate hadn't rescued me from the ruthless Captain John."

"What happened?" I asked breathlessly.

"We were caught unsuspected, and Captain John's crew boarded our ship. He seized on me in the lower deck of the ship. He threatened my life in trade for possession of the ship. I refused, and he stabbed me with his sword."

Dennan rubbed his leg. "The sword of my first mate, Michael, pierced Captain John's heart. I owe Michael my life."

Suddenly, I felt remorse for telling Dennan that if he were the prince, he should take advantage of the opportunity to help his people. He was doing just that. He was the Robin Hood of his time.

I brushed my fingertips over the scar above his eye. "How long ago did you get this?"

Dennan closed his eyes at my touch. "Two years ago when I was eighteen, I was helping a woman who was being attacked. A man struck me from behind. I didn't feel the pain from the knife until I was nearly blinded by the blood pouring into my eye."

I lowered my hand. "You are the most amazing man I've ever met."

Dennan slowly opened his eyes. "I'm sorry I didn't tell you I was the prince."

"I understand why you didn't. You didn't want me to tell anyone who you were."

He leaned in close. "It worked to my advantage that you weren't from here and didn't recognize me."

I stared at his mouth. "Yes, that worked out nicely."

"How do you view me now, Miss Brinlee? Does the highwayman you met at the pond win your heart, or does the prince?"

"You've already won my heart, no matter who you are."

He moved even nearer, until his lips hovered above mine.

Overwhelmed that I was about to be kissed by the prince, I asked, "Are you sure you want to do this?"

"More than you know."

His mouth captured mine in a hungry kiss. I let my fingers slide to the back of his neck and tangle themselves in his hair.

I'm kissing Prince Charming! I thought. Then, my brain cruelly reminded me, *But you're not Cinderella.*

I turned my face away from Dennan's. "Stop."

"Why?" He gently turned me back to him and kissed me soundly on the lips.

"I'm not Cinderella." I tried to push him away.

He kissed me again.

Sigh. "The world will hate me," I mumbled against his mouth.

He chuckled. "Then, Black Rider will fight the world."

I couldn't help but smile.

He smiled back. "I love you, Brinlee."

I froze. *Really? Did I hear him right?*

"Why do you love me?" I asked. "Is it the curious girl from the pond that you fell in love with? Or is it the girl who's trying so hard to fit into this elegant world?"

"I love everything about you." He brushed a stray curl from the side of my cheek, and I almost swooned in the magic of the moment. "I love that you're different. I love the way you make me smile. I love your passion for life."

This cannot be happening.

"I'm having a bit of a post-modern moment right now," I said. "I'm in a dream, and when I wake up everything is going to disappear."

"You've been running through my dreams all day," he joked, using another one of our pick-up lines.

"There is so much about me that you don't know," I said. *Like the fact that I'm not from this world, for one.* How do you tell someone you're from a different world, a different time?

"I know everything I need to know."

My heart began to break, and I couldn't look into his eyes. With the absence of my father, and every other failed relationship in my life, I had stopped keeping track of how many times I'd had my heart broken. And now Dennan had come out of nowhere and stolen it. I should have known better than to fall in love so fast . . . especially with a prince. I had to tell him the truth, no matter how strange it sounded. It was going to come out sooner or later.

"You are supposed to fall in love with Gabriella—not me," I said. "Your happy ending has already been designed."

"Who's Gabriella? The only girl I have been arranged to marry is Camilla, King Edwin's daughter, but that was before I met you."

I felt a twinge of jealousy. "Was she the beautiful blond girl I saw standing near the platform?"

"Yes. Her family has been friends of mine for as long as I can remember. Her father and mine always agreed that we'd marry if circumstances permitted."

"She's perfect." Like a beautiful Barbie doll.

Dennan put his finger under my chin to lift my face to his. "I've never loved Camilla. I love you."

My cheeks went red. "Dennan, this will never work."

"It's because I'm the prince, isn't it?" He frowned.

"No. Well, I don't know." I pinched the bridge of my nose. "It's complicated."

"I was afraid to tell you. I didn't want you to see me any different than before." He stepped back and ran a hand through his hair.

"It doesn't change how I feel about you." I grabbed his arm so he wouldn't step farther away. "I'm just a little confused right now."

He put his hands on my waist and pulled me against his chest. There wasn't an inch of space between us. "Let me explain something," he said. "I love you, and there is nothing confusing about that."

I wanted to remember everything about him—the feel of his chest under my palms, the way he smelled, the sound of his voice, his handsome face, and the taste of his kiss. All of my senses would have an imprint of him. Every fiber of my being would remember his effect on me.

"I can't resist you anymore." He licked his lips. "If you deny me one of your kisses, I'll go mad."

"Forgive me."

"Never," he grumbled and gave me a quick kiss. He stopped and held up two fingers. "Two things. First, you will dance with me the rest of the night, because I cannot endure seeing you in the arms of another man."

"Sir Henry is my date," I reminded him.

"He will have to find another date." Dennan tapped my nose with his finger. "I asked you first when I made you promise to go to the ball if I found you a dress. Second—" he raised his two fingers "—I want you to meet my parents."

And say what? Hi, Your Royal Highnesses, my name is Brinlee. I came here through a magic door from Idaho, and I'm in love with your son, the prince of Fenmore Falls.

Yikes!

Chapter 22

Cinderella

Germany, 1812

The prince saw the carriage stop before the gate, and thought that a foreign princess was arriving. He himself walked down the steps, helped Cinderella out, and escorted her into the hall. Many thousand lights shone upon her, and she was so beautiful that everyone there was amazed. The sisters stood there, angry that someone was more beautiful than they were, but they had no idea that it was Cinderella, who they thought was lying at home in the ashes. The prince danced with Cinderella and paid her every royal honor. He thought to himself, "I am supposed to choose myself a bride. I will have no one but her."

However long she had suffered in ashes and sorrow, Cinderella was now living in splendor and joy. As midnight approached, before the clock struck twelve, she stood up, bowed, and said that she had to go, in spite of the prince's requests for her to stay. The prince escorted her out. Her carriage stood there waiting for her. And she rode away just as splendidly as she had come.

Meeting the King and Queen

The king and queen were charming and kind. King Nathaniel was so much like his son, both in rugged, handsome looks and the way he acted as if he couldn't wait until he was free from his responsibilities at the castle. The king didn't have the imposing attitude of a typical royal—in fact, he was reserved and humble. He leaned against a pillar on the platform, and I watched him pull at the neck of his shirt like he was uncomfortable in the formal attire. With his gentle manners and cowboy grin, he looked like the kind of man who would've preferred riding his horse to attending a ball.

The queen, a stunning beauty, exuded her regality and majestic lineage. Though not arrogant, she stood tall and confident.

"She's beautiful, Dennan," she said as soon as he made the introductions.

"Yes, she is." His hand was at my back, giving me some much-needed confidence.

"You did good, Son." The king slapped Dennan on the back.

The queen took my hand as she asked, "Where are you from, my dear?"

I was touched by her kindness. "I'm staying with some friends at Sherwood Manor." Of course, I would only tell them what they needed to know—or what was easy to explain.

"Mom, Dad, you can talk to Brinlee later," Dennan said as he began to nudge me away. "At the moment, I intend to dance with her and own every bit of her attention."

While we walked away, I said, mostly to myself, "That wasn't so bad."

"My parents already love you." Dennan kept his hand at my back, and I thrilled at the jealous looks of the other girls who watched us walk out onto the dance floor.

"How could they not love you?" He tipped his head close to my ear. "They see what I see."

Somehow, I restrained myself from begging him to keep me in this kingdom forever.

"I think I preferred our dance from last week when we were alone." He held me in the dance position, but a little closer than the norm.

I wanted to lean my head on his shoulder, but I remembered my manners. "This shindig is a lot different than dancing in the grass."

He laughed. "Shindig? I love how you speak." He whispered against my temple, "At least this way I can show you off to everyone."

I looked across the room and saw dozens of pairs of eyes on me. There would definitely be talk throughout the kingdom and the surrounding kingdoms of my connection to the prince. I even saw Dennan's intended, the beautiful Princess Camilla, give me the evil eye from across the room.

"You look beautiful, Brinlee. As soon as my grandmother showed me this dress, I knew it was for you," Dennan said.

"Where is she?" I scanned the area where the king and queen stood.

"Grandmother doesn't come to these shindigs anymore." I smiled at his adaptation to my modern word. "Since Grandfather died and my father became king, she prefers to remain quietly in her quarters of the castle."

"Tell her thank you for me."

"She was more than thrilled to help. She's been trying to get me to fall in love ever since I can remember. She never agreed to the prearranged marriage. I just never had the desire to look elsewhere. Other things were more important to me."

He leaned in closer and placed his lips on my cheek. My eyelids fluttered closed.

"Don't look now, but Lady Catherine is watching you like a snake," Dennan whispered.

I opened my eyes and turned to see her glaring at me. If looks could kill, I'd be dead. Icy fear gripped my heart. Lady Catherine had proven she would go to great lengths to arrange Gabriella's inheritance and strip her of her happiness, so I knew the woman would do anything in her power to destroy my happiness too.

"Has Lady Catherine given you any more reason to suspect her of devious activities?" Dennan asked.

I had temporarily forgotten where I was and that I was dancing with him, given that Lady Catherine had her cold hand around my heart.

I turned back to him. "Not anymore than before. She's as wicked as usual."

"Did you tell her about meeting me?"

"I only told my two friends, Katie and Amanda, but I didn't tell them you were the prince. They'll figure it out, though."

"Nobody can know I'm Black Rider," he said.

"What should I tell them?"

He looked past my shoulder for a moment. "Do you trust them?"

"Katie and Amanda? I trust them completely."

He looked back at me. "Tell no one else."

"Of course."

"Tell your friends the importance of being discreet about this information."

"Dennan." I slid my hand up to his shoulder. "Don't worry. They won't tell anybody."

"I need to locate the traitors of this kingdom. I can't let my identity affect my efforts."

"Yes, sir." I did a silly salute with my fingers to my head.

Dennan smiled, making his dimple pop. "Let's talk about something else. Let's talk about how lovely you look tonight."

"Hmm, that's much better." I winked.

His low laugh rumbled in his throat. "Do I sense that you enjoy being suitably dressed, as opposed to when I found you by the pond?"

"If it means dancing with you at the castle, then the answer is yes."

Dennan's eyes sparkled. "Are you saying you aren't too disappointed to learn that I am the prince?"

I moved my hand up and touched the nape of his neck. "I couldn't have been more pleased."

I probably shouldn't have said it, but I couldn't help it. At least I didn't declare my love to him, which I was tempted to do. I was not going to make promises that were impossible to keep.

Later in the evening, though, I found it difficult to pretend. I couldn't let Dennan continue to believe this would last forever. I needed to get away. Being near him only made me forget the fact that I wasn't part of the story. It almost made me believe I was Cinderella.

"Dennan, I'm not feeling very well," I lied.

"Do you need a drink or some fresh air? Let's go outside for a minute." He placed his hand at my back and led me to the balcony again. The crowd parted so we could pass.

Once we were outside, he asked if I was all right. I suppressed my guilt when I saw his loving expression.

"It's been a lot to take in." I put my hand to my head. "Perhaps if I go home and rest, I'll feel better."

"Are you sure?"

I nodded. "I'm sorry. I thought my headache would go away, but its only getting worse."

"I'll fetch a carriage to take you home."

"Thank you, Dennan. That would be great." If I traveled home alone, no one could ask me questions along the way.

He took a step closer but didn't try to touch me. "Are you sure you're all right? Did I say something wrong?"

Pain squeezed my heart, and I held back the tears that sprang to my eyes. "No, you didn't say anything wrong." I grabbed his hands but kept my focus on the ground. "Thank you for giving me the best night of my life. I will never forget it."

"Brinlee, look at me."

He squeezed my hands when I didn't respond.

My gaze finally met his, and I could see my reflection in the moisture clouding his eyes.

Dennan knew. He knew I was saying goodbye.

I blinked away my tears, knowing I had to be honest now. "I'm going home, and this will be the last time I will ever see you."

"What are you saying?"

The tears rolled down my cheeks. "I'm sorry, Dennan. I'm so, so sorry."

"I don't understand. You said it didn't matter that I am the prince—you were even happy about it."

"It's my fault. I should never have opened the door."

Now he'll think I am nuts. That's good. It will give him a reason to break up with me.

"Don't apologize." He kissed my tear-stained cheeks. "I wouldn't trade anything for the world."

Why does he have to be so perfect?

"I wouldn't either," I said.

Ignoring all reason, I raised my mouth to his and kissed him one last time. Dennan wrapped his arms around me, and I felt the sadness of departure in our embrace. He kissed me just like our first kiss after he lectured me about kissing William. He kissed me like he did when we danced next to the cliff. He kissed me like every magical kiss we had ever shared, and I returned his kiss with all the passion I felt, because after this, I would never feel his kiss again.

When I couldn't stand the ache in my chest anymore, I stepped away from his arms. "Goodbye, Dennan. Don't come after me."

I ran out the doors and didn't look back.

Chapter 23

Run, Run as Fast as You Can

I didn't just run from my problems—I also ran for my high school track team. I loved running and was good at it.

One year, my school counselor called my mother because she thought I was training too hard. I explained to her, and again to my mother (who understood my motivation since she was a control freak too), that my 5:00 AM practice and my 8:00 PM practice after team practice weren't a problem. I was only doing light conditioning.

What I didn't tell them was how good it felt to run eight miles and then eight miles again to numb everything I felt. The farther I ran, the farther away my problems seemed.

Like I said before, maybe my love for running away had something to do with my father.

Day 16

Dennan didn't follow me that night when I left the castle. And no, I didn't leave my glass slipper on the steps. I'm not Cinderella, remember?

It had been two days since the ball, and nothing could ease the pain in my heart. I missed Dennan with an ache so deep I could barely endure it. All I could do was pound on the magic door in the kitchen and beg it to release me.

Lady Catherine didn't say a word to me when she came home from the ball, which felt worse than if she'd yelled at me. I feared she was planning something evil, so I didn't go anywhere but my bedroom or the kitchen.

William was in charge of inspecting the servants' work, but recently his attention seemed excessive. Almost everywhere I went he'd be there, lurking in the corner. I didn't even have to see him to know he was there—my skin crawled either way.

That Sunday, two days after the ball, I had a restless night. I dreamed of dancing with Dennan at the castle. But then the ballroom went dark, and I found myself running down a long hallway. Instead of the red gown, I now wore my sweatpants and T-shirt. Suddenly, I was racing toward the magic door at Sherwood Manor. I ran as fast as I could, but the door got farther and farther away. A flight of stairs appeared unexpectedly, and I fell down it and lay at the bottom.

In the dream, my shoulder ached and my hands were scraped. I assessed my injuries and realized I was wearing the red gown. It was torn at my shoulder, and the entire dress was damaged by mud. When I rubbed at the pain in the back of my neck, my hand came back covered in blood. I looked at the floor and found I was surrounded by a pool of dark red.

"Brinlee," I heard Dennan shouting from the distance.

"Dennan," I tried to scream, but my voice didn't work.

Lady Catherine approached, holding a knife in her hand. As I lay in the puddle of blood, she sneered, "Sleep tight, Cinderella."

Her voice rang in my ears as I screamed.

My shout woke me, and I jerked upright in bed. I looked around to make sure I wasn't still dreaming. My heart pounded furiously. I rubbed the back of my neck, thankful the wound wasn't there.

Feeling unsettled, I wondered what the frightening dream meant. Maybe Lady Catherine was even more of a threat to me than I had imagined. I shuddered at the thought.

Knowing I wouldn't fall back to sleep, I got up to find Fred. When I took a step out my bedroom door, the friendly dog was nestled comfortably in the hallway a few steps from my door, as if guarding my room.

"There you are," I said as I scratched him behind the ears. I sat down and scooped him into my lap. "Will it always hurt this much?" Stubborn tears crept from the corners of my eyes as I thought about Dennan. I hugged Fred closer to ease my sorrow.

Suddenly, I heard a commotion coming from Lady Catherine's bedroom. I put Fred down, then crept down the hall and stood just outside Catherine's closed door. I knew it was pretty stupid, but I had to hear what they were talking about.

"It's not enough," I heard Lady Catherine exclaim.

"Milady, there is no more to be found," William replied.

"The ingredient is vital," she cried out. "Do what you must!"

Ingredient for what? I wondered.

"Yes, milady." William's voice and footsteps were close to the door.

Oh no!

To escape, I ran around the closest corner and took the attic stairs two at a time. I had never been in the attic before, but I figured it would be a good place to hide. I stilled myself against a wall and listened. My panting was the only sound I could hear, so I relaxed a bit. Moonlight shone through the small windows, allowing me to look around the wide room. I stared at the unexpected treasures. This was not like the attic where I lived at Nana's house. This was a shrine of history. There wasn't a trunk or box in sight, and the walls were covered with tapestries. Tucked at each end of the long attic room were curtained windows, and curtains in the same fabric hung over what I presumed to be doors at either side.

I stepped beneath one of the towering tapestries. My hand brushed against the tattered cloth, and I watched as it rippled against the wall with my movement. I looked closely at the intricate stitching. Amazing!

One tapestry showed a knight standing next to his horse. I stepped nearer, enchanted by the artwork. There was something different about this tapestry. The images on the other tapestries were busy, with groups of men fighting at war, but this one was plain and brilliant. When I moved my hand to touch the material, instead of stopping at the wall behind the tapestry, my hand went beyond the wall. I eagerly pulled back the tapestry and stepped into a hidden compartment—an alcove behind the tapestry of the solo knight.

Finding something so mysterious, I felt all Nancy Drew. Just sayin'.

The only light in the small alcove came through a small opening that would be unnoticed if the tapestry was pulled back. It was too small to be a window. When I peered through the opening, I was looking directly down into the entrance hall of Sherwood Manor. I could see the foyer and anyone coming in or going out of the house.

"Wow!" I gasped out loud. *This is awesome!*

Just as I shook my head in disbelief, Lady Catherine appeared in the foyer. I watched the dark-haired woman walk to the far end of the room and stop to stand in front of an empty wall.

All right, wicked stepmother, what are you doing out of bed in the middle of the night?

She looked over her shoulder as if making sure she was alone. Then, she placed her hands on two different spots on the wall and pushed. The wall moved forward, revealing a passage. She stepped through the entrance and disappeared, and the wall closed, looking just as it had before she touched it.

"Holy crap," I muttered.

There were definitely strange things about this house, and Lady Catherine was number one. She simply couldn't be trusted. Well, the evil stepmother wasn't going to win in this story, not while I was here. It was time to use my CSI skills to solve this mystery. Lady Catherine wouldn't know what hit her.

Day 17

I crept back to my bedroom that night and waited for the sun to rise. When the rest of the household woke up, I left my bedroom. As usual, I spent the day helping the servants, though I got a little tired due to lack of sleep.

That evening, I stood at my bedroom window and stared into the sky. I wrung my hands nervously, anticipating the few short hours until I could inspect Lady Catherine's secret passageway. I'd gone to the foyer once during the day, but I didn't dare try to open the wall with other people nearby.

Someone knocked on my door.

"I don't need your help tonight, Katie," I said.

Another knock.

I moved to the door. "Katie, don't worry about me. Go home and get some sleep."

When the door slowly opened, I froze. Dennan stood on the threshold. I couldn't believe my eyes.

"What are you doing here?" I asked.

He took a step into the room and closed the door with his foot.

Oh man! He was even more gorgeous than I remembered.

"How did you get in here?"

He was coming closer, no hesitation in his stride. "Your friend Katie let me in."

"You shouldn't be here." What I meant to say was that he shouldn't be here when it had been so hard to forget him.

"I was worried about you." He reached out to touch my arm.

I stepped away. "You just came to check on me?"

"I know you told me not to follow you, but I had to make sure you were all right." Dennan tilted his head. "You seemed overly troubled about Lady Catherine that night."

I dropped my eyes and fidgeted with the fabric of my dress. "Thank you, Dennan."

He reached out again to touch my arm. This time I didn't back off. "Are you all right?" he asked, his thumb caressing my skin.

I nodded but changed my mind and slowly shook my head. "Something bad is happening in this place. I can feel it."

I told Dennan about Lady Catherine's hidden passageway, and how she was arranging Gabriella's marriage so she could maintain control over the girl's inheritance.

Dennan also had new information about Lady Catherine. He said the lord of the manor, Gabriella's father, had been gone for many years but returned with Catherine, only to be confined to his sick bed a few weeks later. No one knew where Catherine came from. Dennan had often wondered if she had traitorous connections, since she obviously wasn't from the kingdom of Fenmore Falls.

"That's why you were always so close to Sherwood Manor," I said suddenly. "You were spying on Lady Catherine."

"I don't know if she is a traitor, but nothing has proven otherwise."

This was probably bigger than I thought.

"Where is your friend Gabriella right now?" Dennan asked.

"She's at my house."

"Let me help you." He still had hold of my arm and gently squeezed it.

I needed him to protect me, so I said, "I'd love your help."

"What do you want me to do?"

"Can you come by tomorrow at noon? That way, we can see where Lady Catherine goes every day."

Dennan squinted. "I'm leaving tomorrow for two days for a peace gathering—part of my royal duties. How about Thursday?"

"That will work. I'll see what I can find out before then."

He grew serious. "Be careful. Don't do anything foolish."

"Okay."

He put his hand behind my head and pulled me close. "I don't want to see you get hurt."

"I'll be fine."

I heard only his steady breath until he asked, "Why did you leave me, Brinlee?"

Even though I'd tried to avoid it by talking about Lady Catherine, I knew this conversation was coming.

Dennan kissed the top of my head. "Why did you run away?"

Because that's what I do. I run away from everything.

"Please don't leave me," he said.

I didn't make him any promises, but I did reach up and give him a kiss.

Just one kiss, I thought. *Just one very long, very magical kiss.*

Chapter 24

Cinderella
Germany, 1812

"Listen," said the mother secretly. 'Take this knife, and if the slipper is too tight, just cut off part of your foot. It will hurt a little, but what harm is that? The pain will soon pass, and then one of you will be queen." Then the oldest one went to her bedroom and tried on the slipper. The front of her foot went in, but her heel was too large, so she took the knife and cut part of it off, so she could force her foot into the slipper. Then she went out to the prince, and when he saw that she was wearing the slipper, he said that she was to be his bride. He escorted her to his carriage and was going to drive away with her. When he arrived at the gate, the two pigeons were perched above, and they called out:

Rook di goo, rook di goo!
There's blood in the shoe.
The shoe is too tight,
This bride is not right!

The prince bent over and looked at the slipper. Blood was streaming from it. He saw that he had been deceived, and he took the false bride back.

Did you read that? The evil stepmother told her daughter to cut part of her heel off so the slipper would fit. *How gross is that?* The mother said the pain would soon pass and her daughter would be queen. In other words she was saying, "The reward is worth any sacrifice."

If you ask me, the Brothers Grimm had a sick twisted sense of what a fairy tale should be.

Days 18 and 19

You know that feeling you get when someone is watching you? Well, even in an empty room, I could feel eyes all around me. I could even hear voices sometimes. Sensing that someone was behind me, I'd turn around to find nobody there.

Tuesday night, another strange thing happened. Not only was I unable to find the hairbrush I always placed near my wash bowl, but I could have sworn I saw the shadow of a person when I entered my bedroom that night. When I looked again, the shadow was gone.

Because of these weird events, I decided Wednesday was the day I would find out what was in the secret passageway. Dennan had told me to wait for him before I did anything, but I couldn't stand around waiting for more creepy things to happen.

Just past noon on Wednesday, I gathered my courage. After making sure Lady Catherine had left in the carriage with William, I went to the foyer and stood in the spot where I'd seen her three nights before. I mimicked how she held her hands on the wall, one above the head and slightly to the right, and the other hand straight out. I gave a little push and the wall moved to reveal a narrow spiral staircase. Before I could think twice, I stepped into the secret hallway and onto the first step. The wall closed behind me, but I kept moving. There was no turning back now.

When I reached the fourth floor, I opened the door. The room was large but crowded with books and glass jars. Thick books lay on the floor, overflowed from bookshelves, and were piled high on a table in the middle of the room. I had to step around stacks of books and dozens of glass jars to get to the giant table.

At first glance, the books looked like dictionaries, but I soon realized they were medical books. The pages described and illustrated various medical procedures from the past, like purging, cold bathing, and bloodletting—things modern doctors would never try.

Why would Lady Catherine have a bunch of medical books?

The jars in the room were filled with powder, some dark gray and some white. I picked up a jar that sat by my foot. I removed the lid and took a sniff of the powder, but couldn't detect a scent. What was it they said about poison? Did it have a scent or not?

Remind me to never leave my drink unattended again. Lady Catherine will probably slip something in it.

I continued to roam around the room, flipping through pages of books that lay open on the floor. Maybe Lady Catherine was studying medicine, or was already a practicing physician. Since female doctors would've been scorned and rejected in this era, she would've been required to practice in private. She probably left at noon every day to visit patients.

Yeah. Uh-huh. You just keep on thinking that, Brinlee.

Since Lady Catherine was usually gone for about an hour, I left the tower a little before 1:00. I hurried down the stairs and placed my left hand high on the wall and my right hand straight out to my side, mirroring the spots on the other side of the wall. The wall shifted and allowed me back into the foyer, then closed behind me.

As I headed toward the kitchen, I heard the carriage wheels crunching on the gravel, signaling Lady Catherine's return. Just for kicks, I sneaked up to the attic and peeked through the spy hole behind the tapestries. I watched as Catherine entered the foyer and went straight to the secret door. William joined her, and they both passed through the secret door and climbed the steps to the tower.

Tomorrow I would find out where they went every day when they left the manor. Tomorrow I would solve this mystery. This is where the story gets good. As my grandmother always said, "Buckle your seat belts and grab some good snacks, because the plot just thickened."

Day 20

Dennan returned Thursday an hour before noon and met me outside the kitchen door as planned. I wore my pink sweatpants, white T-shirt, and purple slippers, which were still dirty from my run on my first day there. I knew our mission could be dangerous, and I didn't want a long dress to get in my way.

On a side note, I had a hard time getting my modern clothes. I couldn't tell Katie what I was up to because she would try to stop me, so I threatened to tell Krys about the poems she'd written about him. That worked, and she found my clothes hidden in a closet in one of the spare rooms. Sneaky girl. Now, back to the real story . . .

Dennan gave me the once-over. "Why are you wearing those clothes?"

"Why aren't you wearing your mask?" I retorted. Even though I loved to see his handsome face, I had missed the mystery of the highwayman.

"Touché." He grinned. "I remember the first time we met. I couldn't understand why you dressed so funny."

I shrugged. "We dress a little differently where I come from."

He folded his arms across his chest, studying me. "It suits you."

I looked away bashfully. "Thanks for coming."

"Why wouldn't I come?"

"I don't know. It's still hard for me to believe you really exist, let alone you wanting to help me."

"I'll always be here for you, Brinlee." He reached for my hand. "You know that, right?"

I threaded my fingers through his. "Yes."

Dennan came closer to bow his head to mine. "I know you don't feel the same, but I want you to know how much I care about you."

No, don't say it.

His forehead touched mine. "I love you, Brinlee. I'll stand up with you forever."

I began to move away, but he held my hands firmly to halt my retreat. "What's wrong?"

"I need to go home. Too many things are wrong where I am concerned.

"What do you mean?".

"I need to solve the mysteries of Sherwood Manor, and then maybe I'll be able to go home."

"Why can't you go home whenever you want?"

I shook my head. "I just need to figure out what's going on."

"Okay," Dennan said hesitantly.

"You probably think I'm crazy, but I promise there are strange things that don't make sense in this house."

"I don't think you're crazy." He gently touched my face.

"Things have started to disappear from my room. Little things like my hairbrush, and I always feel like I'm being watched. During the night I'll wake up feeling like someone is in my room, but nobody is there."

He cursed under his breath. "I can't let you stay here if you are in danger."

"I don't think I'm in danger. It's more like someone is trying to scare me."

"Why would someone want to scare you?"

"Maybe they're trying to scare me away from finding the truth."

"You shouldn't stay here anymore, regardless," Dennan said. "With what you have told me, it can't be safe."

"But I have to stay! I'm so close to finding the answers. That's why I wanted you to come with me today. I need your help."

Dennan frowned but said, "Of course I'll help you. Where do we start?"

"I went up to the fourth-floor tower."

"I thought I told you not to do anything foolish." His voice was serious but his face was teasing.

"I was careful, and I went while Lady Catherine was gone."

"What did you find?"

"A bunch of medical books, and jars filled with some kind of powder."

"What kind of powder? What did it look like?"

"I don't know. It looked like dirty flour."

"What time did you say Lady Catherine leaves?" Dennan asked.

"At noon."

He looked up into the sky. "It's just about noon."

I had an idea. "Come with me." I pulled on his hand.

"Where are we going?"

"Lady Catherine always goes to the tower before she leaves." I talked over my shoulder as I led him to the front of the house where there were no servants. "We're going to watch her from the attic."

Cautiously, we entered the foyer and quickly climbed the steps to the attic. If someone saw the prince in the house, things would go from bad to worse.

When we reached the attic, I showed him the tapestry and the small peephole hidden behind it.

He stepped closer to the hole. "We have some leper's squints at the castle."

"What do you call them?"

"Leper's squints. Many old houses, including the castle, have them. There's even one in my bedroom."

"That's a little creepy."

"The squints come in handy. If the king becomes ill, he can still wander through the back halls and observe the business of the house by peering through these squints."

"Maybe that's why I always feel someone's watching me," I said. "There's probably a leper's squint in my bedroom."

"The castle has a secret passageway like this house, only it leads to an old chapel. The history is that lepers couldn't come into the castle—they could only enter through the leper door and look through the squint overlooking the chapel."

Fascinating. "You're quite the expert."

He smiled. "There's more. Most castles had a priest's hole. It was a secret room, and priests used it whenever they or someone in the royal family needed to hide."

"Let me guess. You were skilled at hide-and-seek when you were a kid."

He laughed. "Yes, I was a very curious kid."

I stepped up to the leper's squint and peered down into the foyer. Dennan had moved right behind me to peek over my shoulder.

"Do you see Lady Catherine?" he asked softly.

"Not yet." My body tingled at his closeness.

"What do you think she carries in the parcel?" His voice was right by my ear.

"Probably something poisonous."

Dennan wrapped one arm around my waist. "I'll help you get to the bottom of this. Here, let me see."

With his arm still around me, he leaned his head close to mine so he could see out of the peephole. Out of the corner of my eye, I stared at the handsome man who stood so close to me. I watched his long eyelashes lower as he squinted to see through the hole. It felt incredible to be so near to him and to be held by him. I didn't want the moment to end.

"Do you see her?" I asked.

"She's coming!" Dennan whispered. After several seconds of anticipation, he added, "She's going through the secret door."

"William should be coming."

I leaned my head closer, and Dennan tilted his head so I could take a turn looking through the squint. With him so close, it was difficult to concentrate.

I saw William walk across the marble floor and stand next to the secret door in the foyer below us. He waited as if guarding the entrance.

"There he is." I moved so Dennan could see.

"Is he the man who kissed you?" Dennan asked with disgust.

"Do you mean the one who kissed me before you did?" I teased.

"I want you to stay away from him." Dennan looked straight at me, clearly not in the mood for teasing. "From what you've told me, I don't like him."

"Don't worry, I stay as far away from him as possible."

Dennan peered through the squint again. "Here comes Lady Catherine."

I turned and pulled on his arm. "Hurry, let's follow them."

Thankfully no one saw us leave the manor, and Dennan's horse was waiting for us near the pond. Once we mounted him, we easily caught up with Lady Catherine's carriage. Using Dennan's knowledge of the back roads, we kept hidden in the trees as we followed.

I was riding behind Dennan with my arms wrapped securely around his waist. "So, how did the peace gathering go?" I asked. It was a little off subject, but I had to get my mind off how nice his abs felt under my hands.

"It went fairly well. I explained to King Edwin why I cannot marry his daughter, and we discussed other options to manage peace between our kingdoms."

"That's what the meeting was about?"

I could feel the kingdom's scowling eyes on me—after all, I was the reason for any concern for Fenmore Falls' safety because of the broken engagement. I felt awful.

Dennan placed his hand on mine. "It was inevitable, Brinlee. The engagement was never made public. It was only an alternative."

I was touched that he would change his future for me, but I couldn't let him keep thinking our relationship could go any further.

"Dennan—" I began.

"Look," he interrupted, pointing to Lady Catherine's carriage.

I watched as they turned left onto a path that was concealed by vegetation. "Where does that road go?" I whispered.

"I don't know. I've never come across it before."

I shivered and gripped the front of Dennan's shirt. He placed his hand over my clenched fists.

"I won't let anything happen to you."

I rested my chin on his shoulder. "I know."

We rode a little farther, and then he said, "It looks like the trees are starting to open up."

We rounded a bend in the trail, and sure enough there was a clearing. Dennan steered his horse farther into the trees so we could remain unseen.

Seeing a tall, run-down house in the middle of the pasture, I asked. "What is that?"

The house leaned to one side and looked as if it would blow over with a slight breeze. Each wall of the building was made from a different color of wood, and each wall inclined inward. There were gaps between some of the boards.

Two other carriages sat in front of the old house. One driver was slumped in his seat, but I could see no one in or near the other vehicle. Dennan and I watched William park Lady Catherine's carriage next to the others and help her out. The two of them stepped toward the house.

I could feel adrenaline pumping through my veins. "What are they doing? And what do we do now?"

"We just wait," Dennan replied.

"We can't wait. We might not get this chance again. We have to see what they're up to."

"We don't know what's in that house yet. Remember, I promised to keep you safe."

"Please, Dennan. I have to find out what's going on."

He sighed. "All right then, here's the plan. Stay close to me. If at any moment I think it is dangerous, we leave. Agreed?"

"Agreed." I held up my right hand as if swearing an oath.

We got off his horse and quietly approached the side door of the house. We kept out of sight of the lone driver, who looked asleep.

As Dennan pushed the creaky door open, I held my breath and hung tightly to his hand. We stepped into a wall of cobwebs and onto a floor blanketed with dust.

There was shuffling on the floor just above us. Several people shouted as if arguing, but I couldn't pick out any words. After a few minutes, it sounded like the voices were moving to another part of the house, so Dennan led me by the hand and we quietly climbed the stairs to the second floor.

We carefully walked down the hall and into a room lit by open windows. Two tables were pushed up against the wall, each covered with medical instruments. There were syringes, tweezers, bowls, rags, and bottles of liquid. Then I saw a basin of blood collecting the drops that fell from a cloth hanging over the edge of the table. I gasped and covered my mouth.

At the same time, I heard a moan from the room next to us.

"We should get out of here," Dennan said.

With my hand still at my mouth, I shook my head no.

He glanced back at the medical instruments. "I don't feel good about this." Then he looked at the closed door leading to the next room. "But I told you I would help you, so let's solve this mystery."

I nodded. We approached the door, and Dennan carefully turned the doorknob. We stepped into the room and saw a gray-haired man with a beard. He lay on a dirty mattress on the floor. He appeared very ill and malnourished. When the man heard our soft footsteps, he cringed. He may not have been more than fifty, but his condition made him seem much older.

I let my hand slip out of Dennan's and walked toward the man, my concern for him trumping any worry for my safety. Once the man turned in my direction, his eyes grew wide and his cracked lips stretched into a wide grin.

"A . . . A . . . Abby?" he said hoarsely.

By the loving look on his face, it was clear he was calling out to someone he loved. And he obviously thought I was that special person.

Then, it dawned on me.

I took his outstretched, shaky hand and turned back to Dennan. "He thinks I'm Gabby," I said. "This must be Gabriella's father."

Chapter 25

Rashin-Coatie
Scotland, 1901

So the bird sings:

Clippit feet an' paret taes is on the saidle set
But bonnie feet an' braw feet sits in the kitchen neuk.

*The prince turned his horse and rode home, and went straight
to his father's kitchen, and there sat Rashin-Coatie. He kent her at
once, she was so bonnie; and when she tried on the shoe it fitted her,
and so the prince married Rashin-Coatie, and they lived happy, and
built a house for the red calf, who had been so kind to her.*

Day 20 (continued)

"This is your friend's father?" Dennan exclaimed.

The ill man spoke to me again. "Abby, is that you?"

I patted his hand, which clung to mine. "It's going to be all right."

I looked at Dennan, this time with tears rolling down my cheeks.
"We need to find Gabby."

Dennan moved to the foot of the bed and said gently, "Sir, who
are you? Where are you from?"

The man's gaze never left my face. "Sherwood Manor," he slowly answered.

If this was Gabriella's dad, why was he confined in a rundown house behind a mountain, and what role did Lady Catherine have in hiding him here?

"Is Gabby your daughter? Is that who you're calling for?"

His eyes twinkled as he nodded at me, but suddenly he looked terrified and shrunk up against the wall.

"What's wrong?" I asked.

The man trembled while struggling to wrap his ragged sheets around his thin arms.

Dennan placed his hand on my shoulder. "We need to get help. He's sick."

From behind us, a familiar voice said, "Yes, he's a very sick man. You should leave immediately."

Lady Catherine. I rose from the edge of the bed and grabbed Dennan's forearm in a death grip.

The woman stood in the doorway. Her cold gaze examined Dennan and me slowly from head to toe as her lips curled in disgust. "Your Highness," she acknowledged Dennan in a mocking tone.

He stepped forward. "You will be punished for your crimes."

"Tsk, tsk. The absentee prince attempts to play his role as a ruler," she sneered. "You would be wise to leave the leadership to the nobles and carry on with your juvenile frolicking in the forest."

A burly man stepped into the room behind Lady Catherine, and I saw the shadow of another man in the hallway. Besides William, how many other men were in the house?

"You will never find me guilty of anything," Lady Catherine said under her breath.

Dennan started toward her in anger, but I held onto his arm. "She's only trying to bait you."

"How charming," Lady Catherine said scornfully. "The damsel in distress rescues the great prince of Fenmore Falls, or should I say Black Rider."

She knows. How does she know?

"Leave Brinlee out of this," Dennan growled through his teeth.

"Brinlee is part of this, if you like it or not." Lady Catherine turned beady eyes toward me. "Why do you think I let you stay at my house when I didn't even know who you were, Miss Brinlee from Idaho?"

I felt nauseous as I realized I was part of her malicious crimes.

"When Isaac informed me that he saw Black Rider in the forest with a strange girl," Lady Catherine went on, "I knew it was you the first moment I saw you." She spoke to the prince again. "I used Miss Brinlee to distract you from your goal. You were getting too close to discovering what we were doing."

Dennan looked at me. I thought I saw a bit of doubt in his eyes.

"When Black Rider couldn't be killed by pirates," Lady Catherine continued, "don't you think I took every precaution of deterring you when you were on land?"

My hand tightened on Dennan's arm. I shook my head and pled with him with my eyes. He must have sensed my sincerity, because he drew me closer.

"Do you really know who this girl is?" Lady Catherine cocked her head to one shoulder while looking at the prince. "She's from a far different place than you could ever imagine."

How much does she know?

"There are many secret doors in Sherwood Manor, Miss Brinlee," Lady Catherine snapped.

I gasped. She knew about the magic door. She knew where I came from. That meant she knew where Gabby was.

Now my blood was boiling. "I know exactly what you're doing, and you won't get away with it," I shouted.

"Well, Miss Brinlee, we'll just have to see." Lady Catherine practically hissed. But underneath her confident exterior, I knew she was afraid of how much I knew.

Two could play at this game, especially when one had read a lot of mysteries. "I know that if Gabriella realized her father was still alive, you wouldn't have control of her wealth. You only kept him alive to get his money. He wouldn't willingly give it to you, and there was no other way to legally get it."

When Lady Catherine narrowed her eyes, I could tell I was right. Suddenly, something rushed into my mind like a flood breaking through a dam.

"Gabriella's father never married you, did he?" I said.

Lady Catherine didn't answer, but I could see the truth in her bitter, dark eyes.

"Gabriella's father would never marry you," I continued. "You drugged him and brought him here because he was worth more alive than dead. You drugged him every day to keep him weak so you could control him."

Lady Catherine glanced at Gabby's father, who lay huddled on the far side of his bed. "As soon as Cinderella's marriage is planned and completed, I will have no more use for him."

That's right. If Gabby marries before she turns nineteen, Sherwood Manor's wealth will fall to Lady Catherine as Gabby's self-appointed guardian.

"And you need the money to get people to help you try to take over the kingdom," I guessed.

Ooh, I am getting good at this investigation stuff.

"The king will hear about this," Dennan said angrily.

Lady Catherine's mouth formed a thin line. "You will never live to tell your father."

"Brinlee, when I say run, you run." I could barely hear Dennan's whisper as he brushed his mouth across my ear.

My heart was beating hard. What was he going to do?

He released me and took a step toward Catherine. At the same time, the large man also took a step closer, and the other man from the hallway stepped into the room. He was just as big as the first.

The next moment happened so fast. Dennan told me to run, and I ran the only place I could—through the door to the adjacent room. I heard fist hitting face and a groan, but I didn't stop. I ran through the hallway and down the steps. When I came to the door leading outside, I stopped with my hand on the doorknob. *Wait, I can't just leave Dennan. He needs my help. I'm done running away.*

I turned and saw William standing behind me. I gasped.

"Hello, Miss Brinlee. What a pleasure to find you all to myself."

I tried to step back, but with the door shut, there was nowhere to go. At the look in William's eyes, I felt pure terror for the first time in my life. I ran past him and toward the hallway.

Suddenly, I realized I was living my recurring nightmare where I ran down a long hallway in my modern clothes. Just like my dream, I couldn't run fast enough or find another door that led outside.

My heart raced as I heard William's rapid footsteps behind me. He firmly grabbed my neck, and I crumpled to the floor in pain.

"You're not getting away from me that easily," he said.

I fought back and kicked him as hard as I could, but he threw me to the floor and pinned me. "I always knew you were spirited," he snarled.

He took a handful of my hair and forced me up. Then, he grabbed my arm and pushed me through the front door and toward the forest. We passed the carriage driver, who I now realized was dead—no doubt murdered by one of Lady Catherine's accomplices.

William dragged me into the forest. Certain "Do not let him take you into a forest" was on the top-ten list of things not to let your kidnapper do, I found the strength to wrench from his grip and run.

"Help!" I yelled.

I retraced my steps back toward the house, but William was on me in a flash. He grabbed me even before my mouth had time to finish a scream.

He raised his hand and struck me in the face. "Shut up!"

I cried out as the sting wrapped across my face.

"Make another sound, and I'll slice your throat." William showed me the knife in his hand.

"Brinlee!" Dennan's voice was far away.

I wanted to yell to him, but William brought his knife under my chin. When I felt warm blood drizzle down my neck, I stood silent and still, not even swallowing. Long seconds passed. Then, like a beacon tower above the waves of the sea, Dennan ran toward us.

He came! He really came for me.

"Don't take one step closer." William tightened his hand around my arm and pressed his knife to my neck again.

Tears rolled down my face, and I could see tears in Dennan's eyes. I knew he'd seen the blood trickling down the front of my shirt.

"You will not kill her!" he shouted.

This is so déjà vu. Just like the first time we met and Dennan saved me. Only he was Black Rider then. But I digress . . .

"Let Brinlee go, and I give my word you will leave a free man," he offered.

William gave a sinister laugh. "Your word!" He waved his knife in the air. "Of what worth is your word? The entire royal family are imposters. Your word means nothing."

I watched the wavering knife. If I was quick, I could grab it. Dennan's desperate gaze met mine, and I understood his silent urging to remain still. He wanted me to do nothing—he wanted to be my champion. I winked to let him know I understood.

"My word is worth a lot more than you can imagine," Dennan said to William. "I'll bestow on you a wealthy man's inheritance if you release her to me."

"How do I know you won't just kill me after I release her?" William asked harshly.

Dennan didn't answer. I knew he wanted to kill William even more than I wanted to.

"Besides, I don't think I'm ready to give her up," William said. He leaned his face into my hair and inhaled. "Your fragrance haunts my dreams," he whispered to me. "Just as in my dreams, I can smell myself on you."

That's so disgusting.

"You've been avoiding me ever since our first kiss," William spoke against my ear. "I am determined to finish what we started."

I clenched my fists. It took every ounce of my self-control to not punch the pervert.

"You see, Brinlee," William said in a low voice, "there's something about you—something that makes a man want you more than anything else in the world."

He used his knife to brush the hair away from my neck. With the knife, he pulled at the sleeve of my shirt, and I heard the sound of cloth tearing. He placed his lips on my bare skin with a soft kiss. "Do you think it was easy for me to stand by and watch the prince have his liberties with you while you danced with him that night at the cliffs?"

My skin crawled like spiders where William touched me. I didn't know how much more I could take.

"I kept close tabs on you through the squints in your private chambers." He kissed my neck again. "I was ever attentive of your whereabouts, and now my fantasy will be fulfilled."

"You'll never be rewarded with the affections I have been granted," Dennan shouted tauntingly. "You could only dream of being the kind of lover she's already had."

My eyes went wide and I blushed, but Dennan's words had the desired result when William raised his knife again in the air and yelled, "She will be mine, and I kill anyone who stands in my way."

The blade of his knife arced through the air. With a nod of Dennan's head as encouragement, I bent my head sideways and swung my elbow into William's midsection.

What was it that Sandra Bullock said to remember for self-defense in the movie *Miss Congeniality*? SING: Solar plexus, instep, nose, groin. I learned some cool moves from watching that show a few too many times. Anyway, I elbowed William in the solar plexus, then stomped on his foot, punched him in the nose, and turned and kneed him in the groin. *Oh yeah!* Take that, Ponytail Man!

My efforts distracted him, and I twisted out of his grasp. He struck at me with the knife. The wild blow tangled in the thick of my hair and only grazed the back of my shoulder.

I reached for Dennan but lost my balance and fell sidelong into the dirt. He leaped forward and thrust me behind him. Like a madman, William swung wildly at Dennan's body. His eyes burned with a strange glare. He yelled foul words and then struck again.

"No!" I screamed as I collapsed at the foot of a nearby tree.

Dennan stepped away from the thrusting knife and seized the arm that held it. With a maniac's strength, William barreled his body into Dennan's. They fell, but Dennan managed to hold onto William's knife arm and keep the blade away.

When they fell, William landed on the knife. It pierced him in the chest, and his breath expelled in a *whoosh.* He lay silent.

"Dennan!" I cried.

He got up and ran to where I lay on the ground. He knelt beside me and kissed the top of my head. "Are you all right?"

"I think I'm cut," I said through my tears.

Besides the seeping wound at my neck, I felt a sharp pain on the top of my shoulder.

Dennan gently brushed my hair away from the back of my neck. "Brinlee, I'm so sorry. I shouldn't have—"

"This wasn't your fault." I looked back at him. He forced a smile but obviously felt guilty. "I'm fine. Everything will be okay."

He took off his shirt and tore strips from the fabric, then loosely bandaged my wounds.

"What happened?" I asked, looking at his bare chest. "How did you get away?"

He stilled his hands and gave me the half grin that showed the dimple I loved. "I knew the minute I saw those two that they were trained to kill, not fight. So, I did what I do best and fought."

"Just like that?"

Dennan was checking my bandages but looked up to laugh. "Yes, just like that." He winked. "You underestimate me."

I grew solemn realizing what might've happened if he hadn't shown up. "Thank you, Dennan, for saving me again."

He moved to kneel in front of me and placed his hands on my shoulders. "I told you I wouldn't let anything happen to you. I'll always be here for you, Brinlee."

Can't I stay here with him forever?

He gathered me into his arms and kissed me tenderly. Tears of relief ran down my cheeks. With Dennan cradling me in his arms, everything was all right.

Soon, he helped me up and we walked back to the house. I laid my head on his bare shoulder, in the place that seemed to be made specifically for me.

"I need to detain the criminals, and then I'll take you home." Dennan kissed the top of my head.

"I'm going with you." I didn't want to be left alone.

He nodded. We passed the carriage with the driver, who we now could see was dead.

"How many people were in the house?" I asked Dennan.

"Only the two besides Lady Catherine."

"Why did they kill the man in the carriage?" I wondered.

"Criminals don't trust anyone—not even each other."

Sad, but true.

I held Dennan's arm and we walked into the house. We climbed the stairs and entered the bedroom, where Lady Catherine was tied to the table and the two men were knocked out cold on the floor.

My attention went to Gabby's father, who was huddled on the bed. I tried to put my hand on his shoulder, but he pulled away.

"It's all right." I scooted closer. "It's over now. We're going to take you home."

He slowly peered over his shoulder at me. When recognition lit his eyes, he swiftly moved and wrapped his arms around me.

I was too stunned to respond.

Dennan moved to stand beside me. "Are you all right?"

"Yes. He thinks I'm his daughter."

I put my arms around the older man. I never had a father to hug, and it felt nice, even if he was only Gabby's father.

I looked at Dennan. "It's all right. Go take care of Lady Catherine."

"I'll be right back," he said, but he didn't budge.

"I promise I'll be fine. Go."

He took Lady Catherine to the carriage first and then returned for her two henchmen. Dennan tied all three of them in the carriage so they couldn't escape.

When he came back for me, I told him I didn't want to leave Gabby's father.

Dennan stood by me and placed a hand on the older man's shoulder. "Sir, we'll be back with people who can help you."

The man looked up and said feebly, "Take care of her."

Is he talking about me or Gabby?

"Don't worry," Dennan said. "I'll take her home."

"Home," the man mumbled. He looked off in the distance, probably forgetting where home was.

"We'll be back," I told him. "I promise."

He looked at me with those bright hazel eyes. He reached out to touch my cheek. "So much like your mother."

He misses Gabby's mother. So sweet.

"Stay here," I told the man.

Dennan helped me up. Before we left the room, I looked back at Gabby's father one more time. He seemed to be thinking of a place far away, and he had a small smile on his lips.

I need to find Gabriella, I thought. *He needs his daughter.*

"Will he be okay?" I asked as Dennan helped me onto his horse.

"We'll send help as soon as we can. Right now I must get you home. Your safety and well-being take precedence over any other matter."

Home. Now that the mystery was solved, would I be able to go home?

With that thought, I left the mysterious house in the woods. It was like walking out of a nightmare.

Chapter 26

Magic Doors

When I was younger, my grandmother often told me stories about secret doors. They always sounded so magical. I dreamed of entering them and visiting places that only existed in storybooks.

In one story Nana told me, a boy walked through a magic door, leaving breadcrumbs to mark his trail. He got lost and entered another realm. He had to adapt to his new environment, but along the way he found love.

The story was enchanting. I especially loved how Nana told it, as if it were real. I always wondered if the boy ever made it back home, or if he stayed in that world forever.

Day 20 (continued . . . again)

What did Lady Catherine mean about other secret doors in the manor? Were there more than the one in the kitchen and the one that led to the tower? Sherwood Manor was crawling with mystery.

Dennan tied a piece of his white shirt to a tree on the main road to mark the secret path. Then, we hurried back to Sherwood Manor on his horse. I rode in front and leaned my head back on Dennan's chest, my injured neck throbbing with every bounce.

As we galloped onto the path behind Sherwood Manor, Krys was leaving the stables.

"Young man!" Dennan shouted.

Clearly alarmed at our haggard condition, the servant backed away from our approach.

"I am in need of your assistance, by order of the prince of Fenmore Falls," Dennan explained.

Krys must've suddenly recognized Dennan, because he bowed his head and said, "Yes, Your Highness."

Dennan stopped his horse in front of the servant. "Please make your way quickly to the castle and tell my father that I apprehended the people who were conspiring to corrupt the kingdom. There is also a sick man in need of assistance. Just off the main road, a white shirt tied to a tree marks a secret path. Tell my father to have his men follow that path, where they will find the ill man in a rundown building. They will also find the conspirators tied in a carriage out front."

Krys nodded. "Yes, Your Highness." He turned in the direction of the stables.

Dennan hopped off his horse and reached for me. I painfully slid into his arms and let him carry me to the kitchen door.

Once we stepped inside the kitchen, Miss Brenda shrieked and dropped the bowl she held in her hands. She'd never been to the castle and didn't know Dennan was the prince. I'd probably shriek too if I saw a shirtless man walk into my house carrying a girl.

Katie, who was also in the kitchen, quickly approached us. "What has happened?" she asked.

"Brinlee is hurt," Dennan explained. "Can you bring some water and bandages up to her bedroom?"

Katie nodded and quickly began to acquire the necessary items.

"What is going on, and who is this?" Miss Brenda asked with authority.

Katie tugged on Miss Brenda's arm. "This is Prince Channing," she said.

The woman's mouth fell open, but no words came out.

Dennan didn't wait for an official introduction. He made way to the hall and climbed the stairs to my bedroom, where he carefully lowered me onto my bed.

"Don't go," I pled as he released me. "I need you to hold me."

He sat on the bed, and I nestled in the shelter of his embrace.

My mom would freak if she saw this—me sitting on my bed with a shirtless boy.

"Your arms are my castle," I whispered as I raised my head from Dennan's chest and peered up at him. "You're everything I ever dreamed of." *Even more.*

I was getting sappy. It was the shock talking.

Dennan smoothed my hair. "And, how long have you been dreaming of me? Because I can't stop thinking about you, even when I'm awake."

"I've had you in my head since I was ten years old," I said quietly. It was the complete and honest truth. "I've been in love with you and your life for almost eight years. My heart has your name written all over it."

This was it! It was now or never. Dennan needed to know the truth—the whole crazy truth.

"You are half of the best love story ever told," I continued. "You are the superstar of this enchanted fairy tale. You are Prince Charming."

Dennan's brow furrowed. "I don't understand. I'm Prince Channing."

"I don't even understand it anymore," I said. "Everything has turned upside down."

I sat up and moved the pillows on my bed, then held up the Cinderella book that had traveled with me to this fairy-tale land.

"This will explain everything. This is Gabriella." I tapped on the book. "Well, it's Cinderella, but Gabriella's stepsisters call her Cinderella because of the cinder that is always on her dress from her work in the kitchen."

Dennan stared dumbfounded at the book.

I turned to the first page. "Read the story, and then you'll see."
He gave me a strange look and began to read:

Once upon a time there was a very good and pretty girl named Ella, who lived with her stepmother. This woman had two daughters of her own, and neither she nor the daughters had any love for poor Ella. They were proud and selfish, and were jealous of her because she was so pretty, and had sweet, gentle ways which made a strong contrast with their coarse, ill-bred manners.

Dennan looked up at me, I knew he didn't understand, and I didn't blame him.
"Don't you see that it's talking about Gabby and her evil stepmother and stepsisters?" I asked.
"It's just a story," he muttered.
I turned a couple of pages. "Read this."

The king's son waited for her at the door, at least three-quarters of an hour, and when she arrived, he again led her into the ballroom. He danced with her every time, and kept by her side the whole evening. When the first stroke of midnight sounded, she stopped dancing, at once left the side of the King's son, rushed across the room, and flew downstairs. The King's son ran after her, but was too late. The only trace of her was a glass slipper.

"This is you." I pointed at the book. "You're Prince Charming."
"Where did you get this?" he asked.
"It's a story about you," I said. "Your story lives on every bookshelf and in every heart in the human world." I stopped, allowing my words to sink in.
After several seconds of silence, Dennan said, "I don't know what you mean, Brinlee."

"There's something else," I said softly.

He looked up from the book.

I dropped my next bombshell. "I'm not from here."

"I know you're not from here. You already told me you're only a visitor at Sherwood Manor."

"That's not exactly what I meant." I paused. "Yes, I don't live here or anywhere near here. The truth is, I don't actually even live in this time period."

He only stared at me.

"Dennan, I'm not from this world. I'm from a future world that only dreams about your world. I don't know how I got here, but I'm caught in the middle of something I'm not."

When he didn't respond, I continued to explain. "One day Gabby brought me through some kind of magical door, and I entered your world. At first, I thought it was a dream, but when I didn't wake up from the dream, I realized I was actually in a different dimension. I've been living this fantasy ever since."

I grasped his hands, which still clutched the book. "I don't expect you to understand or even believe me. The only thing that matters right now is that I find a way to get back home so I can find Gabby. She needs to know that her father is alive."

Dennan still didn't move or speak. I couldn't imagine what he must be thinking, but I was positive he had classified me as crazy.

"Maybe someday you'll understand," I said. "It may not be tomorrow or the next day, but someday it will make sense. And now I have to leave." I felt as if my heart was being ripped from my chest. "I have to find Gabby."

Dennan moved his head slowly to meet my eyes.

"Thank you, Dennan—for everything. You'll always live in my dreams."

I turned and raced out the bedroom door. In the hallway, I bumped into Katie, who carried several rags and a bowl of water.

"Miss Brinlee, where are you going?"

"I have to go home to find Gabby."

"Are you leaving?" she asked. "When Miss Gabriella left, she never returned, and now you are leaving?"

"I think I found Gabby's father."

Katie's eyes widened.

"I know it's crazy," I went on, "but Lady Catherine has been hiding him in an abandoned house a little ways from here."

Katie shook her head. "No. Miss Gabby's father is dead."

I touched Katie's arm. "That's why I need to find Gabby, so she can find out." Down deep, I felt my conscience burning. "I need to help her come back to see her father." It was my destiny.

I gave Katie a quick hug and whispered goodbye. Just like with Dennan, time would help her understand why I had to leave.

I dashed to the kitchen and toward the magic door. Fred lay on the floor near the hearth, and I stopped to pet my faithful friend one last time. "I'm sure going to miss you."

Lady Catherine's haunting words replayed in my mind. *There are many secret doors in Sherwood Manor, Miss Brinlee.*

"I hope this works." I mimicked how I saw Lady Catherine hold her hands on the wall, one hand up and slightly to the right, and the other one straight to the side. My right fingers grazed the top of the doorframe, while my left hand touched the wooden hearth. I felt a raised bump on the doorframe and one on the hearth. When I pushed both buttons simultaneously, I heard the click of a deadbolt opening.

I turned the doorknob and pushed the door ajar. I could see into my attic bedroom. *It worked!*

After one last glance at Fred, I swung the door wide open and stepped into my room.

Back in Idaho. Back home.

Chapter 27

Secret Kingdom

My mother never talked about when my father left. Did it feel like her heart had been ripped out? Is that why she never wanted to talk about it—because she didn't want to relive it?

Sometimes I heard her crying in her room at night. Her sadness brought back a memory of my father singing to me when I was sad. It was a wistful song about a secret kingdom. I would watch his eyes, which were so much like mine, grow wet as he sang.

When I was ten and received a DVD of *The Slipper and the Rose,* I finally found the song. It was called "Secret Kingdom."

In that secret kingdom that you see
Should the make believe become reality?
With no scepter in your hand
No dominion to command
Could you be content with only me?
(Image Entertainment, 1976)

Idaho

I didn't even think about propping the door open, and it closed behind me. I raced into my grandmother's farmhouse to find Gabby.

I took the stairs two at a time from my attic bedroom down to the kitchen. As I skidded into the room, the two people sitting at the table looked startled.

I hurried over to Cassidy and gathered her into my arms.

Her eyes were wide. "Brinlee?"

I squeezed her tighter, holding fast to the idea that I was really home.

"Ow,'" Cass complained. I loosened my grip.

"What happened?" She pointed to my bandaged shoulder. "Are you all right?"

"It's just a scratch. I'm fine."

I looked at the other person sitting at the table. It was Gabby, whose life I had swapped. The girl who left me on the wrong side of the door. The girl who was the cause of all my hazards. The girl who allowed me to have the most magical experience of my life.

I smiled at her, and she smiled back. A wave of understanding passed between us. "You come from a very strange world, Gabby."

Her grin widened. "I could say the same to you."

I noted her modern, casual attire—jeans and a T-shirt. Her hair was in a ponytail, and her nails were polished a bright pink.

"Oh, Brinlee, I'm so glad you're back." Cass grabbed my hands and jumped up excitedly.

My attention shifted back to my beautiful sister. My heart ached with how much I had missed her.

"Gabby and I have had so much fun," she said. "When she told me that you two decided to exchange places, kind of like a foreign-exchange summer thing, I was more than thrilled to guide her around. We've been everywhere."

Cass's rambling, which reminded me of how I could ramble, made me extra glad to be home. I took a deep breath and listened to her report of Gabby's introduction to Idaho.

"She's even met Shane and his friends," Cass continued. "He asked about you, of course, along with calling every day to see if you were back. But one of his friends, Lyle, likes Gabby, so we went to the movies with them. Gabby enjoys every little thing in this little town. It has been fun to see her so excited about such small things. In fact, just yesterday . . ."

Cassidy's words trailed off. She stood with her mouth open. Her eyes, along with Gabby's, were transfixed at something behind me.

I turned to see what they were staring at. There, standing in the kitchen of my grandmother's farmhouse in Idaho, was Dennan— still shirtless, and looking every bit like a lost puppy. *Oh my!*

"Dennan?!" I exclaimed.

"Brinlee."

"You followed me," I said, though it was obvious.

He stepped forward so he was directly in front of me. "You left."

"I had to."

Is he really standing here? In my grandmother's kitchen? Right now? Somebody pinch me.

He frowned. "Why did you leave?"

"I had to find Gabby."

As soon as her name was spoken, the girl stood and said, "You must be Prince Channing. I saw you one time when I visited the castle with my stepsisters."

Everything seemed to move in slow motion as I watched Dennan look at beautiful Gabriella for the first time. I could see the recognition in his eyes and something else, perhaps appreciation or attraction.

Fine, I'll admit it—I'm jealous.

He was looking at the woman who would eventually be his wife. They would live happily ever after, and everything would be perfect.

Except, I would fade away miserable and alone.

Now look who is being the love glum.

"Yes, and you must be Miss Gabriella." Dennan bowed politely.

She dipped into a perfect curtsy and elegantly swished her gorgeous ponytail back behind her shoulder. "It is an honor to meet you, Your Highness."

It's an honor to meet you, Your Highness, I mimicked in my mind with a nasal voice.

Gabby was beautiful and perfect, and Dennan was charming and wonderful. I knew the two main characters of the world's greatest love story had to meet, but all I could feel was pain, jealousy, and rage. I wished the prince and Cinderella could have met somewhere other than right in front of me.

"You're a prince?" my sister shrieked.

Dennan chuckled. "Yes, I'm the prince of Fenmore Falls."

"B–b–but, uh, how did you get here?" Cass stuttered.

Obviously my sister didn't know that Gabby and I had switched places via, well, paranormal means.

Dennan looked at me, then said, "I followed Brinlee."

"You followed me?" I was touched.

"I saw you open the door in the kitchen. I couldn't figure out how to open it until I remembered seeing Lady Catherine open her secret door. I simply copied what she did."

Why did it take him only two minutes to figure out what I couldn't figure out in three weeks? *So unfair.*

"We all entered through a door in the attic," Gabby told Cass.

My sister scrunched her nose. "In the attic?"

"You see, Cass," Gabby began, "I'm from a place that doesn't exist in your world. You could say that I live in a fairy tale. There is a little bit of magic in that enchanted world, and I discovered a magic door in my home."

Gabby looked at me as she continued to explain to Cass. "Three weeks ago, I opened that door and stepped into your world, which is far different from mine. That's the night I met your sister in the attic."

I felt goosebumps run along my arms at the memory.

"You're saying you simply stepped through a door into Brinlee's bedroom?" Cassidy didn't hide her sarcasm.

I reached for my sister's hand. "She's telling the truth, Cass. Gabby is from a storybook world, and she and I switched places."

"I'm sorry you got stuck on the other side," Gabby said to me. "I couldn't open the door from my side."

"I thought you locked me out on purpose." I didn't know how many times that thought had crossed my mind.

Gabby shook her head. "I tried several times to pry the door open, but it wouldn't budge."

"Wait a minute!" Cass demanded. "You're telling me that you live in a different world and came here through a magical door, and that my sister has been trapped on the other side in your world?"

Gabby nodded.

"Who are you?" Cass asked her.

Gabby was silent a moment then said, "Some people call me Cinderella."

Cassidy looked at me, then at Dennan, and then at Gabby again. "You're telling me you're the real Cinderella from the story?"

"That's what I've discovered," Gabby said.

"So, that's why you wanted to read all of the books about Cinderella?" Cass wondered.

"When Brinlee told me I was from a book, I had to find out everything I could about my story," Gabby said.

Seeming a little calmer, Cass looked at me. "Did you really take the place of Cinderella?"

"Yes."

"And you're the prince?" Cass asked Dennan, who had stood quietly listening.

He nodded.

With the stall in conversation, I remembered why I'd returned. I looked at Gabby. "You have to go back. Your father needs you."

"My father?"

I grabbed both of her shoulders. "Your father is alive."

Gabby shook her head. "My father is dead. This cannot be true."

"He's sick, but he is alive."

Dennan finally spoke up. "Brinlee and I found him. Lady Catherine had hidden him not far from Sherwood Manor."

"My father is alive?" Gabby's eyes teared up.

"There isn't time to tell you more," I said. "You must hurry to him. He needs you."

"Yes, yes. I must go now." She quickly moved to climb the stairs to the attic.

We all followed. I went first, then Dennan, and then Cass. My sister looked dazed and bewildered—understandably so.

"This is what we're going to do," I said when we reached the attic. I looked at Gabby and then at Dennan, who stood close by me. "Cassidy and I will say goodbye, and then the two of you will step back into storybook land." *And I'll spend the rest of my life in therapy.*

Dennan leaned forward and said in a low voice, just inches from my ear, "I'm not going anywhere without you."

I was mortified by his nearness. What would his future wife think? I looked at him. "I don't belong there."

He spoke again, this time quiet enough that only I could hear. "You belong where I am."

My heart pitter-pattered. *Curse you, traitorous heart.*

"I can't open it," Gabby shouted from behind the boxes.

I hadn't noticed she had gone to open the magic door. I squeezed through the towers of dusty boxes and approached the door. Gabby pulled and yanked on the doorknob.

"Did you not leave the door propped open? I don't know how to open it from this side." She slammed her palm on the wood. "I've tried everything."

I stepped to the door. "Oh yes, it will work. Cinderella and Prince Charming have to get through this door."

I put my right hand above the doorframe and my left hand to the side, but felt nothing. I switched hands. Still nothing.

Come on! Why isn't this working?

"Perhaps the levers are on the back of the door." Dennan stood next to me. He peeked behind the leaning door and located the necessary buttons on the back side of it—one on the top right and one straight to the left.

What a relief. I turned hard at the doorknob and almost fell back as the door opened easily.

"No way," Cass gasped behind me.

Dennan chuckled. "I never would've believed it if I didn't see it."

"I'm just glad you're all going insane like me," I said.

"You have to come with us," Gabby begged me.

"You don't need me." *And I don't need to be near Dennan anymore with the feelings I'm feeling.*

"Come with me," Dennan gently whispered.

For so long, I'd dreamed of love. With Dennan so close but so unattainable, I felt as if I was letting go of my dreams. I knew I couldn't hold onto them forever, but I'd need them when he was gone. They were all I had, and I wasn't ready to let go of them yet.

"Please, Brinlee," Gabby said. "Help me find my father."

I knew I needed to help her. Nothing else mattered—not even the devastation of my heart.

"All right, I'll go." I glanced back at my sister, who looked perplexed. "I'll be back by tomorrow. Tell Nana not to worry."

"Where are you going?" Cass slowly asked.

I looked at Gabby and answered my sister. "I'm going to help Gabby see her father, and then I'm going to help her get ready for the ball."

Yes, that was what I was going to do. I was going to make sure this fairy tale ended right—with Cinderella and Prince Charming dancing at the ball.

"Tell Nana I'll be back as soon as I can," I said.

Cass nodded numbly.

So, one last time, along with Cinderella and Prince Charming, I stepped into Cinderella's kitchen in Sherwood Manor. With every effort I had made to leave the house in the first place, I was right back where I started.

Chapter 28

"Tell Him Anything But Not That I Love Him"

This song says it all.

Don't let him know
Why I must leave him
Why I must go so far away
For if he knew how much I love him
No power on earth could make him stay.
(The Slipper and the Rose, Image Entertainment, 1976)

Back at Sherwood Manor

"Where is my father?" Gabriella asked as soon as we stepped through the door.

"He's not far away," I said. "Dennan can take you on his horse."

"No, I'll ride my own horse. I'll get there much faster."

I followed her outside to the stables. She mounted the beautiful brown mare that excitedly whinnied at her arrival. Dennan climbed onto his own horse and reached for my hand to help me up.

This was my chance to leave. "I'll stay here and make sure the stepsisters aren't part of their mother's plans," I said.

With a deep frown, Dennan dismounted his horse and firmly grabbed my waist. He easily lifted me onto his mare. "I'm not leaving without you."

He climbed onto the horse and sat directly behind me. He kept one hand tightly around my waist, while the other held firmly to the reins. My heart pounded. It was hopeless to try to ignore my feelings for Dennan, just like it was impossible to stay away from deep-fried Twinkies. So good, but so bad for you.

"Follow me," he said to Gabby.

His horse broke into a mad gallop, and I had no choice but to lean on Dennan's chest for support. He wrapped his arms more securely around my waist, and I could feel the thumping of his heart against my back.

Everything about him was magical. He had the strength of heroes and champions, and the good looks of princes and models. *Yeah, he's pretty much perfect.*

I closed my eyes, blocking out everything except the man behind me. I pretended he was Prince Charming. I ignored the fact that I wanted to live in a pretend world and therefore must be deluded. For a moment, I disregarded what my head told me and listened to what my heart was shouting. I gave in to the inescapable truth—that I loved Dennan. I loved him, and now I had to find a way to leave him.

He said nothing as we rode toward the house in the woods. I wondered what he was thinking, what questions he had. He hadn't said much at Nana's house. How did he rationalize all of this in his mind?

When we arrived in the clearing, a company of royal guardsmen stood near the rundown house. Obviously, Krys had gotten word to the king.

Dennan halted in front of the line of men. "Did you find the old man inside?" he asked a tall guard who stood in front.

"Yes, Your Highness." He bowed his head. "We have placed him in the far coach under the shade of trees." The guard pointed to his right.

Gabby slid off her horse and ran to the sheltered carriage. Two guardsmen tried to intercept her.

"Let her pass," Dennan ordered.

The men moved to let her pass.

I felt awkward sitting so close to the prince while his guardsmen stared at us. I still wore my sweatpants and T-shirt, and Dennan was shirtless.

"What about the dead body in the woods?" he asked. "Have you located him?"

"Yes, Your Highness," the man answered again. "He has been recovered."

"And the woman and the two men locked in the carriage?"

"Already on their way to the castle for tribunal."

"Very well," Dennan said. "You may finish your post and return to the castle."

"Yes, Your Highness." The man bowed. The rest of the sentinels scattered like ants.

Dennan guided his horse toward Gabby, then dismounted and gently lifted me to the ground. I quickly moved away to avoid being close to him.

I approached the carriage and saw Gabby bent over her father.

"I love you, Daddy," she said through her tears. "Everything is going to be okay."

Her father smiled up her. Gabby patted his hand and smoothed the gray hair away from his forehead.

Dennan placed his hand on my back. My cheeks were wet, and I didn't know when I had started crying. I wiped the tears away.

"You did this," he whispered in my ear. His thumb rubbed gentle circles on my lower back. "You found her father."

My heart warmed. I had finally discovered the purpose of this dream. I had found Gabby's father. Seeing them together was worth every unhappiness I would face. Gabby was back home, exactly where she needed to be—she was in the right place at the right time.

It made me think of my own father. Where was he, and why couldn't I have the wonderful interchange Gabby was having with her father? Maybe I could search for him. Didn't I deserve to find my own dad?

Even more than wanting to locate my father, I realized how much I needed my mother. I yearned for her to wrap me in her arms and promise me everything would be all right. Leaving Dennan would be awful, but right now I wanted nothing more than my mother. Sure we had our tough times, but sometimes a girl just wanted her mom.

Chapter 29

Cinderella
Germany, 1857

She danced until evening, and then she wanted to go home. But the prince said, "I will go along and escort you," for he wanted to see to whom the beautiful girl belonged. However, she eluded him and jumped into the pigeon coop. The prince waited until her father came, and then he told him that the unknown girl had jumped into the pigeon coop.

The old man thought, "Could it be Cinderella?"

He had them bring him an ax and a pick so that he could break the pigeon coop apart, but no one was inside. When they got home Cinderella was lying in the ashes, dressed in her dirty clothes. A dim little oil-lamp was burning in the fireplace. Cinderella had quickly jumped down from the back of the pigeon coop and had run to the hazel tree. There she had taken off her beautiful clothes and laid them on the grave, and the bird had taken them away again. Then, dressed in her gray smock, she had returned to the ashes in the kitchen.

Day 21—Last Night in Fenmore Falls

"I can't believe we're in the castle." Gabby twirled in front of the mirror in her lavender gown and matching mask.

"You look lovely," I said. We were in a luxurious room of the castle, getting ready for the ball that evening.

The day before, when the guardsmen brought Gabby's father to the castle, all the residents of Sherwood Manor were invited to join us. Katie brought her sister and mother, Miss Brenda came, Fanny and Rose came (after proving they weren't involved in their mother's crimes), and Krys and Henry drove the carriages. We were like one big happy family.

With the best medical treatment in the kingdom, Gabby's father was recovering nicely. I didn't visit him, though, because seeing him made me feel a new sadness about my own father. I knew the two situations were different, but I still felt as if I'd lost my father again.

Now, pushing aside thoughts of my father, I said to Gabby, "I don't think your sneakers will be appropriate."

She lifted the hem of her skirt and stuck out the toe of her white tennis shoe. "You're probably right."

"At least you got rid of the jeans." I giggled.

She shrugged her shoulders. "What can I say? I was born out of time. I'd much rather be dressed in pants than a skirt and corset."

"I'm with you on that one."

I moved to stand in front of her so she'd look at me instead of her reflection. "But this is where you belong. You are Cinderella."

"It's different somehow," she said. "I've read the stories, and I know who I'm supposed to be. But that's not who I am."

I opened my mouth to argue, but I knew how she felt. It was hard being who you were told to be.

"The prince and I do not have a fascination with one another," she said. "Feelings can't appear out of thin air."

"Give it time. You'll see he's the man you were born to love."

"I've changed, Brinlee. Seeing what I've seen has given me a new view of things."

I grabbed Gabby's shoulders. "You're Cinderella and he's Prince Charming, for crying out loud. You were made for each other."

"I don't know."

"Just promise you'll give it a chance."

Gabby grinned. "Fine, as long as you will come to the ball."

"What?"

"Don't leave yet. Stay for the ball."

"What do you mean? Of course I'm staying for the dance." I stepped back and lifted the skirt of my red ball gown.

She gave me a pointed look. "I know you'll take the first opportunity to run away."

She was right, of course, since I planned to sneak away during the ball and go home to the twenty-first century. *She must be psychic. Either that or I'm really easy to read.*

"I will not run away," I fibbed.

"Stay, Brinlee, please."

"If I promise to dance, do you promise to be Cinderella?"

"Yes." She thrust her hand toward me.

"Agreed." I felt guilty as I shook her hand. She hadn't specified *where* I had to dance. I would dance at home in Idaho, when I needed my dreams to dance me away to the memories of a faraway land.

"Miss Gabby, Miss Brinlee, can we come in?" Katie asked from the other side of the closed door.

Gabby sprinted to the door and opened it wide for her chambermaids, Katie and Amanda, who were more like her sisters to her than servants.

"You two look amazing," Gabby exclaimed to the two blond-haired beauties dressed in their ball gowns.

"You look like princesses," Katie said as she and Amanda entered the room.

I couldn't help the moisture from flooding my eyes. These girls—these figments of my imagination—were the best friends I'd ever had. When I passed through the magic door, it would be almost as hard to leave them behind as it would be to leave Dennan.

The four of us jumped when a knock sounded at the door.

"Sorry." Dennan cleared his throat. He stood grandly in the doorway wearing a green jacket, with his hair combed back. "I hate to interrupt, but I searched my mother's closet in search of shoes for four damsels in distress."

He stepped into the room, and when he moved to the side, his grandmother also entered.

"Girls, you look radiant," she said with a smile.

I was delighted to see her again. My fairy godmother, as I liked to think of her, had made it possible for Katie, Amanda, and me to go to the ball the week before, and now she was helping us again, as well as Gabby.

"Shoes make the dress, is what I always say." She flicked her hand.

Four servants walked in, each carrying a basket of shoes. Gabby Amanda, and Katie gasped excitedly and began looking through the selection of shoes.

Dennan said to me, "You look magnificent."

I kept my eyes on my girlfriends. "Thank you," I said flatly, my hands fidgeting at his nearness.

He placed his hand on my lower back, sending shivers down my spine and goosebumps up my arms. I was grateful my curls hung low to cover my still-bandaged neck, or he would've seen the flush on my skin.

I felt his breath on my neck as he said, "Red is my favorite color on you."

I looked down at his mother's stunning red dress. "Thank you."

"I need to talk to you." His mouth was just inches from my ear, his hand still on my back.

Not going to happen. Being alone with him only spelled T-R-O-U-B-L-E, so I pretended not to hear him.

He huffed and grabbed my arm. "Thus, I *will* speak with you." He led me out the door and continued his mad pace down the hall. After pulling me around a corner, he finally let go of my arm. He turned to face the opposite wall and began to rub his temples.

"Dennan . . ." I started, wanting to apologize. I couldn't stand to see him upset.

He abruptly turned and held my face between his hands. "Don't talk." He held my face hard.

I saw the conflict and passion in his eyes, causing tears to spring to my own. Oh, how I loved this man! He was more beautiful than I could comprehend, and I'd never understand how I held his heart the same way he held mine.

His grip softened as he began to trace my lips with his thumb. I closed my eyes and heard him mumble, "Just one kiss."

He pressed me against the wall. I gasped slightly, and he took full advantage of my parted lips. Tears escaped from my closed eyes. I would tuck this moment away in my heart until the day I died.

Soon, my shattering heart interrupted my bliss. I tried to push away from Dennan.

"Don't go, Brinlee."

He knew me well. He'd recognized my fear when he followed me through the magic door. I remembered the adamant look he gave as he said he wasn't going anywhere without me.

My tears fell freely now. It was too late to save myself, but it wasn't fair to let him continue to feel something for me.

"Dennan . . ." I started.

It was evident by his clenched jaw and tight grasp that he wasn't going to let me go easily.

"I wasn't looking for a change in my life," he said. "I used to run in circles, taking one step forward and two steps back."

Stop, please stop.

"I didn't count on you." Tears streamed down his cheeks. "From the moment I found you in the forest, you sneaked right into my heart." He tucked a stray hair behind my ear. "I remember every look on your face. Everything you do or say takes my breath away."

If a heart can break twice in the course of a minute, mine broke again.

"I saw myself deep in your eyes," Dennan said. "You saw the man, hidden under a stupid disguise. Everything I thought I knew has been redefined by you."

This isn't fair! I screamed in my mind.

"Does love do this to you?" he asked.

What could I say? I knew if I opened my mouth I would confess my love for him.

"I know exactly where I want to be, and I know exactly who I want to be with. I want to be with you, Brinlee. I love you! It doesn't matter where you're from or if you came from a different world. I love you!"

"Dennan, please." I wanted to cover my ears. It couldn't end this way.

"Why do you fight it, Brinlee? I can see the same love in your eyes."

I shook my head and felt tears drip from my chin.

"I've decided what to do," he said after a few seconds of silence. "You once told me to mind my duty." I watched as his body straightened a little. "I acknowledge my duty and will use my power to help my people. For far too long I have run away from what I now understand was my privilege, not my burden."

I found my voice. "I'm proud of you, Dennan. You'll make a great king one day."

"Thank you for believing in me." He leaned in close. "You saw in me what I couldn't."

"It wasn't me."

He drew in a deep breath. "I love you, Brinlee."

If I didn't free myself now, in another moment I would say the words I could never take back. "I'm sorry," I cried.

This time when I squirmed out of his arms, he didn't try to stop me. I turned and rushed down the hall, holding my sobs until I had turned half a dozen corners and was lost and alone. I sank to the floor and held my knees tightly to my chest. I cried until I had nothing left to cry.

When I finally made it back to my room, Gabby and the others had left for the ball.

A servant came to the door and handed me a note. It said:

Brinlee,

We are certain you will be escorted to the ballroom by the prince, so we've gone along early in hopes of witnessing the commencement.

On the bed are the most exquisite shoes. They match your dress perfectly. Slip them on and join us as soon as you can.

Your sister,

Gabby

I looked at the shoes. As if in a dream, I slowly walked forward and picked them up. They were the glass slippers from the Cinderella story. Yes, they really were made of glass.

I held the slippers close to my heart and sighed.

Chapter 30

Lists

Women love to make lists, especially at night when things come crashing into their minds all at once. If it's not homework lists, it's project lists. If it's not shopping lists, it's to-do lists. Everything is categorized in lists. It's what girls do!

My mother was the queen of lists. If it wasn't on the list, it wasn't important. One time my sister added an item to Mom's list. She got furious and grounded Cass for two weeks—no phone, no computer, no TV, and no reading (whose mother does that?).

I asked Cass what she'd added to Mom's to-do list. She handed me the list, and I read what she'd written with a pink gel pen, between Mom's entries in black ballpoint:

Go on a date.

Checklist to Leave Fenmore Falls

I made a list of my own:

1. Say goodbye to Dennan. *Check.*
2. Leave a note on the bed next to the glass slippers. *Check.*
3. Walk away from Fenmore Falls forever. *Hardest thing I will ever have to do.*

I left the red gown next to the glass slippers and changed into my pink sweatpants and T-shirt. Then I left the room and quickly descended the steps of the castle. The monotone chime of the castle clock urged me on. *Ding-dong, ding-dong.*

As I made my way outside, the music from the open windows of the ballroom whispered across the breeze. Oh, how I wanted to be there, dancing with Dennan!

I found Gabby's horse in the stable and managed to saddle her, then climbed on her back and reined her away from the castle. Once she seemed to sense where we were going, I urged her into a full gallop down the dusty road toward Sherwood Manor. With each hoof beat, my heart thumped hard in my chest.

I felt like a character in a sad movie—the kind of movie you feel compelled to finish watching even though you know the ending will be bad. Like when both Romeo and Juliet die, or when Amanda Seyfried's character marries someone else besides Channing Tatum in *Dear John.* And no matter how many times you watch *Titanic,* Leonardo DiCaprio's character still dies.

How much can one heart take? I whispered.

I replayed in my mind the note I left for Dennan:

Prince Channing,

   How can I explain? I apologize for giving you with the wrong impression of my intentions. I will treasure every memory with you, but not in the same way you will. I let things go too far, and your recent affections have been misguided.

   Please understand why I must leave you. I simply do not love you. I'm sorry!

Brinlee

P.S. Don't ever lose your sense of wonder.

It was a lie—all of it! Well, not the part about treasuring every memory of him.

My words would bring him despair, but they would make it easier for him to move on. I had to leave him, because I did love him.

When Gabby's horse brought me back to Sherwood Manor, I ran across the yard and hurried into the kitchen. With trembling hands, I pushed the buttons on the magic door and then turned the knob. I pulled the door open and stepped into my room.

I almost reached the bed before I crumpled to the floor. I buried my head in my hands and wept.

Step 3. Walk away from Fenmore Falls forever. *Check.*

Chapter 31

My Epitaph

Charles Dickens wrote a novel called *Little Dorrit*. The inscription on a character's tombstone gave me an idea for mine.

Here lie the mortal remains of [BRINLEE AMBER ATWOOD],
Never anything worth mentioning,
Who died [when she was only 17],
Of a broken heart,
Requesting with [her] last breath that the word [DENNAN]
Might be inscribed over [her] ashes,
Which was accordingly directed to be done,
By [Her] afflicted [mother].

There's No Place Like Home

"Brinlee," a soothing voice said.

I looked up to see my mother. I reached up and pulled her in for a hug. She didn't ask any questions or say a word. She just held me tight while my heart dived into complete blackness.

When the sun seeped through my windows the next morning, I awoke to find my mother lying next to me on my bed, and my sister at my feet. Nana was sleeping soundly on the tattered couch.

My mother's eyes opened. "How are you, honey?"

"I'll be all right."

She placed her hand on my cheek. "I'm so, so sorry, Brinlee."

The pain rose sharply to my chest, and I wondered if the memories would always hurt so much.

Cass and Nana awoke from our stirring.

My mother smiled sweetly. "It may not help to hear this, but I know exactly how you feel."

"Mom, I know you feel heartache because Daddy left you, but this is different," I retorted. "You didn't fall in love with someone from a storybook."

"You might be surprised."

I frowned. "What do you mean?"

Nana stood up and came to sit on the bed. "There's more to this story than you know, Brinlee."

"What are you guys talking about?"

My mother glanced at Nana and then back at me. "Many travelers have passed through Fenmore Falls' door. The attic door has always served as a gate between our two worlds."

"What? And you're just telling me now?" I asked angrily. I looked at Cass. "Did you know about this?"

"No. Mom just told me yesterday."

I glared at my mother. "Why didn't you tell us about this before?"

"Ever since the door sealed shut after your father returned to Fenmore Falls, there was no reason to confuse you with what would've sounded unbelievable anyway."

"We had a right to know." I folded my arms in a huff.

"Yes, I should have told you. I was just so frustrated that your father left us. I wanted to spare you girls from the same painful outcome."

I touched my throbbing head. "Daddy is from Fenmore Falls?"

"Yes. He often returned home to take care of his late mother's manor, but the last time he never came back. The door was sealed, and nobody could enter or exit."

Could it be true? Was there a greater connection to the mysterious land of Fenmore Falls?

I stood up from the bed "Let me see Daddy's locket."

"What do you mean?" My mother joined me in walking to the bedroom door.

"Mom, I need to see the locket." I felt dizzy. *What if, just what if?* I leaned on the wall for support.

"Stay here. I'll go get it." My mother hurried down the stairs.

When she came back, she handed me the locket. I opened it and stared at the picture of my father in the tiny frame. His stunning hazel eyes were so like those of the man I met yesterday.

"There's still more I should tell you two." My mother looked at Cassidy and then back at me. "Your father went back to Fenmore Falls with your sister."

"Wait a minute. What?" I blinked slowly.

At my side now, Cass asked, "We have a sister?"

"Yes, Gabriella is your older sister."

Gabby is my sister? Seriously? No wonder I often had memories of another girl in my childhood.

Crash!

Before I could act in response to the new announcement, a tower of boxes plummeted to the ground next to the magic door.

"Sorry . . . so sorry," said a velvety female voice.

From the cloud of dust emerged none other than the queen of Fenmore Falls. Her yellow tresses bounced along her shoulders, and with her serene beauty, she looked as if she had walked out of the pages of a storybook.

"Aurora!" Nana hurried to the queen and gathered her into an embrace. "My Sleeping Beauty!"

My mouth dropped open. Was this Aurora of the Sleeping Beauty tale?

To add to my astonishment, my mother joined Nana and wrapped her arms lovingly around the queen.

"Abby," the queen said in a familiar tone. "It's been too long."

"Yes, it has," my mother replied.

"Are these your daughters?" The queen looked at me with recognition. "They've grown into beautiful young women."

"Yes, this is Brinlee, and this is Cassidy." My mother pointed to each of us in turn.

"Yes, one of your sweet daughters has managed to break my son's heart." The queen smiled, but her words were serious.

I lowered my eyes in shame. If only she knew how my own heart was breaking.

"Do you mean Dennan?" my mother asked.

Please let this nightmare end. I can't take it anymore.

"You see, my son shared with me the note that Brinlee left, explaining that she did not love him," the queen said. "When I saw her leave the castle, I knew I must investigate the matter. After all, I had seen her love for my son mirrored in her eyes."

I was mortified and wished for a hole in the floor to swallow me up.

"I realized Brinlee had not been forthright with the prince," the queen continued. "I suspected she might come from the imaginary land I knew in my youth. So, I visited Sherwood Manor and entered through the magic door—the same door where I once discovered a faraway land. Here I hoped to find my son's true love."

How many people had passed through the door? It seemed as though everything I'd believed to be my imagination was reality.

The queen stepped closer and reached for my hand. "He loves you. He's completely heartbroken that you're gone."

"He can't . . ." I trembled. "He can't love me."

"Brinlee, it's okay." My mother stood next to the queen.

"How can you talk, Mom?" I struck back at what hurt the most. "You've always told me that daydreams are just the cruel invention of a disappointed reality."

"I know what I said, but you must listen with your heart for what lies hidden." My mother looked sad. "More than anything, love teaches our heart to sing."

"It's not a question of my love for him. It's whether I belong where he does, because I'm not Cinderella."

"And I'm not Sleeping Beauty," the queen interjected. "Yes, I was a princess who was cursed to sleep a deathly eternal slumber, but I fell in love with a humble man from a place called Idaho and chose the outcome of my own fairy tale."

Nana finally spoke up. "And I may be Dorothy who once survived a tornado by entering through the realm of an enchanted door, but I selected my own happily ever after."

I knew it! I knew Nana was the REAL Dorothy. Awesome!

"You see, we do understand what you're going through," my mother said. "Even I met your father through the magic door."

My father!

"Mom," I exclaimed. "I know where Daddy is."

She gasped.

"He couldn't come back home because Lady Catherine drugged him and held him captive in an old house. She used him for his money and to get Sherwood Manor."

When I saw Gabby's father for the first time, he'd breathlessly said the name Abby. I thought he was calling for Gabby, when in truth he wanted my mother—Abby. Obviously, I had reminded him of her.

"Daddy didn't abandon us!" I cried. "He couldn't come back!"

My mother's eyes were wide. "Could it be true?"

I held up the open locket. "Mom, this is the man I saw yesterday when I found Lady Catherine."

My mother took the necklace in her hands and traced the picture with her finger.

"Abby, it's true," the queen said. "Your husband was brought to the castle yesterday. He is receiving the best medical care in the kingdom."

My mother's hands rose to cover her mouth as tears fell down her face. "Jack."

The queen wrapped an arm around my mother. "I should have recognized something was wrong when you didn't visit for these long years. I assumed you had moved on with your life and forgotten about the land of Fenmore Falls."

No wonder I had felt strangely connected to Gabby's father. He was my father, too! I couldn't believe I had inadvertently saved my own father from the evil Lady Catherine.

My mother dropped her hands to her sides. "I must go to him."

"We should all go," Nana declared.

This was all happening so fast.

"Including you," my grandmother said to me.

"But I'm not Cinderella."

"Cinderella is only a shell, a character in a story," Nana explained. "You are the only one who can define who you really are—not the fairy tale."

"But . . ." I closed my eyes. "What if Dennan doesn't want me?"

"Only you can break the shell, Brinlee." Nana touched my cheek. "Find the love within yourself."

Was it possible? Could I actually live happily ever after with Dennan? What if this was supposed to happen? Maybe, possibly, my dreams would actually come true.

Excited, I passed through the magic door again, this time with my whimsical grandmother, my anxious mother, my apprehensive sister, and the queen of Fenmore Falls.

Epilogue

Fair, Brown, and Trembling
Ireland, 1890

"Well," said the son of the king of Omanya, "when I find the lady that shoe will fit, I'll fight for her, never fear, before I leave her to any of you."

They visited every place where a woman was to be found, and left not a house in the kingdom they did not search, to know could they find the woman the shoe would fit, not caring whether she was rich or poor, of high or low degree . . . she belonged of right to the son of the king of Omanya.

Two Months Later—First Day of My Senior Year

Mr. Simms's Biology class could not have been more boring. I had already suffered through Algebra and was hoping my next class, History, would be a little more exciting.

When the bell rang, I gathered my books and headed to my next class. I always chose a seat in the back. I didn't even look up until I had sat down and moved my backpack to the floor.

"Hello, Brinlee."

I startled and looked to my right. "Dennan!"

The dimple in his cheek deepened as he laughed. "You're so cute when you jump."

"Har, har. You're so funny." I impulsively reached up to play with the locket at my neck, the one with my father's picture.

Now that my father and Gabby were home with us in Idaho, I never wanted him to leave my side. When I had to go to school, I took the locket with me and wore it close to my heart.

"So, do I look out of place?" Dennan sat at the desk next to me and looked down at his gray T-shirt and stonewashed jeans.

His chin-length hair was shaggy, he had that scar above his eye, and he was a twenty-year-old prince attending a public high school in Idaho. You'd think people would be terrified of him, but he made the look work, and every girl in the school tried to flirt with him.

"You fit right in," I said, delighting in the fact that he was mine.

He reached over and lifted my hand to his lips. "I'm glad my parents allowed me join you for a while and experience your world."

"Me too."

When my mom, my grandma, my sister Cassidy, and I had gone back to Fenmore Falls—with the queen in tow—I was afraid of how Dennan would receive me because of my letter. After all, I had lied to him and said I didn't love him. But when I arrived at the castle, he showered me with kisses and made me promise to never run away again. I also took an oath to love him forever.

Yep, I said it. I told him the four-letter word I had been holding back for so long.

Even though a classroom probably wasn't the most romantic setting, I leaned across the space between our two desks and planted a firm kiss on Dennan's mouth. "I love you," I said.

"Mmm, I love you too." He leaned in for another kiss.

"History class won't be so boring with you here."

He looked serious. "I will always be here for you." His mouth quirked into a grin. "Even to save you from a boring History class."

"You're my knight in shining armor."

"You've got that right."

"And I'm a damsel in need of saving." I placed the back of my hand to my forehead, feigning a faint.

"I'm always saving you." He waved his hand as if to say I wasn't worth his effort.

I stood to move from my desk. "Fine, I see how you are."

"Wait." Dennan jumped up to grab me around the waist. "Don't ever leave me."

I turned around to put my hands on the sides of his face. "Never."

"Good, because I think I'm liking this world of yours, and I'd be disappointed to leave."

"So, I guess it's a good thing I replaced Cinderella in your world?"

He kissed one corner of my mouth and then the other. "It's a very good thing."

"I love you, Dennan—Prince Channing of Fenmore Falls." I wove my fingers through his hair. "I've loved you since I was ten. I loved you when I dreamed of Prince Charming, and I've loved you since the day I met Black Rider."

As I finally told him how I felt, my heart swelled with happiness. The truth echoed through every fiber in my body. This was my fairy tale, and it was better than anything I had ever created in my dreams. In fact, everything I'd thought was fiction had turned out to be real. In addition to falling in love with Prince Charming, who was also the son of the supposed Sleeping Beauty in a fairy-tale land called Fenmore Falls, I'd also discovered that my grandmother was the girl who fell out of the sky and landed on the Wicked Witch of the West.

What else was there to discover? Was my father the same Jack who climbed a beanstalk looking for treasure and adventure? What about Nana's friends, Miss Wendy and Allie? Was their background just as colorful?

I guess that's a story for another day.

For those of you who like to read the last page of a book first, you really don't want to find out how this story ends yet. Trust me on this. Now go on, turn back to chapter 1 and get reading!

About the Author

Tarrah Montgomery has loved writing stories since she was a child. She earned her associate degree from Ricks College and her bachelor of science in education from Utah State University. Tarrah currently lives in Snowflake, Arizona, with her husband and young children. She loves to travel with her husband, and many of her story ideas have come from seeing the ancient castles and architecture around the world. Some of her adventures have taken her to Paris, London, Rome, Germany, Austria, Switzerland, Czech Republic, South Korea, and Thailand. When not writing, Tarrah teaches preschool and enjoys reading, traveling, spending time with her family, and playing the piano. *I'm Not Cinderella* is her first novel, with several more to follow in The Princess Chronicles. Check out the upcoming sequels at tarrahmontgomery@blogspot. com. Tarrah loves to hear from her readers, and you can contact her at tarrahmont@gmail.com.